SO EASY TO REMEMBER . . .
SO HARD TO FORGET

For a piercing moment, they both froze, their hearts pounding as one. Then his arms clasped her in an encompassing embrace and her lips strained hungrily for his. His kiss burned through her, searing into her a truth she could not deny. His strength flowed into her, forging the bond that had ever existed between them with an iron existence.

But one fact marred this idyllic scene. The man who held Emmaline in his arms was not the one she was to wed in two short days. So when he said, "The best course would be for both of us to forget the past few minutes ever occurred," she had to agree, "We must."

So much easier said than done!

LEIGH HASKELL explored castles, museums and cold cities while based in Germany. She now lives with her husband and two sons in northeast Ohio and studies historically preserved homes.

The Paragon Bride

Leigh Haskell

A SIGNET BOOK

NEW AMERICAN LIBRARY

A DIVISION OF PENGUIN BOOKS USA INC.

1

"Keep a sharp eye, the both of you," cautioned the dowager Countess of Langdon. "Today we shall find her, the illusive bride-to-be. You may depend upon it." She nodded emphatically, setting her second chin to wiggling and the suspiciously bright-auburn curls beneath her bonnet to quivering. Receiving no response, the elderly but by no means frail lady sniffed. "Apparently, neither of you credit my prediction. Have I ever read the tea leaves incorrectly? I daresay not."

Nicolas Ransom reined in his big grey gelding to match the pace of her carriage. The countess's bewigged coachman and liveried footmen were properly without expression. But Nicolas exchanged glances with his cousin Cecil, prospective bridegroom and grandson of the redoubtable countess, who rode beside him. Cecil's gaze was bleak with forbearance, Nicolas's dark with vexation. For a moment, Nicolas was tempted to speak, to point out tersely that the countess's inkling had produced not a single candidate for the unknown bride-to-be in a fortnight, but he thought better of the urge. When his great-aunt Minerva set her mind, neither heaven nor earth could upend her determination. The square angle of his jaw hardened and he slowed his horse to a walk alongside the landaulet, resigned to the fool's chase.

It was the fashionable hour of five in the afternoon, and a line of carriages wound slowly through Hyde Park. Although many a passing young lady peered coyly from beneath a stylish bonnet at the intriguing and powerful form of Nicolas Ransom, he returned none of the flirtation. In his tall beaver hat, his perfectly cut, deep-blue coat, and his fawn-colored trousers, he looked the typical London dandy. Yet his expression belied the first impression.

The relaxed, carefree attitude so obvious in other gentlemen of leisure was noticeably missing in Nicolas. His every movement was tense and his form well-honed as an officer of the King's Dragoons. This gave rise to the gossip that Ransom was a former military man, mayhap cashiered from the corps, for he refused to confirm or deny the speculation, or to boast of any heroics. Others whispered that his bronzed complexion and ebony hair proved the theory that his well-born father had married a gypsy or a Spaniard. Little was known of his background in a society that could recite family histories back to the Norman Conquest. The puzzle surrounding him made him the more attractive to certain adventuresome mamas who were willing to risk a taint in his heritage for the cachet of his mystery.

Yet Nicolas remained immune to their matchmaking. His gaze, usually as direct and demanding as that of a falcon, was pensive and betrayed not a little restiveness. He had pressing business that demanded his immediate attention. And here he sat on his big gray, idling away time that he could ill afford to squander.

But just when his patience began to wear thin, he chanced to gaze at his great-aunt Minerva, her brown eyes bright with hope as she scanned the passing carriages through her quizzing glass. His fondness for her melted the ice of his anger, and Nicolas breathed deeply and remained silent.

His cousin Cecil, who at three-and-twenty was six years the younger and a century the less wise, did speak up.

"Grandmama," Cecil moaned dramatically, "must you drag me 'round London in this foolish quest? I've Lady Cavendish's rout to attend this evening."

The countess gave a decidedly unladylike snort. "And a mere three hours to dress. I doubt it can be done in your case, Cecil. And what a scandal, were you to attend completely *déshabillé*."

She winked ironically at Nicolas, who could not contain a smile. Cecil had been known to threaten disaster when his cravat would not submit to his valet's ministrations.

"Laugh if you must, Grandmama," Cecil mumbled, fighting petulance. "But I have espied any number of fetching young ladies, and all you can say is that 'tis not she. I fear we shall waste my precious time and never find this . . . this paragon you seek."

"Patience, my boy," the countess said serenely. "She is here somewhere. We have only to spot her. The tea leaves were ever so precise. A dove nibbling cherries will be the sign."

Cecil groaned, but Nicolas merely shook his head. Lady Minerva would not relent until her prophecy was fulfilled. And in his genuine affection for her, he hadn't the heart to deny her attempt.

When the gray gelding whinnied and danced skittishly, longing to gallop, Nicolas constrained the horse firmly but with rueful empathy.

Emmaline Hazlett glanced about the teeming street, her blue eyes shining, unable to contain her exuberance.

"Uncle Markham, this is quite the most exciting place in the world. I am ever so grateful you consented to bring me with you."

Her guardian, the vicar, frowned at her and kept up his resolute pace. Emmaline considered that she should be further grateful that his parsimony prevented yet another hiring of a hackney, else she would be denied the simple pleasure of window-gazing.

She glanced at him from under her bonnet, weighing the risk of his sharp tongue against an overwhelming desire. As usual with Emmaline, discretion lost the battle to whim. She decided to chance the request.

"Might we proceed more at leisure?" she asked wistfully.

The vicar growled under his breath. "You have twitted me overlong to visit London. And when from the goodness of my heart I relent, you rail at me needlessly. Hurry along and do not bother me with talk of leisure. You will be only the more distracted by the frivolities in these shops, useless items that are no concern of yours."

From long practice, Emmaline knew that any retort would earn her more trouble than was worth. Yet she stewed. Her guardian possessed the personality of a withered lemon: unpleasantly pinched and everlastingly sour.

Her long-awaited "visit to London" had been proving most frustrating. It had begun with an uncomfortable five-hour coach ride from the village of Bevindale, where they lived. Then, eager to feast her own eyes on sights she had but read about, she found herself stuck with a limited view from a closed hackney as they made their way to the Paddington home of her guardian's elderly aunt. In truth, she suspected that Markham had succumbed to her repeated pleas only to spare himself the complaints of the poor woman. She had been forced to listen politely for two hours while the vicar buried himself in another room, going over his aunt's accounts.

Now, as quickly as he could secure his monthly supply of his special blend of tea, they would be returning to Bevindale by night coach. Emmaline felt for all the world like a child who had been given a whiff of plum tart and then denied even a taste of the treat.

Deliberately, she slowed her pace. Gazing longingly at the smart displays, she drank in the alluring glimpses of silk and lace, of trimmed bonnets and sleek leather boots as they passed the windows of the fashionable shops. All around her, St. James's Street was bustling with activity, and Emmaline felt her pulse quicken with the pace.

"Will you kindly," the vicar said in acid tones, "cease your infernal dawdling?"

His complaint was interrupted by a trio of street urchins who encircled him, clamoring for a penny.

"Here," he said sharply, waving his bony arms. "Away with you! Earn your money, like good Christians. Off, off!"

The children scattered, making rude gestures, while Markham scowled.

"Disgusting sight! Filthy little beggars, with no sense of decorum, no respect for their elders. Imagine, harassing a man of the cloth! They should be swept from the streets like the refuse they are."

"Surely they do not choose their plight," Emmaline said mildly, hiding her irritation.

"Do not apologize for them, miss. You merely add to my vexations. I knew I never should have agreed to this ludicrous plan in the first. You rightly should have remained in Paddington for the afternoon. If not for your mewling, I should have left you there. If your reputation is ruined, you shall have only yourself to blame."

Emmaline peered at him wryly. "My reputation? Who could be a more proper chaperon than you, Uncle?"

"Look about you," the vicar answered, entirely missing her irony. "Do you see any other respectable women in the streets? These shops are the province of dandies and libertines. If not for the fact that Baskin Brothers is the only purveyor of decent teas in this Gomorrah, I myself should never set foot in this street. And as for you . . . May I simply remind you that should this news reach Bevindale, there is a great possibility that Mr. Cooper will withdraw his generous offer for you? You will never catch another husband; not even a pauper will have you. Think on that, my headstrong young lady. Think on that when you scheme to bedevil me with more of your whining."

The vicar, his rigid beaked nose twitching with righteousness, pushed on through the crowd, his beloved tea his only objective.

Emmaline bit at her full lips to suppress a bitter reply. There was no justice in the fact that merely appearing upon a questionable street could ruin her reputation. And even so, in what manner could the country villagers, who never ventured beyond the southern meadow, hear about her ruination? Like so many of her guardian's rules, she could not fathom a reason for this one. She did know that securing a proper—read "wealthy"—husband for her was to Markham his most important task. In truth, the vicar lived for the day on which he could hand her over to the highest bidder.

Thus far, the complacent Mr. Will Cooper was, in the vicar's estimation, leading the pack. At six-and-thirty, Cooper was exactly twice Emmaline's age, a dyed-in-the-wool bachelor who had seen the error of his ways and wished to breed hands for his sheep farm. She supposed that he was presentable, in a rough, elemental manner. A tall, powerful man, he carried himself uneasily, as if apologetic for his massive appearance. Yet the very thought of the man, with his measured speech and the slight odor of foul raw wool that constantly clung to him, brought a shudder to Emmaline's spine. Her most pressing mental exercise of late had been weighing which was the lesser of two evils: servitude to the vicar or to the farmer. Since she had not fully decided, she had been holding them both at arm's length—a strenuous task indeed.

Shaking thoughts of her dilemma from her mind,

Emmaline returned her gaze to the shops and hoped Baskin Brothers was far enough away to allow her a few more moments of vicarious enjoyment.

Too soon, they arrived at that establishment. The vicar barged in, but a street seller cut off Emmaline's path.

" 'Ave a trimmin' for yer bonnet, dearie?" a toothless old woman asked, waving a basket of feathers, silk flowers, and other sundries.

Emmaline smiled appreciatively and on impulse reached for a cluster of bright-red wax cherries. Trimmed bonnets were considered unnecessary frivolity in the vicarage. Nonetheless, the gaiety of the small cluster symbolized for her the bright sauciness of London, and Emmaline knew she must have the trimming.

"Emmaline," her guardian barked from inside the shop, "stop dawdling and come here immediately."

Knowing she would undoubtedly pay the price for her "extravagance" later, Emmaline dropped a coin in the old woman's hand and pinned the cherries to the brim of her sedate gray bonnet.

With a lilt to her step, she entered the shop. As she breathed deeply, she became aware of her surroundings and found herself actually smiling.

The shop spilled forth its fragrances, with its seductive wares: rich coffees, fragrant teas, and piquant spices. Emmaline's senses reveled in the experience.

"Ah, Vicar Markham," a jolly voice called. "So good to see you once more. And I daresay you have brought a young lady with you."

The plump woman in black bombazine and a snowy lace cap approached Emmaline with friendly bonhomie. When it was apparent her curiosity would not dissolve, the vicar grudgingly turned from his pursuit of Darjeeling and souchong varieties.

"My ward, Miss Emmaline Hazlett," he muttered,

annoyed at the intrusion. Then his eyes narrowed and he addressed only the girl. "And what, pray tell, is that ridiculous gewgaw sprouting on your bonnet?"

"My dear vicar," said the other woman. "Why, 'tis a quite cunning spray of cherries, to be sure. Now allow me to assist you in your selection. Then I must speak to your ever-so-charming ward in her ever-so-charming bonnet."

The vicar opened his mouth, then promptly shut it, with a glance at Emmaline that said the subject would not fade away with the woman's blithe dismissal, but merely be postponed.

At the same moment, the friendly woman turned her attention toward Emmaline. "Welcome, my dear. I am the Widow Dorn, proprietress of this establishment. You seem pleased with what you see in my shop, and I must say, that pleases me."

"Aye, 'tis a lovely place," Emmaline agreed, her face lighting with enjoyment. "Such marvelous aromas! I am put in mind of home. Not Bevindale, naturally, but India, where I spent my younger days."

"From a mysterious land to a sleepy village," the widow speculated. "However did you manage the change?"

"Not well," Emmaline admitted with a wry smile.

The widow laughed once more. "Since I have not had the pleasure of meeting you ere now, I take 'tis your first journey to London."

"Yes, if one discounts the journey from India to Bevindale. At that time, I was most distraught to be leaving my parents and did not so much as glance at the sights as we passed through the city."

"And how have you found London this time?"

Emmaline considered. Even through the restricted view from the hired hackney, she had been agape at the fine houses and broad squares, the crowds and heavy traffic, gawking like any country girl. She had sensed a vitality that alternately thrilled and frightened her.

"I have thoroughly enjoyed what I have seen," she replied at last. " 'Tis ever so noisesome, and yet 'tis like the heartbeat of some powerful beast. One does not know whether the beast is tame or wild, and yet, I vow, the uncertainty adds to the excitement."

For a moment, the Widow Dorn appeared startled; then she scrutinized Emmaline shrewdly and gave a broad smile. "How unusual to hear such a view from one your age. Quite refreshing to discover in one young lady both intellect and beauty."

Emmaline blinked in amazement. Surely the woman's eyesight was failing. She had no illusions about her appearance. Her drab walking dress of dove gray was far more serviceable than fashionable. The vicar frowned mightily on "ostentation," and therefore Emmaline's costume sported no decoration save the black closures of her pelisse, and now, to be sure, the cluster of wax cherries perched defiantly on the brim of her matching bonnet. She presumed that the widow was merely showing a kindness and made no reply.

The vicar decided upon his selections, carefully watching as a clerk measured out his tea.

The widow gazed bemusedly at Emmaline. "I hope I shall see your ward again next month, Vicar. I daresay London agrees with her."

Impatiently, Markham fluttered his bony hand. "Forgive me, dear lady," he said, clearly uncaring as to whether she would or not, "but my ward is quite out of her element. Our quiet village suits her far better. And she is nearly engaged to be married there. Assuming, that is, that she comes to her senses and forgets about useless frivolities."

His dour glance at her bonnet undid Emmaline's determination to ignore him. He finally had succeeded in spoiling her London visit. In her heart, Emmaline rebelled. She despised the continuous stultification to which she was subjected. Even an innocent longing for a clever bonnet was considered unseemly and wasteful. It was a bare wonder she was ever allowed to leave the confines of the village, even once. Surely that imprisonment was not what her parents had in mind when they appointed Edwin Markham as her guardian.

Fate cruelly had intervened in her young life, uprooting her from exotic India and her family. She had consoled herself that her father had no notion that his clergyman had over the years become a dour, uncompromising curmudgeon. She could not bear to think her dear papa had knowingly abandoned her to such a sentence: spending her school holidays in the silent, musty vicarage with, as her only companions, a querulous housekeeper and a man who tolerated her presence so ungraciously.

And since her schooling at Miss Calder's had concluded, the oppressive air of the vicarage had threatened to suffocate her. She had been given chores the housekeeper deemed too unpleasant to perform herself. Her life was an endless round of scrubbing hearthstones, fire stoves, and chamber-pots. London had promised to be a breath of salvation, and Emmaline's heart wrenched to realize the visit would be but another long disappointment, only because Markham's penurious character would deny her even the pleasure of observing.

Yet, at last, she lifted her chin, her blue-eyed gaze once more direct. She had overcome the harshest setback of her young life, and the experience had left her strong-willed and of an independent mind. This disappointment would not be her undoing.

"Best wishes on your betrothal, my dear," the widow murmured, but an odd trace of regret tainted her felicitations.

And hearing that intonation, slight and subtle as it was rendered, Emmaline knew with a sudden, blinding clarity that a life in Bevindale would be a death sentence for her. She yearned in a shocking manner for the stimulating pace of the city she had but glimpsed. The notion that she might never have what she craved was an unbearably cold stone on her heart.

The cruelly exotic scents of cinnamon, vanilla, saffron, and nutmeg assaulted her. In Bevindale, such spices were considered vaguely hedonistic. Once again, she was allowed a whiff, but prevented from ever partaking.

When the vicar called grumpily for her, she followed him out of the shop, the wonderful aromas still taunting her.

"Grandmama," Cecil groaned once more, "we've been 'round the park a dozen times. Surely you will concede defeat. Mayhap you read the tea leaves upside-down."

"I am never wrong." The countess gestured to her grand-nephew. "Remind this dolt, Nicolas. Just a month ago, after a quite ordinary cup of tea, I chanced to peer at the leaves. Did I not summon you immediately? And did I not predict that Lady Hampton's youngest daughter was about to elope with the second groomsman? And was I not astoundingly accurate?"

Despite his impatience, Nicolas could not suppress a grin. "Indeed, Auntie. Indeed, you were."

Diplomatically, he refrained from adding that the entire affair came as a surprise only to Lady Hampton herself, who incredibly had not heard of her young hellion's ongoing scandalous behavior behind the stables. Most of the countess's prophecies ran along the same lines. Nicolas suspected she took fragments of gossip, mixed them with bits of speculation, and threw in a pinch of shrewd reckoning to read her predictions. Yet she never added grist to the mill concerning his own hazy background. Indeed, she delighted in keeping a gleeful silence with her cronies, no matter they hinted extravagantly. For this he was grateful and oddly touched, and so he went along with her readings from the tea leaves. Indulging his aunt was one of his few weaknesses.

"Then," the countess continued with a smug titter, "the very next week, did I not foresee your bride, Cecil, the perfect wife for you?"

Cecil paused, then slowly removed his tall beaver hat. The pale sunlight filtering into the park glinted in his fair hair and lit his face theatrically.

"Grandmama," he murmured, his mouth trembling slightly, "I have told you on numerous occasions, my life is in turmoil. I am not in the market for a wife. If you persist in this folly, I—I cannot be responsible for the depths of my melancholy. Mayhap I shall do something foolish again."

Rolling her eyes, Lady Minerva groaned. "I beg of you, Cecil, spare me such nonsense. I shall quite lose my patience with you."

Nicolas took pity on his cousin's downcast expression. "Perhaps 'tis too soon to search for a bride for Cecil. He is young, and forgive me, Auntie, there is time enough—"

"Nicolas!" Lady Minerva blinked rapidly, wounded. "Must I remind you, of all people, how little time on this earth is afforded to the men of this family? My dear Alfred's most aching desire was that the earldom stay in direct succession. Indeed, I have pledged my life to just this aim. Pray, do not make my task more difficult than it is proving already."

Her reproach pricked at his conscience. "I am sorry, Auntie," he said quietly. "Do forgive me."

Lady Minerva halted in midpout and regarded him fondly. "How can I not? We are too affectionate a family to vex one another. And as soon as we have found Cecil's bride, I shall read the leaves to find the perfect woman for you. No, no, do not bother to thank me. You know I love you too dearly to see you alone and unhappy."

At this comment, Nicolas prudently turned away. He was the last man in London to afford or desire a bride, perfect or not. He told himself that he refrained from argument with his aunt's unshakable notions for one reason: to avoid inevitable defeat at the hands of her incomprehensible logic. Yet, reluctantly, he owned only to himself that his fondness for her was the stanchion of his restraint. He would let Cecil try to distract her from her fantasy.

"And as for you, dear Cecil, think on it. You, fulfilling the dying wish of your grandsire; you, the envy of every man in England; you, the handsome, the dashing ninth Earl of Langdon with this vision of beauty, your countess, at your side, reigning over the *haut ton.*"

Cecil's stubbornness abruptly softened and a dreamlike haze hovered in his eyes. "By Jupiter, you are perfectly correct, Grandmama. 'Tis my—my *destiny.*"

Nicolas barely succeeded in stifling a groan. The countess's notions alone he could tolerate. But add to it Cecil's mercurial romanticism and the two of them should certainly drive him mad. He closed his eyes briefly and prayed for an early deliverance from this folly, only the latest of Lady Minerva's many intrigues.

Yet his prayer went long unanswered. An hour of tenacious perusal revealed only the same young ladies who sallied forth daily with their sharp-eyed mamas. No idealistic paragon appeared. No dove nibbling cherries appeared. Undaunted, Lady Minerva pledged to try a more auspicious day, while Nicolas shifted restlessly in the saddle and stifled his despair.

Later, the countess was to remember having seen the letters SJ, for St. James's Street, in the leaves and to rejoice at her uncanny luck. For she insisted on stopping by Baskin Brothers on the way home.

"Grandmama, I have no time for this foolishness.

'Tis Humble's duty to keep you supplied with tea."

"Hush, Cecil. I cannot trust the man to . . . Cecil!"
Lady Minerva gasped, fluttering her head. "Look!
'Tis she!"

Nicolas, hoping against hope that this bedeviling
waste of his time was over, peered in the direction
that his aunt was so frantically gesturing. He saw
a trim young woman in a modest, pale-gray walking
dress, accompanied by a spare, unbending country
vicar. His experienced eye noted that her bonnet
was at least three seasons old and her hairdress
unassumingly simple. He turned back to his aunt,
staring at her incredulously.

"This is the paragon?"

Lady Minerva took no notice of his ironic tone.
"Oh, yes, indeed. She bears the sign of which I
spoke. Look at her bonnet: a dove gray and, upon
my word, a cluster of cherries! Cecil, is she not the
loveliest of creatures?"

"Ah, my vision of beauty," sighed Cecil
ecstatically, and Nicolas observed them closely to
see if the rare London sun had blinded their eyes.
Finally, he grimaced in puzzlement.

"From this distance, she appears a comely young
woman, I own. But a paragon, Auntie?"

Lady Minerva smiled knowingly. "Ah, there is
where I have the advantage over you, Nicolas. The
tea leaves have told me what you cannot yet
perceive. 'Tis a quite extraordinary young lady
before us. She must be, for she is the one. The one
and the only bride."

"Ye gods, Grandmama, I must meet her. But however shall we manage an introduction?"

The countess beamed with complete confidence.
"Leave all to your grandmama, dear boy. I have a
scheme."

On this occasion, Nicolas' groan would not be
denied. He shook his head in foreboding at Lady
Minerva's next move.

2

Emmaline trained her gaze firmly toward the pavement upon leaving Baskin Brothers, as she did not wish to be distracted by the tantalizing arrays in the shop windows. The startling discovery still captured her thoughts: life in Bevindale, whether shackled to the vicar or to Will Cooper, would lead her to an emotional gallows. She shuddered at the very prospect.

Yet what choice had she? Her life was shaped, would continue to be shaped for all eternity, it seemed, by a series of keepers. First, her father had deemed she come to England and had passed her on to the vicar. now, that ill-humored man was intent upon passing her to the sheep farmer. No one would dream of asking her how *she* would chart her life.

In fairness, Emmaline owned that ere now, she had never considered the question herself, accepting her fate much as Cooper's animals did at shearing season. But the vibrancy of London had struck her like a slow-swinging hammer, chipping away at her none-too-solid resignation. Now she chafed openly at her constrictions. Near desperation, she suddenly grasped at a means, shocking but necessary, to free herself: to escape her fate, she must run away.

Yet even as the thought caromed in her mind, she knew it was a doomed plan. She had naught but a few pennies in her reticule, doled out reluctantly once a month by the vicar. And she had no other funds upon which to draw. In an almost daily accusation, the vicar had reminded her that the moneys her parents had settled on her had dribbled away long ago, eroded by her schooling fees. Emmaline was, in essence, trapped with scarcely a farthing to her name.

Occupied with her frustrating thoughts, she took no notice of the landaulet until, with a vast jingling of harnesses, the carriage drew alongside.

"Vicar," called a woman's voice. "I say, Vicar."

So imperious was the tone, so accustomed to instant obedience, that even her guardian halted and peered at the source.

"Madam?" Markham replied, rather curtly.

Emmaline, stirred by curiosity, relinquished her self-possession to regard the woman. Certainly no longer young, nor even mid-aged, she nonetheless retained a lingering handsomeness. With jewels twinkling about her neck and upon every finger, she bore testimony to wealth and position. She was expensively dressed in a tightly laced gold brocade that suited her demeanor and age. And yet, by the audaciously red curls and lively brown eyes, Emmaline detected a humor and warm eccentricity in the woman. She found herself smiling.

"I must say, Vicar, I am most put out that you fail to remember me," said the woman with a shadow of a pout. "Yet 'twas nigh a year ago we met, and I am of a forgiving nature. I shall refresh your poor memory: I am Lady Garwin, dowager Countess of Langdon."

The vicar frowned. "I assure you, milady, we never have been introduced. You are mistaken."

The woman, although seated, drew herself up regally. "And I assure you, my good sir, I never am mistaken. 'Twas at Bath you made my acquaintance, in late July. Or mayhap early August. You were collecting alms for the poor."

Reddening in annoyance, the vicar tightened his lips, his next words escaping in sharp chops. "Never in my life have I begged for funds."

The countess looked askance, then raised her

quizzing glass and peered at Markham down her aquiline nose. "I own to a small flew in my speech. 'Begged' is a word of the masses, and you are obviously a gentleman. But, by Jupiter, 'tis you I encountered. I have no doubt. I recall for quite a good reason, dear sir. I pledged fifty pounds to your charity. Then, before I could deliver the amount, I was summoned unexpectedly back to London by my grandson here."

For the first time, Emmaline noticed that two riders had halted on the far side of the landaulet. The one nearest the countess, whom she called her grandson, sat quite still in the saddle, his tall hat clutched before him. And to Emmaline's surprise, she saw that his eyes were focused with deep interest upon her. Unaccustomed to male attention, she blushed and glanced away without thinking. Finally, she summoned the courage to return his tentative appraisal.

The countess's grandson was young and handsome in a gentle, poetic manner. His fair hair ruffled softly in the slight breeze, and he smiled hesitantly at Emmaline. Once again flustered, she averted her gaze.

This time, the second rider appeared in her view, almost as if he chose to barge in whether she cared to admit him to her perspective or not. So startled was she by his commanding presence, Emmaline forgot to look away.

As she watched, fascinated, he removed his beaver hat with a flourish, a slight and ironic smile on his face. In contrast to the grandson's gentle transparency, this man was an opaque mystery. His hooded eyes relinquished nothing, yet challenged Emmaline in a manner she could not understand. There was no softness in his countenance; each plane—of straight, high-bridged nose, of smooth brow, of firm, square chin—bespoke strength and perhaps even a determination to have his own way. He sat erect but at ease upon his huge gray horse, his broad shoulders perfectly aligned. When Emmaline found her perusal lingering over the solid mass of him, she felt her cheeks flaming in earnest. Yet she could not look away ere she heard her name spoken.

". . . Miss Emmaline Hazlett, my ward."

Realizing she was being presented, Emmaline dropped an unexpectedly wobbly curtsy and forced her attention to the countess.

"Charmed, my dear," Lady Garwin said in an altogether friendly tone.

"We have been shopping for my special blend of teas," the vicar was saying, and despite her discomfort under the gaze of the dark-haired man, Emmaline heard the most astonishing change in Markham's voice.

Blinking, she stared at her guardian. The slight twisting of his lips, which she knew was his rendition of a smile, astounded her. Magically, it seemed, his annoyance had disappeared, replaced by a slightly fawning interest in the countess. Suddenly, Emmaline understood. She had seen this side of the vicar on a small number of occasions, when he hoped to shear a considerable donation from one of the wealthier of his flock.

And with the understanding came a horrified realization. The vicar, his ears having pricked up at the mention of a forgotten donation of a princely fifty pounds, intended to collect on another unfortunate vicar's pledge.

"Uncle," she murmured urgently, plucking at his sleeve, "we must be going, else we shall miss the night coach."

The countess waggled her fingers. "My dear, you must not be planning a return this very evening. An excess of travel is not good for the constitution. No, no, I shall not hear of it. To atone for my neglect in sending your guardian the pledge I made, I insist that you both be my guests for the night."

Reacting to a gesture from her bejeweled hand, one of the footmen jumped off his perch and held open the carriage door.

"So generous of you, my dear Countess," Markam murmured. "The offer of accommodation, that is. But we cannot possibly impose upon you."

Emmaline released a sigh of relief, yet she might have known her guardian better, for he uttered his demur on a rising note, which pleaded embarrassingly for refute.

The countess obliged. "Ah, but I insist, my dear Vicar. In no way will your visit impose. Indeed, I shall be quite honored to welcome you to my home. And quite put out should you refuse."

The vicar threw up his bony hands. "How can a simple country vicar such as I deny so kind a lady?"

Emmaline's eyes widened as she felt the vicar's hand at her back, urging her forward. She stood planted at the spot.

"Come, my dear," said Markham, and then in a harsh whisper meant for her ears only added, "say not a word and come along. Do you understand me? Say not a word."

Emmaline, repelled by his intentions, wished dearly to turn and flee. Yet she recognized his dangerous tone. It brooked no dissent, and she knew that if she mutinied, she would but make a fool of herself, for he would not be swayed as much as an inch in his stance. Indeed, he might well leave her stranded on the street, so eager was he to cash in on the windfall. Emmaline nodded, her only hope being that an opportunity might arise to right his dishonesty.

The footman assisted her into the carriage, and she sat opposite the countess, sinking into the finely tooled leather seat. Her guardian followed, bowing formally to Lady Garwin before beginning to position himself beside Emmaline. The countess patted the seat next to her.

"No, no, sit here, Vicar . . . Markham, you say? Upon my word, I was thinking 'twas more like Hadley, or Henderson." She laughed suddenly, a rich, good-natured sound. "Which merely proves that my memory is naught of which to boast either."

The vicar chortled along with her, his sound grating and unnatural to Emmaline's ears. She cringed, but true to her promise, said not a word.

"Dear me, so befuddled am I by our chance encounter, I have quite neglected my duties," the countess said. "But then, I am not one for formalities with friends."

Emmaline noted with repulsion that the vicar nearly preened.

"This grandson to whom I referred," the countess was saying, "is properly Cecil, Lord Garwin, Earl of Langdon. Cecil, dear, may I present Miss Emmaline Hazlett. And of course, her guardian, Vicar Markham."

The poetic young man bowed from his saddle. "Most delighted," he said eagerly, his gaze never leaving Emmaline's face.

"And this young Spartan," the countess continued, waving fondly to the dark-haired man, "is my great-nephew, Nicolas Ransom."

To Emmaline's mild surprise, his expression softened when the countess spoke. A distinct twinkle lit his eyes as he smiled wryly at his great-aunt's description. The change transformed his visage, by no means erasing the strength in his features, but layering another facet to him. Bemused, Emmaline regarded him with bated interest, realizing that Nicolas Ransom was a most complicated man, and a most intriguing one.

Yet, when he turned to acknowledge her, the gentleness was gone, his expression once more mysterious to her, perhaps even slightly mocking. Emmaline was confused at her disappointment that the barriers about him had gone up after but a glimpse of the man behind them.

"Your servant," he murmured in her direction, and Emmaline heard an irony she was not sure he intended, for it was abundantly clear to her that this man was a servant to no one. And to her astonishment, Emmaline found that trait in him attractive and tantalizing.

The carriage began rolling and she looked away from the riders. By this time, the countess and the vicar were chatting away, thick as thieves. Which, Emmaline reminded herself in some alarm, her guardian literally was. Suddenly, she felt distinctly unwell, and shivered.

"Are you cold, my dear?" asked the countess in concern. "The nights in London can be quite chilly, even in April. Here, take this and wrap it about you."

She pulled a fox-trimmed coach throw from the corner of her seat and Emmaline accepted it gratefully. The robe's soft embrace comforted her; it also hid her shaking hands.

For one accustomed to bland, uneventful days, this one had provided an excess of spicy richness for Emmaline. Her senses never had been so stimulated, her emotions never so provoked. So many unfamiliar thoughts clamored for her attention, she could give rein to none. And so she conscientiously studied the throw on her lap, seeing naught, grateful only that no conversation was expected of her.

Only once did she focus on her surroundings, when the landaulet hit a rut and jostled her. The countess muttered disapprovingly, the coachman turned to apologize, and Emmaline found herself glancing up to her left, where Nicolas Ransom's horse trotted easily.

Ransom stared straight ahead, oblivious to the carriage, seemingly lost in his own thoughts. Watching him, seated so grandly upon his mount, in total command of himself, Emmaline nonetheless detected a hint of the untamed about him. Suddenly she remembered the metaphor she had used with the Widow Dorn when describing her impression of London: one did not know whether the beast were tame or wild, and the uncertainty added to the excitement.

She well might have been describing one Nicolas Ransom.

On the far side of London, in a warren of alleys where the pale sun never penetrated even when it shone, Nicolas Ransom was the subject of other speculation.

"How much does Ransom know?" asked the first, a swarthy Spaniard with a thin mustache, which emphasized the cruelty in his mouth. His attire proclaimed him to be a seaman, as did the location near the docks where he stood, yet his hands were smooth and unblemished, his speech decidedly educated. His gaze darted back and forth through the alley, never once looking at the hackney by which he lingered. So that the burly cabman could not hear, the Spaniard spoke from the side of his mouth, aiming his words like small darts for the ears inside the carriage alone.

"Ransom's awareness has not been determined," replied the other. Safely hidden, the cultured voice still held restraint, as if finding the very act of speaking to the Spaniard repugnant. Repugnant but necessary.

"You assured me we are safe," the Spaniard said sharply, only a hint of accent in his words. "I have waited too long to make foolish mistakes now."

After a long pause, the voice from the hackney spoke again, coldly. "I have served you well ere now, Guillermo, and you have no chance of getting close to Ransom without me. So, pray, do not use such a vexatious tone. We both have the same end in mind. I shall be cautious beyond reproach."

The Spaniard's lips twitched. "For the moment, we must proceed according to your plan. But if I suspect for one moment that your plan will fail, I shall be forced to take my own measures."

"Your measures are undoubtedly too disgusting to imagine," the voice in the carriage muttered. "Just look at you, in those filthy, reeking clothes."

"This is the difference between us, my friend," Guillermo said softly, dangerously. "I am quite willing to disguise myself, to hide where Nicolas would never think to look for me, if it means I may wreak my havoc on the pig. You think too much of your own comfort. Now, give me the purse I have entrusted to you, and pray for your own sake that you have not dipped into the cache yourself."

The Spaniard heard a muttering, which well could have been a curse, then a leather purse was flung at his feet. Before the payment hit the cobbles, an unseen hand rapped on the hackney roof, the cabman cracked his whip, and the vehicle began rolling through the narrow alley.

The occupant of the hackney, indeed even the words they had exchanged, ceased to be of any importance to Guillermo once he snatched up the coins. He focused totally on the future, the attainment of his lifelong goal. The ruination of Nicolas Ransom occupied his mind to the point of obsession.

3

The Langdon town house stood proudly in a long row of tastefully elegant homes in Mayfair. Even to Emmaline's untrained eye, it seemed far the most magnificent of the lot. Of soft rose brick with stone cornices, the Georgian design extended four stories, with tall, graceful windows placed symmetrically six to a floor. The house sat slightly back from the street, with a curved drive up to the entrance. Even before the landaulet stopped rolling, the town-house doors were opened by a pair of bewigged footmen, perfect matches to the ones who handed her carefully down from the carriage. For a moment, she stood uncertainly, staring at the fan window, etched with the Langdon crest, over the entry.

For some reason, that window, perfect and gleaming from a chandelier within, awakened an awe in Emmaline as none of the other trappings of wealth had. She felt suddenly wary, as if once crossing the borders of this new land, she would never view her real world with satisfaction again.

Lord Garwin was at her side, gesturing without words, and she realized he wished her to enter. Her guardian and Lady Garwin were already inside, chirping at each other like contented birds. But, oddly, only when Nicolas Ransom appeared at the other side of her could she move.

"Miss Hazlett," he murmured, and in his tone she heard a command cushioned in an invitation. From a lesser man, such a tone might be offensive. But Emmaline needed the prod to bolster her courage,

28

and strangely, he seemed to recognize her plight. With a deep sigh, she complied.

The foyer, with a floor covered in white marble with pale-blue veining, was larger than the whole of the vicarage. A glorious crystal chandelier, sporting more candles than she used in a year, lit shimmering blue silk walls. A few moments passed before Emmaline noticed a silent maid waiting patiently before her. Emmaline stared at the girl, bewildered.

"Your bonnet and wrap, miss?"

"Oh, yes."

As she untied the ribbons, Emmaline glanced ruefully at her plain walking dress, feeling drab as a mouse. Her clothing, dreary even in the vicarage, seemed a blight in this palace of a home. Impulsively, she detached the cluster of cherries from her bonnet and pinned them at her throat. At the least, a spot of color eased her self-consciousness a bit.

". . . in the music room, Humble," the countess was saying. "And bring sherry. Unless the vicar prefers tea."

"No, no," Markham hastily assured her. "Sherry would be quite refreshing."

Curiously, the countess nodded, as if the vicar had confirmed some notion of hers. Emmaline pondered that reaction for but a moment, until they entered the music room and she near gasped.

The entire population of Bevindale could fit quite easily in the space, hung with delicate French tapestries in cream and blue, a thick Aubusson carpet of the same shades stretching the length of the room. They sat on graceful silk-covered chairs grouped around a huge fireplace, and the countess regarded her guests pleasantly.

"Well, my dear Vicar, I am most anxious to hear how your mission is faring. The alms were for pitiful little orphans, I believe?"

"Uh . . . yes, yes, indeed. The poor tykes.

Homeless and friendless, without decent meals and clothing."

The countess shook her head gravely. "Such a sad fate. Ah, here's Humble. May I pour for you, Vicar?"

"Indeed, good lady."

The elderly majordomo shuffled over, the large silver tray trembling in his hands as he set it clanking on a small table at the countess's knee. She winced and shot him a withering glance, which he blithely ignored.

"Anything more, milady?" Humble said in the exaggerated tones of the near-deaf.

"No, Humble, that will be all. Tell Cook we shall be five at dinner."

"Find a winner, milady?"

"No, Humble, *five at dinner.*"

"Very good, milady."

With an exasperated groan, the countess poured from a cut-glass decanter. "I vow, I should have put that man out to pasture a decade ago. Miss Hazlett?"

Before Emmaline could rise, Cecil bounded to his feet, plucking the glass from his grandmother's hand and offering it to Emmaline with an endearing shyness.

"Thank you, Lord Garwin," Emmaline murmured.

"My pleasure, Miss Hazlett," he answered fervently.

She had rarely tasted wine before and held the stemmed glass uncertainly, watching the others. Cecil regarded her with lapdog eyes, the countess beamed with satisfaction, and Nicolas' features were unreadable. Yet Emmaline detected a glint of amusement in his dark eyes and wondered if he, above all, knew how ill she fitted in this room.

He sat lazily, one booted foot resting on the opposite knee. His black tousled hair gleamed in the candlelight, and even so casually posed, he radiated self-assurance and power. In contrast, she felt alien and inept in this setting. Smiling, he tilted his glass toward her, as if divining her thoughts, as if inviting her to borrow from his strength. Emmaline blinked in confusion and looked away.

How was it possible that a man with whom she had exchanged barely five words could read her so well? Men she had known for years—notably her guardian and Will Cooper, the sheep farmer—had no notion of what she was thinking. And no interest either. Yet, for some reason she felt that to Nicolas she was as plain as ink on paper. And she was not certain she liked the idea.

"I believe a toast is in order," the countess said when all the glasses were filled. "To the great good chance that brought you to our home."

Nicolas laughed, a hearty, melodic sound, and for a horrifying moment Emmaline thought he had seen through her guardian's deception. But the countess dismissed her nephew with good humor.

"Nicolas does not believe in chance."

"On the contrary, Auntie. Many is the time I have placed a wager on chance. Especially when the outcome is all but a foregone conclusion."

It was the first time Emmaline had truly heard his voice in more than two words. The sound of it surrounded her in a rich warmth.

"Indeed." There was an unmistakable challenge in the countess's reply. " 'Tis a trait, I vow, that comes from my side of the family. For I too enjoy a wager now and again. We shall have to choose a sporting event and see who comes up the winner. Have you something in mind, nephew dear?"

Nicolas grinned. "Mayhap I do. Might you be so willing as to put up fifty pounds?"

"Done," the countess agreed with a gleam in her eye. "I always wager in the affirmative, of course."

"Then I shall take the negative, for I believe you will undoubtedly misread the heart of your horse. We are speaking of a horse race, are we not?"

The countess beamed. "I believe we are. And I

shall gladly take your fifty pounds when my horse crosses the finish line."

"Not as gladly as I shall collect the same amount when the said horse balks coming out of the start."

Emmaline peered at them, perplexed. There was an undercurrent of which she had no understanding, as if they uttered familiar words that changed meaning when emerging from their mouths.

"Then, will you drink to chance, Nicolas?"

"By all means, Auntie."

They all raised their glasses and Emmaline took a tentative sip. The sherry was potent, with a pleasant nutty flavor and a warmth that glowed down her throat.

The vicar had drained his portion, and directly the glass left his lips, the countess splashed more sherry to the rim.

"I trust we did not distress you with our talk of wagering, Vicar."

"Oh, no," Markham said hastily, pausing to fish for the correct explanation. "Only in excess is wagering a mistake. Why, even in our parish, the women offer knitted goods as prizes at the annual fair. A penny a chance, and all goes for the welfare of the orphans."

Emmaline stared at him in amazement. For a completely unimaginative man, her guardian was weaving an astounding tale. And, she noted grimly, gently steering the topic of conversation to his purposes.

"Ah, yes, the pitiful orphans," the countess said obligingly. "I am quite moved by your devotion to them."

By now Markham had tossed the third sherry down his throat, and two spots of color appeared high on his cheeks.

" 'Tis my Christian duty," he murmured piously. "One which I take very seriously. Why, my own ward here would be among their dreadful number, had I not in charity taken her into my home."

Emmaline's fingers tightened around the delicate crystal stem until she feared she would break the glass. It was one thing for him to try to fleece these good people of a "donation" to the poor, but quite another to use her as the shears!

"I doubt," she said quietly, pinioning him with her sharp gaze, "that Lady Garwin is interested in such talk."

"On the contrary, my dear. I am most decidedly interested. And may I offer my sympathies on the demise of your parents? If the subject is not exceedingly painful, may I ask how it happened?"

The countess spoke so sincerely, Emmaline in good grace could not deny a response. But before she could offer a reply, her guardian's gaze flickered a warning.

" 'Twas most distressing," he said quickly, what passed for his charm flowing once again. "Mr. Hazlett found his calling in ministering to heathens in India. Six years ago he sent Emmaline back to England to be schooled as a proper young lady at Miss Calder's Academy. As the vicar of Mr. Hazlett's home village, I was most happy to offer his only daughter my hospitality during holidays."

Only the very schooling of which he spoke prevented Emmaline from forgetting her manners and sniffing in disdain.

"And then . . ." Markham's voice dropped dramatically. "Three months after she arrived, her parents were taken with a virulent fever. Imagine, if you will, her total helplessness. No relatives to take her in, and no one to be concerned with her welfare. My heart was moved. As her guardian in England, I took full responsibility for her. She was entirely alone, without a home, without a prospect in the world."

Emmaline regarded him, aghast. Her cheeks flamed with humiliation. And anger. How dare he cheapen her parents' memory with such pathos!

"Oh, you poor child," Cecil blurted, and for the

first time Emmaline was less taken with his gentleness.

She wanted no one's pity; somehow such misplaced emotion diminished the tiny spot still raw in her heart. She knew without question that her parents would agree with her, that they would focus with pride upon the inner fortitude that had carried her through difficult times. So furious was she with the vicar's manipulations, she nearly jumped up, hot accusations trembling on her lips, ready to denouce the vicar for the charlatan he was.

And then she happened to glance at Nicolas. There was cold outrage in his gaze as he regarded Markham, and his mouth curved in ill-hidden disgust. The confirmation of her feelings kept Emmaline in her chair. At least one of them was not taken in by the shameless vicar. With a shaking hand, she took a bolder sip of her sherry, welcoming the burning in her throat as her unspoken words dissolved.

"And you have done quite well by her, I am certain," the countess praised.

A hint of irony tinged her words, Emmaline thought, yet her eyes were innocent. Emmaline stared fixedly at the carpet.

"And now that her schooling is done," Markham continued smugly, "I have succeeded in finding a good match for her."

Startled, the countess asked sharply, "Then she is betrothed?"

Fidgeting at her tone, the vicar mumbled, "Not quite. But I have high expectations that she will be before the summer is out."

Emmaline, her anger successfully controlled for the moment, noticed in puzzlement that the countess all but collapsed in relief. She found herself liking the woman immensely, but she certainly was on the far side of understanding her. Of what interest could the fact of a "pitiful orphan's" near-betrothal be to a countess?

As Emmaline watched, the countess's face lit even as her eyes narrowed with concentration. Abruptly, she addressed Emmaline. "Do you play the pianoforte, my dear?"

Emmaline laughed without mirth. "In a manner of speaking. I fear I am not accomplished."

"'Tis your modesty speaking," the countess insisted heartily. "Do favor Cecil and Nicolas with your repertoire. I must speak to the vicar about the particulars of my donation."

The two men rose and escorted her to the instrument at the far end of the music room. Emmaline, a bit unsteady, realized that the sherry had gone to her head. To give herself time to compose herself, she stretched her fingers nervously, certain that her small talent would desert her and show her to be the fool she felt. Still, any activity that would divert their thoughts from the vicar's telling of her history was one she would grasp. She sat, straight-backed on the stool, and placed her hands delicately upon the keys.

4

While Cecil hovered next to the charming Miss Hazlett at the pianoforte, Nicolas preferred a different perspective. He chose a sturdy settee some distance away and lowered himself into it.

Sipping his third sherry, wishing it were brandy, he regarded the young woman. Her fingers moved tentatively over the keys into a light country air, gaining precision as the tune progressed. At the same time, the slight furrowing of her brow smoothed. Yet she was not at ease. Her dark lashes lowered as she concentrated on the musical pattern.

Emmaline Hazlett had proved somewhat of a surprise to Nicolas. She was far less demure than her outward demeanor suggested. At first glance, he had tagged her as a shy, modest country lass, perhaps overwhelmed by the noise and traffic of London. Her gaze was ofttimes downcast, leading him to assume a gentle passivity in her. His interest heightened when he realized that he had erred in his judgment. The downcast gaze was merely a shield, attempting to hide her internal fire. It was precisely this revelation that prompted Nicolas to make the cryptic wager with his aunt. The surprising Miss Hazlett would not suffer passively the manipulations of even so great an expert as Lady Minerva.

The first time he had witnessed evidence of Emmaline's burning spirit, Nicolas had been intrigued. Her entire appearance transformed, almost glowing, as if the very sun had chosen to favor her with a special beam. He saw that her eyes were blue, but clouded gray; perhaps by the anger inside her, perhaps by the rather dull dress she wore. Uncharacteristically, Nicolas let his mind drift to fancy, wondering if those eyes would take on the clear, bright azure of a midsummer afternoon were she to surround herself with the shades of flowers and sunshine. Like a gentle day in July, she required soft color to set off her own beauty.

Nicolas realized that she was indeed a beauty. Or could be, with her hair, a dark spun-gold, loosed from tight, confining lines. And to what heights could she rise with a decent dressmaker to clothe her in elegant gowns, and with an impassioned husband to tuck primroses in her hair and bring a blush to her creamy cheeks?

Somehow, he could not credit Cecil in that position. Startled by his own thoughts, Nicolas shifted in his seat.

Emmaline had finished the lively air, to which Cecil applauded extravagantly, yet she virtually ignored his excess to peer at Nicolas. He raised his glass in a salute and was favored with a tiny smile, which caused him to catch his breath. She was so lovely when the pain and anger disappeared from her expression, even briefly. What an injustice that she must contend with such disagreeable inner turmoil! Nicolas found himself outraged; whatever ignited that sore wrath in her affronted nature itself.

Or perhaps, he pondered with a narrowed glance at her guardian, it was a case of *who*ever.

"Oh, Miss Hazlett," Cecil enthused, "do play another. You are quite accomplished, indeed. Do you not agree, Grandmama? Grandmama? I say, do you not agree?"

Across the room, the countess paused in her deep discussion with the vicar. "I beg your pardon, Cecil?" she murmured with barely concealed annoyance at the interruption.

"Is Miss Hazlett not marvelously accomplished, Grandmama?"

"Oh, yes. Yes, indeed. The vicar and I are so enjoying our tête-à-tête. You young people go on with your musicale and do not pay us mind."

The countess smiled benevolently at Emmaline until she turned back to the keys. But Nicolas caught the glare his great-aunt then cast upon Cecil, an unspoken message that told the young man she was scheming on his behalf and not to disturb her maneuvering. Nicolas hid a wry smile, far more captivated by this game than he had thought possible.

"I felt it my duty," the vicar said loudly, "to see that Emmaline learned the music of continental composers. She can play from the repertoire of Herr Mozart and Herr van Beethoven, you know. I keep up with fine music, for I find it edifies me immensely. Play, Emmaline." Without so much as a glance at his ward, Markham waved his hand imperiously, a gesture he tried to copy from his new friend the countess, with dismal results.

Nicolas thought the vicar more resembled a fishmonger flapping his wares and fought to suppress a sneer of disgust. He looked up to find Emmaline regarding him.

A glance paused between them; a fleeting contact, but in it, Nicolas felt a bond of taut unity that astounded him. "I despise my guardian as much as you do," her eyes said. "His pathetic aggrandizement is as repulsive to me as to you." And another tone colored her response: she nearly begged forgiveness with one brief glance, as if she wished Nicolas to disassociate her from the vicar and his boorish behavior.

Ransom found himself longing to convey his empathy for her by way of one meaningful look. But he was so long practiced in concealing his deepest thoughts, he had no skill upon which to draw. He noted her disappointment, even opened his mouth to speak what he could not reveal by glance alone. But before he could act, the moment passed.

Emmaline turned her attention once again to the keyboard.

Nicolas was profoundly disturbed, and more by his inability to impart his support or by his desire to do so, he could not decide. This reaction was entirely new to him, and upset his ordered existence. His personal life was so entangled by intrigues not of his own making, he preferred to consign the people he encountered to specific compartments: this one for business contacts, for purposes of commercial success; this one for social acquaintances, to be dealt with politely and good-naturedly. Indeed, even attractive young women had their own divisions: in one category were the marriage-minded daughters of the *haut ton*, with whom to distract himself from his problems by dancing at Almack's and indulging their flirtatious silliness; in the other were more sophisticated women with whom to release his pent-up passion.

The latest figure in that compartment flitted into his mind. With a twinge of guilt, Nicolas knew he must own that he had handled the situation badly. Verity, whose name was near a mockery, for she had more wiles than a vixen, had been in high dudgeon when he called a halt to their assignations. She had proved too much a drain with her outrageous demands; still, he might have controlled his anger and broken with her more diplomatically. Even so, Nicolas had managed similar situations before and knew the rules of disentanglement.

But now, this dilemma with Miss Emmaline Hazlett fit in neither camp he assigned to women. She rendered him uneasy, for he must deal with her on a level that had no preordained rules, and therefore he could not dismiss her casually.

Suddenly the strain of the past weeks, the fatigue he had successfully held at bay for so long, threatened to overtake him. He wiped his mind clean of his roiling thoughts and concentrated on the music. Slowly, a smile inched across his face.

Emmaline had chosen a selection translated for the pianoforte from Beethoven's Symphony in E flat major, popularly known as the Eroica. Wide-held rumor had it that the composer originally dedicated the work to "honor the memory of a great man, Bonaparte." And when the true nature of that arrogant would-be conqueror had become apparent, the dedication had been summarily withdrawn.

Nicolas was captivated by Emmaline's subtle display of irony. What more perfect piece to play at the command of Markham than this, a sly insult relating the pompous vicar to the pompous Napoleon? She played with barely restrained passion that spoke clearly of her soul's response. Nicolas' smile bloomed into a wicked grin, and when Emmaline glanced up from the keys, her eyes danced in merriment.

Abruptly, the grin faded and Nicolas rose. He strode to the small table bearing the sherry decanter, oblivious to the whisperings of the vicar and his great-aunt, and poured himself another drink. Lady Minerva caught his eye for a moment and gave him a furtive wink. Bemused, Nicolas once more returned to the source of the enchanting music.

Standing nearer to Emmaline, Nicolas watched the graceful curve of her fingers as they stroked the keys. She sat so straight upon the stool, leaning forward now and then as the emotion of the melody translated from her soul to her hands. The music surrounded Nicolas, enveloped him, a siren's song he could scarce resist. He downed the sherry in one gulp.

For Edwin Markham, intent on his own purposes, the music held no message, ironic or otherwise. Indeed, he never heard more than the first notes, so eager was he to return to the countess's discussion.

"I am quite moved," she was saying now, "by

your devotion to the disadvantaged of this world. Men like you should be rewarded in proportion to your good work."

He could scarce credit his uncanny luck. Divine intervention alone could explain the coincidence of their meeting. The Almighty had seen how hard His servant labored on earth and had chosen this means to reward His vicar at last. For the first time in his disappointing life, Markham could forgive his Maker for denying him the one desire of his heart.

"You must allow me," the countess continued, peering at him with ingenuous brown eyes, "to aid you in your endeavors. Alas, my health is frail, but my dear late husband left me well-provided. You surely deserve my help, as does your charming ward."

The vicar boldly patted her hand in understanding, his mind speeding with the possibilities.

Perhaps God had realized the injustice at last. For what purpose, divine or earthly, could there be in granting others, far less deserving, favor over himself? Daniel Hazlett, Emmaline's father, was the quintessential example, the one that had lain like a coating of dust in Markham's throat for years. A far younger man, whose studies came as easily as song to a bird, had usurped Markham and his long, debilitating bout with the books. He, Edwin, should have been tapped for future greatness within the Church, not Hazlett. He, Edwin, should have been groomed for the post here in London, with an educated congregation who could appreciate his scholarly interpretation of Divine Will and his inspired leadership.

But it was not to be. He had been banished to Bevindale, to a dull, mean little life, expected to serve dull, mean little villagers. And then Hazlett had the cheek, the unmitigated gall, to throw away blithely the chance Markham would have died for, the chance to climb the ecclesiastical ladder to his deserved rung. Hazlett rejected the grand opportunity and had become a lowly missionary in India. Markham did not like to judge others, but Hazlett's cavalier disregard seemed to him a slap in the face of the Church elders.

In Markham's mind, it was insult of the highest order when Hazlett asked him to be guardian to his daughter. And was it not just like the ungrateful man once again to leave Markham in the lurch, exposing himself and Mary Hazlett to filthy diseases, dying in a foreign hellhole?

The thought of Mary Carnes Hazlett always provoked a deep pang in Edwin's heart. She would be alive today if only she had acknowledged the ardent love Edwin had borne for her. Secretly, Markham had known Mary was the missing ingredient, the final reason he had been passed over by the Church hierarchy. With her behind him, with her social status to boost him, he could have begun the climb and reached heights only imagined. But no. Hazlett had seduced her with his high-flying spiel about bringing the gospel to the heathens. Now she was lost to him forever.

"Tell me something," the countess said casually, "of your ward's background."

Markham grimaced. He saw none of his beloved Mary in Emmaline. She was Hazlett's daughter through and through, from her pale hair and insolent eyes to her inborn disrespect and offensive ingratitude. As a good Christian, he could not in conscience turn her away from his door. And if he needed the moneys settled upon her to repair the vicarage and provide a bit of comfort in his old age, it was far less than Daniel Hazlett owed him for murdering Edwin's woman and his ambition.

"Her father was, I am sorry to say, of little account," he began stiffly. Then his expression mellowed. "But her mother was a fine woman, a lady by both demeanor and title. Mary was the only child of Sir Theobald Carnes of Tewsmore, Kent, and Lady Althea Randolph, daughter of the Earl of

Rainston. Both grandparents have passed on to their rewards. Sad to say, Mary wed far beneath her."

"Hmm." The countess's shrewd eyes regarded him intently. "Vicar, I marvel that we have become such dear friends in so short a time. And I wonder if I may presume upon that friendship to ask a great favor of you."

"Anything, milady," he answered fervently.

"As I have said, my health is declining."

The countess appeared entirely robust to the vicar, but he would not quibble.

"And in my declining health, I do not get out as oft as I like. I need a companion, someone of education and breeding, to stay with me. To read the light novels we ladies are so fond of, to soothe me with tunes upon the pianoforte. I wonder if you would consider allowing me to choose your ward for the position."

Taken aback, Markham had no immediate reply.

"Oh, I know," the countess said, leaning forward beseechingly, "how sorely you will miss her. And I am prepared to compensate you for so great a loss. Let us say, fifteen pounds a month. For your charity, of course."

Speechless, the vicar gaped. One hundred eighty pounds a year! He could retire and never be forced to listen to another tale of woe from sheepherders again.

"Oh, why be penurious?" the countess asked with that casual, regal wave the vicar found so appealing. "Let us say twenty pounds a month and seal the bargain immediately."

The words near tripping his tongue in his eagerness to agree, Markham nodded. "I . . . accept your very generous offer, dear Countess."

"You have made me so happy," Lady Minerva murmured, casting him a sly glance. "I trust Emmaline's near betrothal will not be an obstacle."

The vicar had scarcely remembered Will Cooper,

and the mention of his existence brought Markham up short. Aye, the sheep farmer might well be a problem. Markham had accepted ten pounds in advance as the prospective bridegroom's gift. Cooper was stolid and stubborn and took a handshake bargain none too lightly. But the vicar's spirits buoyed. He would explain that Emmaline's flightiness would prove a poor quality in a wife at any rate. He would even be generous with the man, offering him back his ten pounds and a bonus of five more for his trouble. With the countess's largess near at his disposal, he could afford generosity at last.

"There is no obstacle to your happiness, my dear countess," Markham intoned. "In fact, Emmaline may begin as your companion this very night."

"Splendid," the countess said heartily.

Humble arrived silently and nearly knocked the vicar from his chair with his loud announcement that dinner was served. Then, as the final notes of the Eroica faded, Lady Minerva clapped her plump hands together.

"Nicolas, Cecil, and our charming Miss Hazlett, let us go in to dinner. I have the most marvelous announcement to make to you all."

5

Lady Minerva deemed the vicar should escort her into the dining room. Cecil offered his arm to Emmaline, who placed a trembling hand lightly on his, aware of Nicolas following them closely.

As Cecil chattered, oblivious to her discomfort, Emmaline tried valiantly to murmur the correct responses. But her mind was troubled. She had a deep foreboding that the countess had found out her guardian's scheme, for what other "marvelous announcement" could she make? Even a dull-witted person could scarce fail to perceive the vicar's treachery after a short conversation with him. And Lady Minerva, Emmaline had no doubt, was sharp as a cobbler's tack.

Emmaline shivered. It was mortification enough that Markham had uttered the first lie; the heavens only knew how garishly he had embroidered the tale by now. And after they had taken advantage of the Garwins' hospitality, she dreaded all the more the certain humiliation—perhaps criminal prosecution!—that discovery would bring.

Her mind sped through an assortment of apologies, none of which seemed remotely adequate. She briefly considered approximating an attack of the vapors, to thwart the "announcement." But before she could act upon her desperation, Emmaline found herself seated next to Cecil, at a polished mahogany table gleaming with porcelain and crystal.

Cecil had not ceased talking from the moment they had left the music room, yet Emmaline retained naught of his soliloquy. Yet, when Nicolas spoke, she heard every soft word.

"The day has stretched overlong for you, Miss Hazlett," he murmured. "Has it not?"

Emmaline suppressed a sigh. "Indeed it has."

"The meal will refresh you. My aunt employs one of the finest cooks in all London."

Her throat felt too constricted to allow a morsel to pass, but she nodded politely. "I am certain I shall always remember the experience of this meal."

If Nicolas detected the pale specter of irony in her reply, he gave no sign. Yet, before speaking again, he leaned forward. "I have every confidence," he said softly, "that you will find the evening ending on a pleasant note. That is, should you now relax yourself from the vexations of travel."

There was nothing in his tone or manner to suggest he implied any meaning but the actual statement of fact. Yet, as he sat down across the table from her, Emmaline noted that his gaze never left her and that he smiled encouragingly. Perhaps in Nicolas Ransom she had found an ally who would recommend mercy for her guardian's deceit.

As Emmaline pondered thus, the footmen began serving a terrine of spring leeks, and Humble produced a decanted white burgundy.

The countess motioned to him. "Fetch our best vintage of champagne for dessert, Humble. Ice it well, for I predict we shall have a toast when I make my announcement." She winked at Nicolas and he turned his attention to her and chuckled.

"Auntie, are you still thinking about the wager we made? Do you dare toast your filly's victory before the race has been run?"

Cecil leaned forward eagerly. "I am willing to wager that Grandmama's surprise is the reason she has called for champagne."

The countess lifted her brows in wry amusement. "How very clever of you, Cecil."

"Do tell us now, Grandmama. You know how I love surprises."

"All in good time, my boy. Let us enjoy our meal first. And as for my filly, Nicolas, she will run the race splendidly, mark my words. For tonight, however, I shall be content to savor my uncanny good luck in meeting the vicar and his ward. Such serendipity deserves no less."

Although her words were mild, even complimentary, Emmaline detected a keen light in Lady Minerva's eyes and a quirk to her mouth that left the girl still uneasy. She scarcely tasted the courses that followed—not the tender salmon in dill sauce, nor the roasted joint of lamb, nor the minted peas, nor any other morsel that met her lips. She felt strangely split in two: one part of her responded politely to the table conversation, while another ticked off the moments until Markham's mask should be torn off, revealing the scoundrel he was. When a magnificent chocolate gâteau arrived along with the champagne, Emmaline clutched the folds of her napkin lest her trembling fingers betray her anxiety.

After slicing regally through the chocolate cake, Lady Minerva sampled the wine and a beatific smile lit her broad face.

"Ah, each time I am tempted to take umbrage with the French for foisting that scurrilous Bonaparte upon the world, I have only to sip champagne, and the milk of forgiveness flows through me."

Emmaline merely prayed that her mercy would extend to those at her table.

"Now. For my announcement." She peered at Emmaline intently. "It concerns you, my dear."

Emmaline blanched and felt suddenly faint. But she held her head straight and returned the countess's direct gaze. She might accept her guilt by association, but she would not relinquish her dignity by groveling.

"How is that, my lady?"

Savoring the moment, the countess smiled. "I have requested that you stay on in London with me, as my companion. Your guardian has graciously consented. We will have your things sent up from Bevindale and you will begin in the position this very night."

Despite her strict training at the hands of Miss Calder, Emmaline stared openmouthed.

Cecil jumped up and clapped his hands together. "How perfectly splendid! Oh, indeed, Grandmama, this is a grand surprise. London will welcome Miss Hazlett with open arms. She will be the belle of the *haut ton*. It shall be my honor to escort her to balls and routs and promenades in the park and—"

"Control yourself, Cecil," Lady Minerva said dryly. "I have not announced the Second Coming."

Flustered, Cecil raised his fluted glass. "Forgive me, I am quite overwhelmed with the marvelous news. I propose a toast to the charming Miss Hazlett. The first, I am certain, of many that will be offered to her in the next months."

Nicolas rose and Markham reluctantly followed, visibly annoyed to be cast abruptly into a lesser role. Emmaline gazed from one to another, speechless, allowing the astounding proclamation to sink into her mind. To stay in London, a city that pulsed to her own heartbeat! To escape the unpalatable choice of life with the vicar or life with the sheep farmer! To be a breath away from destruction and then offered paradise!

She was overjoyed, weak with relief. And yet, a tiny nagging thought reminded her that, once again, her fate had been decided for her. It was yet another household to which she had been passed, albeit a golden one.

"Perhaps," Nicolas was saying quietly, "Miss Hazlett should be asked whether or not she desires such a position."

Emmaline glanced up at him and her heart

melted with gratitude and another, richer emotion for which she had no name. She smiled then and found her voice. "Thank you, sir. I shall be pleased to accept."

The next fortnight passed in a dizzying whirl. Emmaline delighted in the accommodations chosen for her, not in the servants' quarters but in the guest wing. The airy room faced eastward, and on fair days the morning light emphasized the elegance of the pink marble mantelpiece, the embroidered blush silk counterpane, and the tiny pink rosebuds on cream-colored wall covering. To meet her personal needs, an abigail was assigned in the form of a cheery young girl named Floss. And before Emmaline scarce settled in, a complex social calendar was being drawn up by Lady Minerva herself, much as Wellington might have plotted his campaign against Bonaparte.

On a rainy afternoon, as she tried to concentrate on a game of whist, Emmaline listened to the countess and Cecil deciding upon the ball at which Emmaline would enter society.

"If only Madame Henriette would use her needle faster," she grumbled, "we might choose Lady Jersey's, Friday next."

"But, Grandmama," Cecil protested, "I have promised Rosetta Cavendish a marvelous surprise at her ball, two nights from then."

Lady Minerva narrowed her eyes. "You did not specify the nature of that surprise, I pray."

"Certainly not. But she has been hinting that she is wounded by my absence from her social events of late. I felt I must soothe her in some manner. She is a dear friend, Grandmama, and her balls are ever so much more entertaining than that of any other hostess in London. 'Twould be an insult to give Lady Jersey the coup of the Season."

"Hmm." The countess paused to consider. "Mayhap you are not the addle-pate I supposed."

Failing to conceal his affronted pout, Cecil sniffed, a vulgarity the countess ignored. "The question becomes academic unless Madame Henriette can deliver the gowns."

At last Emmaline spoke up quietly. "I fear that 'tis my fault your patience is taxed, Lady Minerva, since you so kindly insist on my presence at this ball. I regret that I had not the wardrobe for balls and such to bring up from Bevindale."

"Scarce surprising," the countess replied crustily, slapping down a card. "Undoubtedly that guardian of yours would not know a ball gown from a horse blanket."

Emmaline had noted to her amusement that once the vicar had departed to Bevindale, the countess wasted none of her considerable goodwill upon him. Emmaline herself never spoke against the man, but she ofttimes found herself hiding a smile at Lady Minerva's caustic remarks concerning him.

"Rosetta Cavendish shall be the lucky hostess, then," the countess declared.

Cecil, watching the game from over Emmaline's shoulder, applauded.

To her secret surprise, Emmaline had discovered that she was to be as much a companion to Cecil as to Lady Minerva. At first, the realization left Emmaline slightly uneasy. She was unaccustomed to casual contact with gentlemen and became unnerved when he hung on every word as she read aloud from Mrs. Harvey's novels or leaned eagerly on the pianoforte as she played light tunes. From the conversations he had with his grandmother, she determined that he had all but abandoned his social obligations until the time that Emmaline and Lady Minerva should accompany him. Certainly she could go nowhere without the proper dress. Although four seamstresses had worked furiously the first day of her employment fashioning daytime gowns appropriate for a countess's companion, the more elaborate evening apparel required far longer preparation.

"Henriette is undoubtedly the most competent of modistes. I pray that she is also quick," Lady Minerva grumbled as she reshuffled the cards. " 'Tis most difficult for me to keep a secret from my friends. They all peck at me to know why I am in virtual seclusion. I am anxious to get out and about."

Emmaline glanced up contritely. "Oh, Lady Minerva, surely your health will permit you to attend without me. I dread being the cause of your restriction."

"Do not fret, my dear," she replied, patting Emmaline's hand. "Your come-out shall be well worth the wait."

Emmaline smiled, yet a thread of puzzlement remained. The countess had implied that the existence of her new companion was a secret from her friends. Try as she might, Emmaline could fathom no reason for concealing the fact. And the social life of the entire household was near at a standstill, awaiting her wardrobe. Emmaline did not comprehend all, but she would not protest such a pleasant opportunity for the mere purpose of her own curiosity.

Emmaline handily won the game and Lady Minerva tossed down her cards.

"Well done, my girl . . ." She frowned as the clock struck five times. "Nicolas has not returned. I wonder if he shall be dining with us tonight."

Cecil shook his head. "I believe he mentioned an engagement this evening."

Concealing her disappointment, Emmaline said nothing as she carefully gathered the cards.

"That nephew of mine," the countess muttered. But Emmaline noted that her frown creased more in concern than annoyance. "I believe I shall rest awhile and take tea in my room. Thank you for a rousing game, Emmaline." She rose in her naturally regal manner, gliding across the music room as grandly as a ship setting sail.

Cecil also begged to be excused to dress for dinner, a task that required a span of time longer than the nine-course meal itself.

Emmaline was left alone with her thoughts, which turned, as they had increasingly of late, to Nicolas.

He was the one person whose life seemed the least affected by her presence. Since the day she had arrived, she had seen him infrequently, much to her disappointment. Nicolas was the leveling influence in the household. When Cecil's exuberance grew tiresome, it was Nicolas who tempered the young man's extravagant compliments and plans. Lady Minerva became restless and snappish if more than half a day passed without a brief visit to her rooms by her great-nephew. His arrival seemed to reassure the countess that her domain was safe and happy.

For Emmaline, Nicolas was the reference point around which her day revolved, yet she saw him so rarely. Since Lady Minerva insisted that Emmaline should become accustomed to the social schedule she would eventually keep, they stayed up long into the night adding to Emmaline's education: playing whist, reading gossip sheets, practicing the latest dances with Cecil, and acquainting her with the most dazzling names of the *ton*. Nicolas breakfasted long before she arose in the late morning, and then attended to his business in the City or closeted himself in the library for the day. Occasionally, he would join them for dinner, but often he disappeared in the evening, leaving Emmaline awash with curiosity and not a little regret.

An air of mystery wafted about Nicolas. Casual conversation brought forth few personal details about him, and the one time Emmaline offhandedly questioned Lady Minerva about his background, the countess had been uncharacteristically closemouthed, changing the subject none too smoothly. Naturally, the lack of information served to intrigue Emmaline all the more.

Along with her fascination, Emmaline found true pleasure simply in being with Nicolas, and that fact in itself was a puzzlement to her. He set her at ease, and yet she prickled in a strange but exciting manner when he was near. His conversation was light and amusing, and yet an undertone always colored his words so she was never quite certain she understood the full import of his speech. Again and again she was reminded of her image of the untamed: thrilling and a bit unsettling, and more alluring for the combination.

Sighing, Emmaline finally came out of her reverie. The night ahead promised to disappoint, like champagne, which she had come to savor, gone flat. She had only the sorrow to anticipate, another chance to encounter Nicolas Ransom.

Perhaps, she mused as a gleam lit her azure eyes, it was possible to better the odds of chance. Somewhat taken aback at her bold thoughts, Emmaline nonetheless decided to do a bit of planning of her own.

6

The next morning, Floss roused Emmaline as instructed, just as a pearly light bathed the city. The maid was scarcely awake herself and could not imagine why one who was afforded the luxury of lolling abed until near noon would choose to arise at such an hour. Nonetheless, she assisted Emmaline in her toilette, brushing her long golden hair and arranging it in a smooth coil at the back of her head.

"A fringe is all the fashion, Miss Em," Floss murmured, fighting a yawn. "I could snip a bit 'ere and there . . ."

Emmaline's plan had required all of her boldness. She had none left for new hair arrangements. "I am considering the notion," she demurred. "But, for now, please help me into my clothing."

Floss slipped a simple but elegant day dress of pale-rose jaconet over Emmaline's head and, before Emmaline could protest, added a splash of violet water behind her ears.

"Thank you, Floss," Emmaline said breathlessly. "You may go now."

The early hour had dimmed the abigail's curiosity. She left without further comment, and Emmaline paused but a moment at the pier glass before rushing down to the morning room.

Nicolas was standing beside the remains of his breakfast, preparing to leave. To Emmaline's consternation, her heart leapt at the very sight of him, tall and handsome in his raven kerseymere coat and creamy white stock. He glanced at her with a startled expression.

"Miss Hazlett. You have awakened so early. My aunt is not ill, is she?"

"She is still sleeping," Emmaline hastened to assure him. "I came down . . ."

In sudden dismay, Emmaline realized she was at a loss to explain her unusual appearance at this hour. Her bold plan had proceeded no further than this moment, when she would see Nicolas and bask in his presence. Like a child caught stealing sweets, she clasped her hands behind her back and stumbled over her words.

"I . . . I could not sleep. The sun through my window . . ."

Nicolas smiled. "Had I known you were coming down, I should have delayed to breakfast with you. Unfortunately, my business awaits even now. I must go, but I am anxious to hear how you are enjoying your position. I am dining at home tonight. This evening we shall have a chat."

Composing herself, Emmaline inclined her head. "Indeed. I shall look forward to that."

As he bowed slightly to her and departed, Emmaline felt a flush spreading over her face. How childish, she berated herself. She had not the mind for intrigue, and she was sore afraid she had made quite the fool of herself. What was it about Nicolas Ransom that caused her normal good sense to evaporate like dew in the morning sun?

Throughout the remainder of the morning, Emmaline fretted. What must he think of her? But when Madame Henriette arrived in the afternoon, her acute uneasiness was soon overwhelmed by the task at hand.

"Do stand still, Emmaline," the countess commanded. "Now, Henriette, let us see the deeper blue. I do believe that shade is quite the mode, is it not?"

The modiste and her three assistants hurried to drape Emmaline in a near-finished gown of silk, then stood back as the dressmaker clapped her hands in approval.

"Ah, *oui*, just so. And may I compliment Madame la Comtesse on her clever eye and excellent taste?"

The countess nodded and favored Madame Henriette with a satisfied smile. "Indeed. A simple design suits that particular fabric. Mayhap a pattern of seed pearls should decorate the décolletage and hem."

"Just so, Madame la Comtesse. Just so."

"Now let us see the pea-green sarcenet."

Lady Minerva reclined imperiously upon a cushioned chaise lounge, waving her bejeweled hands, calling out orders, reminding Emmaline of an Oriental queen directing her subjects. And although Emmaline ostensibly was the focus of attention, she noted with some bemusement that Madame Henriette and her assistants looked to the countess for approval as they swirled gowns over Emmaline's head and marked the final fitting.

No fewer than a dozen different dresses had slid over her shoulders in the past hours, some given the nod of approval immediately, more dismissed with a slight frown and orders to alter. At first, Emmaline's wonder and excitement had precluded any opinions of her own. But as the time drew on, she began to shift restlessly, partly because she was growing weary of remaining standing for so long, and partly because her opinion seemed to matter not a whit.

"The pea-green needs more embroidery, I think." Lady Minerva pursed her lips, considering. "And the sleeves are far too long. Shorten them."

"Certainly, Madame la Comtesse."

The modiste was about to add the gown to the sanctioned heap when Emmaline surprised everyone, even herself, by voicing her thoughts.

"No. I do not care at all for that shade."

They all gaped at her, as if she were a statue that

had suddenly spoken. Emmaline felt the weight of their stares, but set her chin resolutely.

"But, Mademoiselle," the modiste protested mildly. "It is a quite fashionable color. Most certainly *haut ton.*"

The assistants nodded in affirmation and Lady Minerva gestured impatiently.

"Miss Hazlett has been buried in an obscure country village far too long. She cannot be expected to understand the latest fashion. Do not forget the sleeves."

Emmaline fixed her with a calm but determined gaze. "Fashion has naught to do with my opinion, Lady Minerva. I do not care for that shade."

The countess regarded her with a keen eye. "Indeed? And if I should like it, despite your objections?"

Emmaline's cheeks flamed. "Forgive me, my lady, I do not wish to appear ungrateful. 'Tis simply that this color reminds me of a soup that was served every Thursday at the vicarage, a vile concoction made of whatever vegetables were left from the past week's marketing. I could not bear to dress in such a color. Even more, I do not believe it flatters me."

Her explanation was met with complete silence. For a moment, Emmaline feared she had offended the countess, and as much regret as that thought caused her, she still could not retract her objection. At last, she detected a slight softening of Lady Minerva's expression.

"What shade would you choose instead?"

Glancing quickly at the gowns yet to be fitted, Emmaline quickly selected an apple-green satin.

"This one is quite lovely, I think."

The modiste peered at the countess and, sensing no rebuke, hurried to arrange the garment around Emmaline. After a long moment, Lady Minerva nodded.

"You are correct, Emmaline. The apple-green will

do. But I would like to see a deep fringe of Brussels lace for the sleeves and over the bodice. Does that meet with your approval?"

Emmaline dared to grin at her. "Indeed it does."

Turning to the modiste, the countess said, "Just as Miss Hazlett wishes. I obviously have underestimated her good taste. And I believe she should decide on the remaining gowns on her own."

Emmaline beamed, gratified that she had earned Lady Minerva's respect. "I am perfectly content with the rest of those chosen. How ever may I thank you, Lady Minerva?"

"Very simply, my dear. By stunning *le beau monde* with your undeniable loveliness."

Madame Henriette assured everyone that such a feat was entirely possible once she had done with her designs. Arrangements were made for delivery, and the dressmaker and her assistants departed, arms piled high with silk and satin. The moment they were out the door, Cecil knocked and was admitted to his grandmother's room.

"By Jupiter, those women were here long enough to clothe half of Mayfair," he began testily. "I have been waiting around with nothing better to do than to read the same gossip sheets ten times over. How soon will Miss Hazlett's wardrobe be completed, Grandmama? There are three balls and six routs this week alone that I shall have to miss. Should I send my regrets to many more hostesses, I shall be considered *persona non grata* throughout the entire city."

Lady Minerva grimaced. "Cecil, I shall reverse my opinion of yesterday. You are becoming quite the lackwit. Have you never heard that absence makes the heart grow fonder? Those hostesses will be wondering why Lord Garwin, once as much a fixture at these events as Grendell's orchestra, has been missing of late."

"Indeed," Cecil blurted petulantly. "They will assume that some scandal has kept me out of sight.

Well you know, Grandmama, that once the *ton* decides a fellow has been touched by scandal—"

"—he becomes all the more desirable at the most elegant events," Lady Minerva finished dryly. "Use your wit, Cecil. They will formulate all manner of reasons for your absence, none as intriguing as the truth. And when in fact you do resume your social rounds, all eyes will be upon you. In good time, when you announce—"

She halted abruptly and glanced at Emmaline, as if remembering her presence at last.

"Cecil, if you please," the countess continued wearily. "If you are so anxious to escape this house, then go to one of your clubs for a while. White's should do. By this hour, most of its patrons will have consumed enough whiskey so that naught that you say will register with them at any rate. Away with you. Go gamble away some of your inheritance and leave me in peace."

Cecil sniffed, mollified. "Very well, Grandmama. If you insist."

He bowed briefly to Emmaline, apparently still miffed that her lack of wardrobe was causing such a crisis in his life. When Lady Minerva begged to be excused to rest before dinner, Emmaline gladly retreated to her own room, summoning Floss.

"About yer 'air, Miss Em . . ." Floss began when Emmaline was seated at the dressing table.

"Floss, I beg you, do not pester," Emmaline replied distractedly. She found herself yet preoccupied by the conversation between Lady Minerva and Cecil.

The exchange had left her quite baffled. Why should the true reason for Cecil's social seclusion be more intriguing than any fantastic suppositions the *ton* could make? The truth was entirely mundane: his grandmama's companion had no suitable evening dresses. And even Emmaline, in her limited sophistication, could imagine any number of speculations that might be made instead.

What was so fascinating about arriving at a ball with a well-attired but socially low-ranking companion?

Suddenly, a bizarre idea took root in her mind. Suppose she were the butt of a cruel joke? The idea was not farfetched. At Miss Calder's Academy for Young Ladies, there had been a few more worldly students from London, who had near unbelievable stories to tell about ladies of dubious judgment who delighted in outrageous behavior. Last Season, one society prankster had been rumored to insist upon invitations for her visiting cousin, Lord Pausentale. When she arrived at a glittering ball, howls of amusement broke forth when she revealed the true name of the guest as Lord Paws-and-Tail, and presented her lapdog bedecked in jeweled collar and satin coat.

Was it possible that Emmaline's acceptance in this household was to be mere a source for the amusement of the *ton*? She knew so little of aristocrats too easily bored with their cushioned lives. If the Garwins had taught her nothing else, she quickly had learned that their conversations contained layers of shading, tones on a scale she had never heard in Bevindale. Would she even recognize a potential cruel prank if she heard rumblings of it coming? Would she be made the jester before she even was aware of her intended role?

Groaning, she remembered that this very morning she had done a fine turn at making the fool of herself, arriving eager and tongue-tied at the breakfast table. Was Nicolas laughing at her naïveté even now? A flame of defiance licked at her soul. If indeed she were to be the butt of a jest, she would not sit demurely by. Her spirit had carried her through far more difficult times and would not desert her now.

"Floss," she said abruptly, "fetch your scissors."

The abigail cooed in excitement, but Emmaline

barely heard her. Even as wispy tendrils fell to her lap, she felt the defiant flame flicker, dampened by her doubt.

Suddenly she yearned to see Nicolas, and was absurdly grateful that he would be dining at home that evening. Although she must own that she had nothing upon which to base her feeling, her intuition told her that she could read the truth in his eyes if only she would look.

With her worry stubbornly refusing to be banished, Emmaline hurried to dress for dinner.

7

The hall clock was chiming the quarter-hour when Emmaline descended the stairs. She had forty-five minutes before Lady Minerva and Cecil would make an appearance for dinner, three-quarters of an hour in which to speak to Nicolas alone. If he were true to his habits, she would find him still in the library.

The carved doors were firmly closed, but a ribbon of light shone beneath the bottom edge. Pausing to slow her breathing, Emmaline finally knocked.

"What is it?" an irritated voice replied, and Emmaline nearly lost her nerve.

According to the tidbits she had picked up from the servants, entrance to this room was strictly forbidden when Ransom was at home. Even Lady Minerva and Cecil honored the dictum, they who seldom followed any rules whatever. But Emmaline's need to see Nicolas, to probe the truth in his eyes, induced her to seek an exception to the custom. With a trembling hand, she pushed open the doors and entered Nicolas' sanctuary.

The library was dark, masculine, a leather and book-lined cave with heavy deep-green velvet curtains closing off tall windows. A bright-burning fire on the hearth attempted to ward off any gloom or foreboding. One solitary lamp burned on Nicolas' desk, illuminating his glower and casting the remainder of the room in shadows.

"I have left strict orders not to be disturbed and . . . Emmaline!"

His stormy expression cleared, erasing the creases in his brow. He did not seem to notice that he had used her Christian name, but Emmaline was fully aware of the slip. Her courage was bolstered by the familiarity.

"I pray you will excuse my intrusion," she began hastily, approaching his desk. "But I have so little opportunity to speak to you in confidence. There are matters I do not understand, and I hoped to be enlightened by you."

Slowly, Nicolas rose, his gaze enveloping her in what felt to Emmaline like a downy embrace.

"You have changed your hair," he commented softly.

Flustered, Emmaline patted the fringe of tendrils curling gently over her forehead. " 'Twas Floss's notion. She would not cease in her persuasion until I had let her snip away."

"The style well becomes you, like a frame surrounding a portrait of loveliness."

Startled, Emmaline glanced at him, only to note that his expression reflected the same surprise at his words that she felt. She flushed to think that he found her lovely, and yet an internal glow, near to happiness, began to warm her.

Nicolas cleared his throat. "I am gratified that Grandmama has accommodated you so well. Your dress is also becoming."

Smoothing the straight lines of her lavender striped-silk dress, Emmaline nodded. "I am indeed fortunate that Lady Minerva is so generous. And that is one reason why I wished to speak to you. There are so many things I fail to understand regarding my position. I thought mayhap you might clarify—"

" 'Ere now, are we done with business, guv'nor?"

The peevish query from a voice she did not recognize caused Emmaline to start. Belatedly, she noticed a man seated in the corner of the library, shrouded in shadow. He stood, shifting restlessly, a compact man half-hidden in a slouching hat and voluminous greatcoat.

Nicolas frowned, casting a swift, appraising glance at Emmaline before speaking. "We are finished. I will speak with you in several days' time."

Shrugging, the strange man moved toward the north window. "Please yerself, guv'nor. But I'd not dally, if I was yerself. This Spaniard was on that ship, sure as roast goose on Christmas. 'E's in London, and an ill wind blows no good, me mum always said. Best you beware—"

"That will do," Nicolas muttered sharply. "Good day."

The curt dismissal seemed not to bother the man. He shrugged once more and, to Emmaline's astonishment, parted the heavy curtains, revealing not a window but a door. Throwing the bolt, he disappeared into the dusk.

Nicolas straightened the papers on his desk, avoiding her puzzled gaze. Since he had not introduced her to his caller, Emmaline assumed she was not meant to see the man. No words came to her, which proved to be just as well, for Nicolas emerged nonchalantly from behind his desk as if the curious exchange had not taken place.

"Come," he said in his usual well-modulated voice. "Let us have wine in the music room. I fear I have been neglecting you woefully. You must tell me all about your days here."

In a moment, he was beside her, his touch light on her arm. Although he smiled reassuringly as he escorted her to the music room and poured a small glass of Madeira for her, Emmaline could not fail to note the tightness around his magnificent dark eyes. It was obvious to her that Nicolas was attempting an air of normality that he did not feel.

Emmaline sat in a chair close to the fireplace, for although spring had arrived in London, the evenings still held a chill remembrance of the season past. Nicolas pulled up another chair opposite her, so close that only a brief space separated his knee from hers.

"So, tell me," he invited, leaning forward. "How may I enlighten you?"

Gazing into his warm, deep-brown eyes, Emmaline nearly forgot her questions. He looked so solid, so secure, his cravat immaculate against the sun-bronzed planes of his face. For a fleeting moment, she wondered why any questions should niggle at her, cozy in the shelter of his attention.

Abruptly, she composed herself. "I understood that I was to be a companion to Lady Minerva. And for what purpose, I pray? She may be lonely, I told myself. Yet not a day goes by that a bushel of calling cards are not left on the hall tray. Perhaps she is not well, I suspected, but no more robust woman exists in London, regardless of age."

Nicolas chuckled, but his gaze never left Emmaline's face. "My great-aunt lives in a family of men. Female companionship is attractive to her."

"So I assumed," Emmaline said, frowning slightly. "But the countess does not lack friends, she merely does not receive them, nor does she attend any of the many social occasions to which she is invited. Even Cecil—Lord Garwin, that is—has curtailed his social calendar to the point that he is becoming surly about the matter."

" 'Tis their decisions, both of them," Nicolas remarked gently.

"You are probably correct. Yet I feel that 'tis not entirely their choices in the matter. I feel that I am the cause, and I am at my wit's end to comprehend why."

Briefly, she told him of the flurry to finish her ball gowns and the quandary over the selection of the ball at which she was to enter society.

"I am not here for a London Season," she finished in bewilderment. "And yet, for all the fuss, I cannot understand why 'tis of such importance that my

wardrobe becomes the bellwether of social
functions in this house."

Regarding her carefully, Nicolas asked, "Have
you spoken to Aunt Minerva on this matter?"

"I have broached the subject. She tells me that
she is not up to attending balls and routs without
a companion to look out for her. My admiration for
the countess's pluck is such that I cannot imagine
her needing anyone to take up the gauntlet in her
cause."

Nicolas' smile faded a bit as he gazed contempla-
tively into the fire. "There are forces," he said
slowly, "against which even so formidable a person
as Aunt Minerva should need a champion."

Astonished, Emmaline stared at him. His mouth
had pulled into a grim line, and she knew in-
stinctively that she and her problem had vanished
from his thoughts for the moment. Suddenly she
remembered the strange man in the library and his
final warning: beware. Was some danger lurking
about the countess? If so, Emmaline near pitied the
rogue who would attempt to harm anyone for
whom Nicolas cared. The heat in his gaze told her
that he would defend his loved ones to the death.

And, just as astounding, she realized that she
yearned to be included in the golden circle of his
caring.

Abruptly, she reminded herself of her purpose in
seeking him out, her desire to learn the truth and
to banish her worries that she was to be the novelty
joke of the Season.

"Mr. Ransom," Emmaline said softly, " 'tis true
that I come from a remote village and am not as
worldly as I might wish. There are customs in the
ton of which I am undoubtedly naive. Yet I assure
you, sir, that I am not foolish, only uninformed. I
have grown fond of Lady Minerva in the short time
I have been here. But I would not like to think that
I am present in her household for any reason other
than to be her companion."

With deep intensity, Emmaline tried to read his reaction to her declaration. She saw a mild surprise in his expression and a flash of what she, to her pleasure, interpreted as respect. And yet there was a small rueful glint in his eyes that alarmed her. The glint quickly passed, but Emmaline felt far less secure in her position.

Nicolas leaned forward and took her hand. "Emmaline," he murmured, and on his lips her name sounded like a poem, "are you happy here?"

His hand enveloped hers so easily, his strong fingers caressing hers. Emmaline had trouble finding her voice.

"I am," she whispered finally.

"Then rest assured that I will see to it that only wonderful things happen for you. Your life may take an unexpected turn. But I promise you that 'twill be only for the best, and only on your decision."

He gave her hand a tender squeeze, and at that moment the bond between them seemed to vibrate, like the string of a harp resonating with a sweet music she felt rather than heard.

"Emmaline, do you have trust in me?"

"I do," she answered without a moment's hesitation.

"Then please erase those lines of worry from your lovely brow. We shall be friends, and when you have doubts, you must come to me for reassurance. Have we a bargain?"

"We do, Mr. Ransom."

He smiled. "You must call me Nicolas. Then I will be certain that you consider me an ally."

Emmaline returned his smile tentatively. "Very well . . . Nicolas."

Voicing his name aloud seemed entirely natural. She found herself wishing to speak it over and over, like an incantation to bring good fortune and joy. His name was still reverberating in her head when a new sound intruded.

"Nicolas, are you in here?" Lady Minerva boomed. "Ah, so you are. I feared you had forgotten your vow to join us at dinner. And Emmaline is here also. Splendid! Fetch the Madeira, Cecil. It seems these two are at least one glass beyond us. We must remedy this situation at once."

At the first echo of the countess's voice, Emmaline had snatched back her hand from Nicolas' gentle grasp. She knew her face flushed guiltily, and she took a sip of her untouched wine to gain time to compose herself. Nicolas stood and cheerfully kissed his aunt's broad cheek, and from the countess's beaming smile, Emmaline deduced that she had not witnessed the intimate moment between her companion and her great-nephew. Concealing a sigh of relief, Emmaline was able to smile a greeting at Lady Minerva.

"Nicolas," the countess said reprovingly, "you are not dressed for dinner. I pray this does not mean you do not intend to join us."

"Indeed it does not, Auntie. If you will excuse me, I shall remedy this situation and return before you have drunk your second glass."

Emmaline's gaze followed Nicolas as he left the room, his walk conveying the same strong purpose she found so appealing in his face. Try as she might, she could not pay full attention to the chatter between Cecil and Lady Minerva. Her thoughts insisted upon returning to the pleasant jolt that had run through her when Nicolas' hand had touched hers.

When at last he returned and they had gone into the dining room, Emmaline was still encompassed in a pleasant haze of remembrance that tarried through all nine, scarce-tasted courses. Not until far later in the evening, when she retired to her room, did she realize an important point.

Far from enlightening her, Nicolas had only added to her puzzlement. He had not denied that she was present in the Garwin household for a reason other than to be companion to Lady Minerva. Indeed, he had all but hinted that there was another purpose to her position here, dismissing her worries with a promise to protect her. The need for protection was ominously clear in the subtle shadings of his replies.

And exactly who was that strange man in the library, and what possible danger threatened the household?

With a rueful sigh, Emmaline finally fell asleep, realizing that Nicolas Ransom had raised far more questions in her mind than he had answered.

Far across London, the man who had seemed so strange to Emmaline was being bombarded by a fusillade of questions himself. The seedy tavern in Covent Garden was filled with a pall of smoke and boisterous voices, amplified by drink. His inquisitor had to shout questions that were better whispered.

"Did you see Ransom tonight?"

Before replying, the man, who gave his name as Lubbock, had a query of his own. "Where's my reward? You promised to pay me."

"And so I shall," Guillermo replied coolly, "when I am certain that you have something of value to sell. You saw Ransom tonight?"

"Aye, that I did."

"And he still assumes you are working for him?"

Lubbock chuckled wickedly. "I am working for 'im, guv'nor. What the gent in question don't know is, I'm also working for yerself."

His answer appeared to amuse him greatly. Lubbock guffawed to the point of choking, finally curing himself by downing a tot of gin and belching loudly.

Guillermo grimaced, repulsed by the crudeness in which Lubbock seemed to delight. "What precisely did you tell him?"

"Just what yer payin' me to tell 'im. That the Spaniard were in London. That 'e came as a seaman, so 'is real name don't show up on any passenger list. That Mr. 'Oity-toity Ransom best beware. I done good, di'nt I, guv? Ain't that worth another tot?''

Ignoring the whining request, Guillermo drummed his smooth fingers on the tabletop, ceasing his unthinking habit when he remembered how filthy the table was. He wiped his hands fastidiously on a clean handkerchief retrieved from his seaman's coat.

"Did Ransom believe you?''

"Aw, 'ow am I to know? 'E never called me a liar, so my guess is 'e did.'' Lubbock peered at the Spaniard shrewdly. "Ye seems a bright gent to me, guv'nor. So if yer aim is to best this Ransom, why tell 'im all this news? Ye went to all the trouble of passin' as a seaman on the journey over, then ye let 'im in on the trick. Meself, I'd never let the gent get wind of me plans.''

With a withering smugness, Guillermo smiled. "And that is precisely the difference between us, Lubbock. I am intelligent and you are not.''

If Lubbock took offense, he swallowed it easily with another gulp of gin.

Guillermo's instincts ran to the secretive, yet he could not resist an opportunity to explain the beauty of his plan. "You see, Lubbock, Ransom is not unintelligent himself. In time, he would have learned that choice bit of information at any rate. He has the funds to pay dearly for what he wants to know.''

The idea seemed to anger Guillermo, for his eyes narrowed to dangerous slits.

"So when he knows you have told him the truth, he comes to trust you, against his better instincts, I would wager. Then when I want to feed him a lie, he will swallow it with no hesitation.''

Scratching his head, Lubbock pondered the answer. Finally he shrugged. "If ye say so. Now, where's me payment?''

Guillermo pushed his chair back from the table.

"You were paid half in advance, and the four gins you just drank made up the remainder of your reward. Be here Tuesday next. If I have another task for you, I shall be here waiting for you."

"Aw, guv'nor," Lubbock protested. "One more tot?"

"Good evening."

"Wait." Lubbock's small eyes darted as he tried mightily to think of a way to wheedle another drink. Suddenly he grinned. "What if I'se to 'ave some information for ye?"

About to rise, Guillermo slowly sat back. "What information is that?"

"First, ye got to pay me."

To Guillermo's disgust, Lubbock sounded near the coquette. "If what you have to say is worth my time," he said evenly, "you shall be paid. Now, out with it, man."

"There's someone new in the 'ouse," Lubbock said, his eyes gleaming eagerly. "A girl, of no more'n eighteen or nineteen years. Right easy on the eyes, too. She ain't no servant. 'Er dress were too fine. Ransom called 'er Emmaline. Lovely name, don't ye think?"

Guillermo frowned, searching his memory for a relative of Ransom's with that name. None came to mind. So someone new, another potential means to cause Ransom's end, had appeared. He smiled, although to anyone watching, the expression might have looked more like a sneer.

"I doubt this information is worth a ha'penny. But since I am generous with those who serve me . . ." He flipped a half-crown on the table as he rose.

Lubbock snatched it up quickly, at the same time signaling for the blowsy barmaid to fill up another glass.

"Thank ye, guv'nor. Thank ye. Tuesday next. Lubbock done a good turn for you tonight, and 'e'll do it again."

Leaning close, Guillermo fixed him with a sharp stare. "You had better. And, Lubbock, let me tell you that if I am crossed, I am just as generous with my vengeance."

Lubbock felt a tiny stab of pain at his throat and realized that the Spaniard held an impressively large knife under his chin. His eyes widened in fear as he nodded his understanding.

"Good," the Spaniard murmured, sliding the knife into a scabbard beneath his coat. Without another word, he melted into the crowd, like a ghost disappearing into a mist.

Beads of sweat had broken on Lubbock's brow, sending dirty streaks down his face. How the gentry plotted murderously against one another was no concern of his. But for all Ransom's privilege, Lubbock would not care to be in that one's shoes while the Spaniard was in town.

8

A mere dozen steps led from the pavement to the door of Cavendish House, but Emmaline felt as if she were climbing to the heights of the Great Pyramid. Every step brought her closer to the thin air surrounding the *ton*, and who knew what they would make of her?

The night wind clutched at her. Emmaline pulled her lace shawl, draped over her head and around her shoulders, even closer. To level her nervousness, she kept her eyes trained on the broad, muscular back of Nicolas, just in front of her, escorting Lady Minerva. Drawing strength from his very presence, she sighed deeply and prepared to enter a foreign world.

"Indeed, you are quite as excited as I am, and little I blame you," Cecil babbled eagerly beside her.

Emmaline realized that her hand had tightened on his arm and that Cecil had misread her apprehension for anticipation. She glanced at him and smiled weakly, a gesture he failed to see, for his cravat was so stiff that he could not turn his head.

At that moment, the grand doors swung open and the light from a thousand candles glittered in the huge, domed vestibule. As they entered and a maidservant delicately lifted her lace shawl from her shoulders, Emmaline stared in trepidation at the slow line of guests moving into the ballroom.

The gentlemen, resplendent in fine tailoring, greeted one another heartily, their gazes all the while darting to appraise the members of the fairer sex among them. The ladies, fetchingly bedecked in a garden of hues, jewels dazzling the eye with every

73

movement, plumes fluttering atop well-coiffed heads, flirted with all and sundry.

Over her better judgment, Emmaline measured herself against them. Her dress, which had been the subject of a three-hour discussion between Madame Henriette and Lady Minerva, seemed unassuming next to the rich palette of satins. Of white silk, with a draped tunic embroidered in pale blue under the bodice and about the edges, her gown was deceivingly simple in design. Floss had proven a veritable artist in her realm, brushing Emmaline's fair hair until it shone like spun gold, then twining a rope of tiny pearls, provided by Lady Minerva, through the coils she fashioned at the back of Emmaline's head. A matching circlet lay around her neck, while pearl teardrops bobbed from her ears.

Although Emmaline had protested the loan of such valuable pieces, she knew she must own that the pearls enhanced the elegant simplicity of her attire. And she had drawn a breath of gratification at the picture she made in the pier glass, her pale complexion but complemented by her adornment.

Yet now, a dove amid tropical parrots, her confidence wavered. She felt the curious stares that followed her every step, and just when she began to feel faint from nerves, she heard Nicolas' calm, even voice.

"I always detest this waiting to be received," he said to his great-aunt. "I am reminded of the horse auction at Tattersall's, and I wonder whether my price has gone up or down since the last ball."

Lady Minerva guffawed, and despite tenseness, Emmaline laughed too. Suddenly the tight coil inside her began to unwind, for she knew that although he had spoken to the countess, never even looking at Emmaline, his droll remark was meant to put her at her ease.

They had reached the arch leading to the ballroom. A footman, without turning his head, began his stentorious announcement.

"Lady Garwin, dowager Countess of Langdon, and Mr. Nicolas Ransom. Lord Garwin, the Earl of Langdon . . ."

Lady Minerva whispered loudly in his ear and he added, ". . . Miss Emmaline Hazlett."

Emmaline, uncomfortably aware of her thumping heart, forced herself to smile as if she had not a care in the world.

"Rosetta, dear," Lady Minerva boomed, allowing her cheek to be kissed by the woman she addressed. "How lovely you look tonight. You remember my great-nephew Nicolas. And here is Cecil, who has been near gnashing his teeth in anticipation of this night . . ."

The men bowed courteously over her hand, then stood back.

The countess smiled in apparent relish of the moment. "And this is Emmaline," she announced, adding smoothly, "my houseguest for the Season."

Near tripping in her astonishment, Emmaline glanced up to stare at Lady Minerva, who affected a blandly innocent smile.

"Perhaps, Rosetta, your family knew hers. Her grandfather was Sir Theobald Carnes of Kent and her grandmother the daughter of Lord Randolph, the Earl of Rainston."

Rosetta Cavendish's gray eyes lit up. "My father knew Lord Randolph well. I believe they hunted grouse in Scotland together."

Emmaline, expecting a doughty matron, was pleased to find that she was mistaken. Rosetta Cavendish, smiling and unperturbed by the bustle about her, seemed to be of some thirty years, with only a few threads of silver in her chestnut hair to disclose her age. She leaned forward to offer Emmaline a delicate hand, the folds of her violet silk gown rustling.

Her warm greeting soothed Emmaline. "Welcome, my dear. We all have been speculating on the Garwins' whereabouts of late. Now I see the

charming reason for their seclusion. But they must
not keep you all to themselves. Come, allow me to
introduce you . . ."

As Lady Cavendish moved to present Emmaline
to the others in her reception line, Emmaline
glanced up at Nicolas. To her surprise and consternation, she saw that his brows were drawn
together in a disbelieving frown, his nearly black
eyes staring at the pearls about her neck. Unbidden,
her hand raised to touch the circlet, and her gesture
broke his concentration.

"Aunt Minerva . . ."

Emmaline heard the mild reproach in his voice
even as she was acknowledging Lady Cavendish's
introductions. Even more pronounced was the
countess's brisk reply.

"Better that your mother's pearls glow from the
warmth of a young lady than lie cold and neglected
in a jewel chest."

Emmaline never heard the names being announced to her, nor did she remember her responses. Her mind reeled with the understanding
that she wore the pearls that had belonged to
Nicolas' mother.

As she glanced at him, she saw that his frown had
relaxed and he displayed no emotion, neither disapproval nor acceptance. Clearly, he had not
noticed the pieces before now, for her shawl had
covered her head and neck. But Emmaline fretted
to think he might assume she had deliberately
hidden them until it was too late for his protest.

"You have indeed made a stir, my dear," Lady
Cavendish murmured, and Emmaline started. But
the soft voice in her ear bore no irony.

"I beg your pardon?"

Rosetta smiled gently. "Ah, well I recall my first
ball. So anxious was I to succeed, I near forgot my
own name. But all is well now. You have passed
inspection."

Emmaline frowned in confusion, causing Rosetta

to laugh. "I have just introduced you to Lady Jersey."

"Oh, yes. A formidably regal lady, indeed. I fear I did not impress her favorably."

"On the contrary, my dear. She has given permission for you to dance, even the waltz. And merely because Lady Minerva has vouched for you. Indeed, you are fortunate in your associations."

Before Emmaline could digest her comment, Cecil hurried over.

"Ah, Rosetta, is she not the most beautiful woman present?" he gushed, showing a toothy grin.

Lady Cavendish paused but a moment before smiling wistfully at the young man. "Indeed, Cecil. Will you show her around until I have done with receiving?"

"Certainly not," Cecil replied with mock disdain. "I shall dance with her before all the dandies espy the catch of the Season."

As Emmaline almost gaped at him, Cecil led her away to the dancing. She wanted to speak to Nicolas, to explain about the pearls. But he had moved away, escorting Lady Minerva to a prominent chair, where she was soon surrounded by her curious friends. He then disappeared into the crowd, and Emmaline was faced with the dance.

A sedate quadrille was beginning. Cecil gently pushed her into place as the music, emanating from Robert Grendell's orchestra in the balcony, flowed over the white-and-gold ballroom.

"Rosetta gives the most wondrous balls," Cecil commented to Emmaline, his eyes blinking rapturously. "When Sir Humphrey was alive, this house was one of the most gloomy in London. But now! I am ever vastly entertained at Rosetta's social events. The more so tonight because you are with me."

A mist had been surging around Emmaline's thoughts since they had entered the ballroom. From the offhanded comments of Lady Minerva and Cecil, she was all the more concerned about her role in their lives. While she had Cecil's full attention, she decided to clear away the fog of her worries.

"Lord Garwin—"

"We have been acquainted near a fortnight. I do believe you might call me Cecil."

"I question the propriety, but very well. Cecil," she began again firmly, "I am flattered by your compliments. But I beg you, do not forget that I am simply your grandmama's companion. I have no social ambitions."

Flushing guiltily, Cecil nodded. "Certainly you do not. I merely hoped that you would enjoy this evening."

"I shall," Emmaline replied impatiently. "But Lord, er, Cecil. I do not understand why Lady Minerva introduced me as her houseguest."

With a confident smile, like a schoolboy certain of the correct answer, Cecil said, "She does not wish to imply that her health is frail. Engaging a companion might give that notion to her friends."

Emmaline had heard the far side of enough regarding Lady Minerva's health. "But she—"

"I will wager that you are curious about all these people," Cecil interrupted none too gracefully. "You have met the formidable Lady Jersey, arbiter of *comme il faut* in the *ton*. There she is now, nodding to Grandmama. One wonders what delicious plots they are hatching. Not to worry, I shall discover their delightful schemes. Ah, and do you see the gentleman quaffing champagne beside them? That is the playwright Sheridan, and a more jolly companion one never meets. I must introduce you to him, Emmaline. I may call you Emmaline, may I not? To preserve Grandmama's pronouncement that you are our houseguest. And over there . . ."

Cecil gossiped on, gaining momentum as he spoke, for he truly relished the tittle-tattle upon which the *beau monde* revolved. Emmaline found that a judicious nod now and again served to convince him of her interest, while leaving her thoughts free to roam.

Her concern, far from being allayed by Cecil, had only been heightened. In a mere half hour's time, the Garwins had made abundantly clear that they expected to present her as a person who belonged in society. She had not been aware that Lady Minerva knew of her maternal grandparents, a fact, she realized, that must have been supplied by her guardian. Emmaline herself had never known them, for they had disapproved their daughter's marriage and cut all ties. Perhaps she had aristocratic blood flowing through her, but she had been raised in humble homes, and was not certain she would be at ease in the *ton*. Yet her pedigree seemed important to the countess.

To what purpose? Emmaline could but surmise that her proposed rise in the world was to be followed by a far more dramatic fall when she was exposed as a poseur.

Before she could ponder further, the dance ended. Almost immediately she was surrounded by a pack of eager young men, begging Cecil for introductions. They closed in on her with eyes shining too brightly, nipping at her with questions and compliments. Just when Emmaline would have pushed through them, a solid figure was at her side.

"Would you care for refreshments?"

Gazing gratefully into Nicolas' twinkling eyes, Emmaline nodded in relief. "Indeed I would."

He steered her artfully away from the disappointed swains, and Emmaline ignored the protests and requests for dances following her.

"Thank you for rescuing me," she murmured. "I now have a deep sympathy for the fox being chased by the hounds."

Nicolas gave a rich, appreciative laugh. "I feared more for the safety of the hounds, fools that they are. It seems I alone saw the fire in the eyes of the vixen. I have no doubt that in another minute you would have dispensed of them quite handily."

Guiding her to an adjacent salon, Nicolas fetched her a glass of champagne, which flowed from a silver fountain in the center of the room.

"Mmm," Emmaline sighed after her first sip. "I vow that of all the luxuries I have enjoyed in London, champagne is my favorite."

She felt a pleasant flush come to her cheeks and wondered if she had been restored by the sparkling wine or by the nearness of Nicolas. In him, both power and grace blended into a unique essence to which Emmaline never failed to respond. Once again, she experienced the unnamed bond between them, a force drawing her to him with a mighty tug. And then, as if to give physical form to that bond, he touched her hand.

Nearly dropping her glass, she started and then blushed at her reaction. All her senses, indeed, her imaginings, were magnified when she was with him.

Nicolas, oddly, also seemed affected. He cleared his throat, uncustomarily ill-at-ease. Emmaline shuddered to think that he must judge her the fool. But if so, he hid his judgment well, for the next moment he was smiling as if nothing had taken place. And yet she detected a tightness about his eyes, an intensity in his gaze that she could not decipher.

"The pearls," she said in a rush. "You are disturbed still by the pearls. I owe you an apology. I vow I should never have accepted the loan of them had I known they belonged to your mother. But Lady Minerva insisted—"

"Quite rightly," he commented. "They were meant to be worn by one who does them justice. And it is I who apologize. I fear I distressed you by my reaction. 'Twas simply a shock to see the set, as I have not laid eyes upon them since . . ."

His mouth drew tight about the remainder of his explanation. Emmaline interpreted his reticence in the sole manner she could.

"I have reminded you painfully of losing your mother," she said softly. "Oh, do say you forgive me, Nicolas."

He seemed about to refute her, then nodded. "It happened so long ago. She died when I was a child of five."

"How terrible! May I ask how?"

His eyes darkened grimly. "Something she ate disagreed with her."

"Oh, I am sorry. What a dreadful fate."

Suddenly he leaned close and grasped her hand purposefully. She felt his fingers tighten about hers as if he wished to reassure her.

"You have nothing to fear from fate. I will protect you as I protect all those whom I . . . for whom I am responsible."

"You consider that you are responsible for me?" Emmaline asked softly.

Nicolas seemed to recover from whatever dark thoughts occupied him, for he then looked upon her gently. "I care deeply for your happiness."

Emmaline's heart lurched, and for a brief moment she thought that she was near to identifying the strange sensitivity he raised in her.

"Would you dance with me?" he murmured.

Distrusting her voice, Emmaline nodded.

The orchestra had swung into a waltz, newly arrived from the ballrooms of Vienna, and before Emmaline could catch her breath, Nicolas led her firmly into the dance.

The music swelled sensuously about them, and Emmaline found herself whirling with him as if they were one entity. Her slippered feet glided over the marble flooring. The banks of lilies and roses lining the ballroom, with colored lamps glowing among the white petals, swirled in her gaze like the bits of glass in a kaleidoscope.

She smiled up at him and suddenly she became aware of their closeness, her hand on his shoulder, his arm circling her waist. His black superfine

evening coat fitted him to perfection, a soft fabric
concealing the power of the man inside. The clean,
starched scent of his cravat filled her nostrils
pleasantly. For a moment, neither spoke, but their
gazes were locked as intimately as their bodies.
Emmaline felt her heart flutter in her breast when,
as if by tacit agreement, they were drawn ever
closer until the dance was near an embrace. In
another moment, their lips would be touching . . .

At last coming to her senses, Emmaline pulled
back, appalled by her boldness. Nicolas, too,
appeared rattled, and Emmaline feared greatly that
she must seem quite the coquette to him. Her foot-
steps faltered and she addressed him beseechingly.

"May we sit for a while?"

Obviously relieved by her suggestion, Nicolas
nodded. He escorted her to the alcove where Lady
Minerva and her cronies were keeping a running
commentary on the guests. For once, Emmaline was
grateful for the distraction of the countess's sharp
wit.

"Lady Melton is looking most buxom tonight,"
she was remarking slyly to Rosetta Cavendish.
"There must be a new modiste in town with
extraordinary skill in aiding nature."

Hiding a grin behind her fan, Rosetta said, "Lady
Minerva, I vow you have not changed in your
absence from society. Ah, here is your lovely houseguest. And I cannot tarry, for the buffet is about to
be served. Will you excuse me, dear Miss Hazlett?
Mayhap I shall call on you Thursday next, and we
shall have a long chat. I do wish to know all about
you."

Emmaline warmed to the sincerity in her voice,
realizing that she would enjoy such a visit. And then
she remembered that despite Lady Minerva's
assertion, she still was merely the companion to the
countess. Briefly, she wondered if Lady Cavendish
would be quite so eager to become acquainted with
her should she learn the truth of her role.

"I am so gratified," the countess said, watching their hostess walk away, "that Humphrey Cavendish had the grace to die while Rosetta still had good years before her."

"Aunt Minerva," Nicolas reproved, but his grin belied his tone.

"I do not apologize for speaking the truth," she snapped in reply. "I knew Humphrey and you did not. He was a mean-spirited old fool, forty years Rosetta's senior. Had her father not arranged the match, she never would have glanced at him twice. But Rosetta was an obedient child—a trait happily lacking in my family, I am glad to say. In the three years since Humphrey's timely death, Rosetta has bloomed. I say, brava!"

She gazed belligerently at Nicolas, and when his grin widened, she too smiled, appeased. "Come sit by me, Emmaline. I shall signal Lady Lindsey when she passes by, for you must meet her. She is—"

"There you are!"

Cecil burst upon them, his expression harried. "Emmaline, where have you been? I have been searching for you for hours, and each time I made to move from the hordes, there was one young thing or another demanding that I dance with her. You must be seen at my side, for when I announce our—"

"Cecil," Lady Minerva barked peevishly. "I vow that your tongue runs thrice as quick as your mind. Do calm yourself. Now fetch me a plate from the buffet. Plover eggs in aspic and lobster claws, certainly. Sliced beef if 'tis not dried out. Go on with you."

With the look of a chastised lapdog, Cecil complied.

Patting Emmaline's hand, Lady Minerva said more gently, "This is your first ball, my dear. One can be overwhelmed unless one takes time to rest between dance sets."

Emmaline sighed in gratitude and glanced up

tentatively at Nicolas. No traces of disturbance lingered in his eyes, and she prayed he had forgotten her impropriety during the waltz, yet she could not deny the feelings that had prompted her to seek his kiss. The beginnings of awareness stirred within her.

Could it be that she was falling in love with Nicolas Ransom? She tasted the notion for substance, not knowing the flavor of love. The emotions inside her seemed akin to the effects of too much champagne. She felt a bit giddy, and joyous and cautious at the same time, as if she stood upon a brink of a tumble that would either free her soul or condemn her to disgrace.

But the warmth from Nicolas' gaze melted her fears, and she was content to savor the uncommon happiness of his presence.

"I fear," he said, smiling wryly, "that when Cecil returns, I shall not have the opportunity to dance with you for the remainder of the evening. Would you dance with me now?"

"Oh, yes," Emmaline replied, not caring that her response was far too eager.

She rose to accept his proffered hand when another set of fingers closed about Nicolas' wrist.

"Nicolas Ransom, I arrived not five minutes ago and have refused a half-dozen requests for a dance so that I may offer the first waltz to you. You would not deny an old friend, would you?"

The woman with the pout in her voice and the invitation in her smile moved smoothly in front of Nicolas.

"Verity," he muttered, the color draining from his face.

Emmaline's breath caught in her throat, for the intruder was the caliber of beauty of which sonnets were written. Her hair was the gold of a caliph's treasure, her eyes the green of emeralds. The deep décolletage of her bloodred gown displayed a startling expanse of creamy bosom, upon which rested a ruby pendant of dramatic proportions. Emmaline felt as pale as a wraith next to her, and her heart sank when she recognized the predatory look in the woman's gaze.

Nicolas struggled mightily to regain his composure, finally murmuring tightly, "Good evening, madam. What mischief brings you to London?"

"You shall quite exhaust me with your enthusiasm," Verity drawled with an arch of her eyebrow. "But I forgive you, knowing how overwhelmed you must be to see me. I have just arrived, and I knew I should find all my dear friends here tonight. Lady Minerva!"

She brushed past Emmaline to buss the countess soundly.

"Oh, dear Lady Minerva, each time I see you I am reminded of my beloved grandmama, God rest her soul. She ever spoke so fondly of her girlhood friend."

"Verity," the countess acknowledged, watching her like a wary cat. "What does bring you to London?"

"Oh . . ." Verity fluttered her hand vaguely. "Shopping, the Season, boredom. I missed my old friends."

"Indeed," Lady Minerva muttered, her expression never wavering.

Suddenly Verity seemed to notice Emmaline. "Nicolas, where are your manners? You have not introduced me to this charming little creature."

"Miss Emmaline Hazlett," he said abruptly, as if reluctant to impart her name. "Aunt Minerva's houseguest. Emmaline, this is Verity, Lady Lockridge."

Forcing a smile, Emmaline nodded politely. "I am pleased to make your acquaintance, Lady Lockridge."

"Oh, no," Verity said sweetly, "the pleasure is all mine." As she measured Emmaline with her gaze, her eyes suddenly hardened. "Well, Nicolas," she purred, "I see you have passed the Ransom pearls onto another. In truth, she wears them better than I. I always considered brighter gems to suit me. Tell me, Nicolas, does she also inherit my place in your . . . affections?"

Emmaline stared openmouthed at the woman. Verity's mild tone had a needling point, the sting of an insult buried under a layer of softness. She was searching for a suitable retort when the looks between Nicolas and Verity stopped her cold.

His eyes smoldered with what Emmaline thought must be anger. But the same burning in Verity's green eyes told a far different story, and Emmaline knew in a moment that there had been a wilder, more primitive emotion than mere affection between them.

And perhaps there still was.

She blanched, her misty fantasies about Nicolas evaporating.

9

Nicolas recognized the challenge in Verity's gaze too well. She thrived on melodrama, and the scent of a rousing great scene stirred her blood noticeably. Determined not to rise to her bait, he clenched his fists at his sides, a great concentration of will alone reining his formidable temper.

"Miss Hazlett graciously consented to wear the pearls tonight," he said through gritted teeth, "to please Aunt Minerva. As you undoubtedly display the Lockridge ruby to please your mother-in-law."

Verity's smile twitched, as Nicolas knew it would, for the Lockridge jewels were a constant bone of contention between the two women. Verity coveted precious gems only slightly more than she cherished her reputation as a coquette.

For a tense moment, there was silence. Finally, Verity gave an elegant shrug of concession. "I do so love to please Freddy's mama. But since the poor dear man has gone from this life, I have not seen her as oft as I'd like. 'Tis entirely too emotional a visit for us both, as we speak incessantly of dear Freddy and miss him all the more."

Her innocent green eyes belied the patent falsehood. Neither woman could bear the other, and the memory of sad, ill-fated Frederick Lockridge suffered a continual shredding at their grasping hands. Nicolas oft had mused grimly that it was not an excessive love of brandy that had killed Freddy; his spirit had been torn asunder by his wife and his mother.

"And besides," Verity continued with an airy wave of her hand, "I have been simply showered with invitations to visit my friends. Should they have had their way, I should still be in Nicolas' favorite country: sunny Spain."

Abruptly, Nicolas started, and a gleam of triumph in Verity's eyes told him that she had received the reaction she sought. She knew full well that he wished never to hear of Spain again, much less to subject Emmaline to tales of the treachery that had been his lot in that country.

"Miss Hazlett," Verity went on, eyeing Nicolas all the while, "has our friend told you about Barcelona?"

"No, he has not."

Emmaline's answer was cool and polite, and Nicolas felt curiously proud of her sangfroid in the face of such open goading. She stood there, composed and beautiful, while only the smallest pursing of her pink mouth betrayed her opinion of Lady Lockridge.

"Shame on him for leaving you in the dark. Oh, the magnificent villa his father had, and the marvelous fiestas he gave! Although Doña Consuelo could be rather . . . unpredictable. Even so, we were quite young and adventuresome. Many's the night we would slip away and—"

"Enough," Nicolas snapped, his temper fraying. "There is nothing quite so tedious as a retelling of very ancient history."

Verity's smile was feline. "Then we should speak of your last visit to Barcelona. Surely a year past could not be considered ancient."

Cecil unknowingly saved Verity's life, for had he not arrived at that moment with a plate of lobster and plover eggs, Nicolas thought he surely would strangle the woman.

"Cecil," Verity squealed, throwing her arms about the startled man and near upending Lady Minerva's dinner into the countess's lap. "Dear boy, I am so happy to see you. Why, you have grown to be quite the dandy. When last I saw you, you were a mere schoolboy, on holiday with your tutor. Your cousin Nicolas was naughty not to have invited you more often. Now, we shall have a lovely waltz together, and you shall acquaint me with the fascinating man you have become."

Obviously overwhelmed and somewhat bewildered, Cecil handed the plate to a tight-lipped Lady Minerva and obligingly led Verity to dance. Nicolas inhaled a deep breath and felt the tension in his chest ease. From the corner of his eye, he noted his aunt's speculative perusal of him, and he attempted a rueful grin.

"Verity is a force unto herself," he muttered.

"Indeed," Lady Minerva retorted. "A storm about to break upon all in her path. And one must stand firm, lest one is blown off-balance by such a force. Were she not the granddaughter of one of my dearest friends . . ."

"Hmm." Nicolas could but imagine the rest of her rumination. But a more pressing urge made him turn to Emmaline, to judge her reaction to the near debacle. To his chagrin, he noted that her cool demeanor was also reflected in her gaze.

Attempting a smile, he murmured, "Perhaps you feel the need of more champagne. I certainly do. Will you join me?"

She hesitated before answering, seeming to take a keen measure of him.

Discomfited, Nicolas realized that she was about to refuse. "Please," he urged gently.

With what appeared to be a reluctant nod, she accepted.

Lady Minerva watched them walk off together, Emmaline graceful in a cloud of white silk, Nicolas with a powerful, protective hand on her elbow. With the experience of more years than she cared to own, she recognized a subtle but definable difference in them tonight. Yet she could not analyze the significance of the change at the moment, for her attention

was caught by another. Rosetta stood somewhat
apart from the dancers, an uncharacteristic frown
creasing her brow.

Setting aside her untouched plate, the countess
rose with unmitigated dignity and approached the
hostess.

"You look troubled, my dear," the countess
began, regarding her shrewdly. "Have you been
ruffled by a little minx misnamed Verity?"

Abashed, Rosetta shook her head. "No. But I did
see—"

"What? Come, come, out with it."

Leaning close to Lady Minerva, Rosetta murmured, "Have you seen Cecil? He is dancing with
Lady Lockridge."

The countess snorted. "No doubt she is in the
lead."

"Yes, but . . ."

Peering keenly at the woman, Lady Minerva
asked, "But what?"

At a momentary loss, Rosetta hesitated, finally
blurting, "I fret over him. He is such an innocent
in many ways, and highly suggestible. I fear that
a worldly wise lady might . . . might break his heart
before he realized it had happened."

Chuckling, Lady Minerva nodded. "Cecil could be
convinced that a pile of rubbish was a pot of gold,
should the words come honey-coated from a rose-
bud mouth. And Verity is quite the Cyprian."

Rosetta blanched and raised a slim hand to her
throat. "Oh, Lady Minerva, I did not mean to imply
that Lady Lockridge was not of quality. Indeed, her
family is renowned and she is received in all the
best homes."

Wondering just who was the innocent in this case,
Lady Minerva patted Rosetta's arm.

"There is a sound reason that the Almighty made
grandmamas, my dear. For no one understands the
feminine wiles better than one who once practiced
them herself. 'Tis the only manner in which men,

who is some matters are the far weaker sex, may be protected."

Gazing away, speaking as if to herself, Lady Minerva added, "My dear Alfred was fond of saying, 'Keep your friends close, and your enemies closer.' A wise man, that, and one whom I shall miss to my dying day. But I have vowed to protect this family as he would have."

She turned back to Rosetta. "Rest your fears, my dear. I shall devise a plan to keep a sharp eye on little Verity."

Rosetta smiled, the faint lines in her brow smoothing. "I pray I have not been too forward in mentioning this to you. My concern for Cecil—"

"—is evident," Lady Minerva finished for her, "and much appreciated. But your worries are in vain, for I think that Verity has her net cast for other fish."

The countess did not fail to note the lack of curiosity in her. Apparently, as long as Cecil was safe from Verity's clutches, Rosetta saw no further reason to fret over the vixen's prey.

"I am relieved that you took no offense to my meddling," Rosetta murmured. "I shall allow you to return to your friends now."

"Hmph. They will be delighted for the opportunity to gossip about the small scandal. The poor crows nearly choked swallowing their comments until I should move out of earshot. My sole consolation is that in a day or two, when a scandal develops among one of them, I shall tear into the gossip without the slightest twinge of guilt."

Rosetta laughed then and with a slight wave of her hand went about her duties with a lighter step.

Eyes narrowed in thought, Lady Minerva glanced from Rosetta's retreating back to the dancing Cecil, indeed being whirled about by Verity, and finally to the dining room, where Nicolas and Emmaline were sharing a glass of champagne.

"I do believe," she muttered thoughtfully to

herself, "that on the morrow I should read the tea leaves again."

Nicolas had said nothing to Emmaline until a few sips of champagne had restored the color to her cheeks. He spent the time searching for the words to smooth the churning that Verity had left in her wake.

"I fear," he began slowly, "that your first ball in London has not met your expectations."

She gratified him with a small, ironic smile. "It has been a most interesting evening."

Her response reassured him, but he sensed that her guardedness remained. "Your understatement is all the more refreshing after Verity's hyperbole."

"I did notice that she is much given to exaggeration," Emmaline commented dryly.

Suddenly Nicolas yearned to clear away the web of innuendo that Verity had woven. That Emmaline see the true nature of his relation to Verity now became of primary importance to him.

"We have known each other since we were children," he said. "Her father was a diplomat of the empire, and mine had set up a thriving trade between Spain and England. In the close British community in Barcelona, we often found ourselves together."

Nicolas paused abruptly. How could mere words do justice to the isolation that had tossed them at each other? He could scarcely understand the frustration and confusion that had intertwined in a tangling pull of emotions in his own home. His father had been a fine man, but his business demanded much of his time and presence. And Doña Consuelo... Verity had been unusually charitable in describing his stepmother as "unpredictable." She had been smotheringly possessive one moment and cruelly detached the next, discarding one mood and donning another with dizzying speed. Small wonder that Verity, equally isolated and equally motherless, had seemed such an appealing companion.

But their paths had veered, for Verity at fifteen had discovered that a dimpled smile and flashing eyes brought her all the attention she craved. Four years the elder, he had nonetheless fallen under her carefully crafted spell. Nicolas shuddered to think how close he had come to offering for her. Although the pain she had caused him had been impressive, he still sighed in relief that he had unmasked her treachery before it was too late.

He might well excuse himself for the folly of youth, but in the past year, long disabused of any illusion he might have sheltered, he had in a weak moment fallen into her arms and her bed. The anger she had provoked in him tonight was directed as much at himself and his foolishness as at Verity and her affectations.

Yet he could not speak any explanation to Emmaline. Such matters were unfit for maidenly ears. Even more, he knew he must own, he dreaded the thought of Emmaline thinking so poorly of him, as she must, were she to know that he had succumbed to Verity's sensual charms.

"Times," he began again, gruff in his inadequacy, "were difficult. I was—"

"You need not tell me more," she said quietly, her eyes clear and so blue, like the brightest summer sky.

A rush of longing flooded through him, stirring up emotions that he thought he had successfully buried earlier that night. Her beauty was near perfect, and so utterly unaffected that his breath caught in his throat each time he looked at her. Amid the brightly gowned women, she moved like a moonbeam, silvery and softly glowing, and he vowed that the Ransom pearls would never touch another neck after nestling in the hollow of hers.

How could such a brief glance arouse such powerful yearnings in him? He wanted to sweep his arms about her and hold her so close that she would become a part of him. He longed to crush his mouth against hers and taste her very soul. Nicolas stood on the brink of falling in love with her. She captured him with her merest gaze, and he was sorely pressed not to wrap her in his embrace then and there and drown in the sweetness of her kiss . . .

With a ragged breath, he struggled to control his urge. Countless times in the past few weeks he had found himself thinking about Emmaline, forcing himself to stay away from her and yet delighting in every small moment she was in his sight. Over the years, circumstances had demanded that Nicolas maintain a rigid control, for his survival and that of his loved ones depended upon his vigilance. And now he was redoubling his efforts, for his feelings for Emmaline had revealed exactly how vulnerable he was.

The means to destroy him might well be through destroying her.

He knew he must perform an excruciating exorcism on himself. He must rid his mind and his heart of cherishing her, for his caring was like a poison to those he loved. He would only expose her to a great and terrifying danger should he allow himself to fall in love with her.

And so he stepped back, throwing a guard about his heart. He could not bear to look at her; a wintery chill seemed to invade him.

Then, in a rustle of satin, Verity was between them, ignoring Emmaline, smiling victoriously at him.

"I could not wait to tell you the marvelous news. I was quite at my wit's end to know what to do. My house is being renovated and I am at the mercy of my friends' hospitality. What do you think, Nicolas? Your dear Aunt Minerva has graciously invited me to stay at your home. Is that not the cap to a perfect evening?"

10

Emmaline awoke to the splash of raindrops on her window, the promise of yet another gloom-ridden day. In the past fortnight since Lady Cavendish's ball, heavy clouds had oft obscured the sun, and the memory of the clear, starry sky on the night of her first ball had faded in her mind. Only the results of that night remained to bedevil her as relentlessly as the rain.

"You awake, Miss Em?" Floss asked cheerily, banging the skuttle as she entered the room.

"Were I not," Emmaline muttered, "I should be, with you knocking about." She pulled the coverlet around her ears.

Piling logs on the hearth, the abigail sniffed. "Ain't we in a snit this morning? And is it any wonder? If you don't get your proper sleep, me mum always says, you'll be right snittish when the cock crows."

With a bleary peek at the mantel clock, Emmaline saw that she had been abed eight hours, but asleep a mere four. Sighing, she burrowed into her pillow. Her rest had been far from peaceful of late.

"As soon as I stoke the fire," Floss promised, "I'll bring you up a fine breakfast. You're looking right peckish."

Emmaline knew she spoke the unpleasant truth. Her appetite had been dulled in the past weeks, no doubt by the near-continual knotting in her stomach. The Garwin household was bristling with animosity, both spoken and silent these days.

"There we are," Floss said with satisfaction,

dusting off her hands. "The room will be right cozy again by the time I come back."

With a brisk swish of skirts, Floss was gone.

Emmaline heard the door latch with a twinge of guilt. Her own sour mood was no excuse to speak sharply to the girl. It was certainly no fault of Floss' that Emmaline's sunny dreams had faded so dismally.

Her last truly happy moment, when Nicolas had held her in his arms at the ball, now seemed but a bittersweet illusion. Since that night, he had affected a polite yet cool demeanor in her presence. The magical bond between them seemed to have snapped—or, more precisely, to have been cut.

Ironically, she saw him far more often than ever, as he rarely left the house alone. He appeared for meals when they dined at home, but seldom joined in the table talk. Rising early, all but avoiding seclusion in the library, he hovered close, yet remained at an emotional distance from them all. When he paid his courtesy visits to his aunt, his conversation was abrupt, his restlessness pronounced. His social life was perfunctory. He accompanied them to all affairs, but in body only; his spirit wandered elsewhere.

For Emmaline, attempting to salve her wounds from his coldness, each night offered a new diversion; a mirthful rout, a boisterous crush, a glittering ball. Determined not to betray her feelings, she threw herself into the merriment, gaining a reputation as the most lively young lady of the Season. Any number of gentlemen sought to partner her in a dance, but the gaiety she professed with them was forced, a mask to disguise her melancholy. And so in the wee hours of the morning, exhausted from dancing, her temples aching from too much champagne and repartee, Emmaline would fall into bed only to find peace eluding her once again.

" 'Ere we are," Floss sang out. She waited until

Emmaline sat up against her pillows and then placed the perfectly set silver tray across Emmaline's lap.

"Mmm, don't the buns smell lovely. Cinnamon, Cook says. Let me pour you a cup of chocolate, Miss Em. That'll put a smile on your face quick enough."

As Floss reached for the pot, Emmaline touched her hand lightly.

"Do forgive me for snapping at you," she murmured. "I fear I have been sharp with you of late, and I apologize."

"Oh, Miss Em, there's naught to forgive. I give thanks every day that 'er ladyship assigned me to you, and not to that one. Nan is near 'round the bend trying to please that one."

As Floss poured the steaming chocolate, Emmaline hid a wry smile. Floss was too well-trained to disparage a lady of the household outright, so she registered her dislike by referring only to "that one." But Emmaline had known from the start of whom Floss spoke. The thorn in everyone's paws these days was Verity.

"Is the chocolate too bitter, Miss Em? 'Ere, let me add some sugar."

Emmaline accepted two spoonfuls in her cup, neglecting to tell Floss that it was not the beverage but the thought of Verity that caused her to grimace.

The woman seemed to delight in creating havoc, whether by her capricious demands of the servants or by the deliberate prodding of everyone else. She hinted extravagantly until she was included in all the Garwin invitations, then spent the next day criticizing the other guests. She teased Cecil into dancing nearly every dance with Emmaline, then feigned a pout because he was ignoring her. She begged Lady Minerva to read the tea leaves for her, hanging on the countess's every word, and then dismissing the entire reading with a disbelieving shrug when no wealthy suitor was mentioned.

But Verity reserved her most sly barbs for Emmaline. She complimented her evening dress, adding sweetly that the color made Emmaline look pale only in bright lighting. Chattering distractingly during a game of whist, she consoled Emmaline for a bad play by commenting that some ladies were simply too fluff-headed for cards. And each time that Emmaline set her chin, refusing to allow Verity's waspish tongue to sting her, Verity would begin waxing nostalgic about Spain and Nicolas.

It was these reminiscences that irked Emmaline the most, for they emphasized the bleakness she felt. And yet there was some measure of solace for her; Nicolas withered Verity with a retort or a sharp glance each time the persistent woman began her nonsense.

Emmaline took secret, wicked pleasure in the fact that Verity could not badger Nicolas. When she leaned into him too closely, when she spoke in innuendos, he simply removed himself, leaving Verity with the pink of frustration on her face. It was a small consolation to Emmaline that while he treated her coolly, he froze Verity on the spot.

And yet, Verity schemed to waylay him. What occurred between them, in private, Emmaline could but conjecture. She kept remembering the raw emotion that had passed between them on the night Verity barged in at Rosetta Cavendish's ball. They had been lovers, of that fact she was painfully certain. The dismal prospect that they might be again filled her with piercing despair.

"Eat a bit, Miss Em," Floss wheedled. "Just a bit. For me."

Obligingly, Emmaline nibbled on the cinnamon bun, sticky and warm from the oven. It had no taste for her.

"That's better. Now tell me about the opera while I pick up. I was too sleepy last night to give proper care to your gown."

Again guiltily, Emmaline remembered that the

clock had been striking four when she rang for Floss to help her undress. Her farcical social life was robbing the maid of sleep also.

" 'Twas quite a gala event," she began, forcing a cheer she did not feel. "Madame Talari sang Cherubino in *The Marriage of Figaro*, and she was in astonishing voice."

She went on to detail the merry confusion of Mozart's opera, where false identities were assumed and true love was thwarted until the final act. In vivid detail, she then described the flashing jewels worn by the ladies in the audience, the handsome figures cut by the gentlemen, and the very opulence of the King's Theatre, with its five tiers of boxes. What she did not explain was that her attention had been constantly interrupted by visitors to the box, coming in at the invitation of Cecil, throughout the entire evening. She had been so anticipating her first opera, having studied the score and read the libretto many times. It seemed the height of rudeness to her that the audience was far more interested in chattering among themselves than in reveling in the magnificence of the music.

But her entire time in London had been marked by disillusion. It seemed a lifetime ago, not a mere month, that she had been so entranced at living in London. Except for the ballrooms of the *beau monde*, she had seen less of the fascinating city than the day she had arrived with her guardian. She was scarce the same eager country girl who had agreed to be companion to the countess, little aware of what her duties would be. She still pondered her true role in the household. After so many social gatherings where she was introduced as a house-guest, she had to keep reminding herself that the designation was an artifice of Lady Minerva's.

And Cecil appeared to have forgotten the distinction altogether. His fawning had grown quite proprietary of late. At the King's Theatre, he had delighted in displaying her to his friends, much like a prize pony he had groomed. Yet when they clamored for her attention, he grandly waved them away, claiming her for himself. He complimented her outrageously and was visibly hurt if she did not accept his paeans to her with exaggerated gratitude. Emmaline was becoming weary of the entire show.

But for Floss' sake, she painted the evening in glowing colors.

"Oh, Miss Em," Floss sighed, clasping her hands to her bosom, "it sounds like a fairy tale, this opera. And love wins at the end."

"Yes," Emmaline agreed softly. "At least it does in the opera."

The thought of love sent a pain to stab her heart. Although she knew that she must be stern with herself, that she must not linger on the memory of Nicolas' arms, or the scent of his starched linen, or the liquid warmth of his eyes, her heart would not obey. As long as she remained in this house, knowing he was as near as the next room yet as far removed from her as if he were in China, the ache inside her would not depart.

And so she began to wonder if she should leave. But where would she go? She still could not live independently, with no means by which to support herself. Despite her protests, Lady Minerva had paid her salary fortnightly as agreed, but it was scarcely enough to purchase a few boxes of sweetmeats, much less on which to live. No, her sole alternative was, as it had ever been, to return to Bevindale, either to the vicar or to Will Cooper. The prospect of such incarceration disgusted her more now that she had tasted the freedom of a reprieve. Yet the distance from Nicolas was a sort of prison, too. Emmaline frowned, more confused and frustrated by her dilemma than ever.

At the very moment that Emmaline was thinking distastefully of Bevindale, she was the subject of discussion in that very town. Edwin Markham had scarcely finished his especially blended tea and his shepherd's pie when his housekeeper reported that a tenacious parishioner demanded an audience.

"Well, who is it?" Markham snapped.

"Will Cooper," she snapped back, "and in as foul a temper as yourself."

With that she stepped aside and the big sheep farmer lumbered into the room. He might have been a decent catch in his day, tall and barrel-chested, his arms well-muscled from wrestling with sheep at the shearing season, his face weathered yet not unpleasantly so. But a life of hard work and solitude had left him little means with which to learn the niceties of conversation. Will Cooper was a man of deliberate action and few words.

"Ain't right," he began without preamble.

"Good day to you, too," Markham said sarcastically. "What are you complaining about now?"

"We had a bargain."

Markham sighed. He thought he had dealt with the problem successfully the week after he had returned from London. Calmly handing over Cooper's money, he had informed the man that his bride-to-be was otherwise engaged.

His anger flared now, and Markham struggled to control the hot reply that sprang to his tongue. There was still another piece of business to be concluded with Mr. Cooper, and he could ill afford to provoke the stubborn farmer.

"Do have a seat, Will," he offered. "Will you take a cup of tea?"

"Nay." Cooper remained standing, stolid and determined.

Drawing a deep breath, the vicar shrugged. "Look here, Will. Emmaline was not the wife for you. Why, she had not even a dowry to bring you! And truth to be told, there is weakness in her stock. Bad ancestry. You would scarcely like to sire children from a weak line, now, would you?"

"She looked strong to me."

"Ah, but looks may deceive, my good fellow. You see, my conscience bothered me. I said to myself, Cooper is an honorable man. I cannot accept his offer knowing that he bargains for tainted goods. What if she gave puny sons, who would be useless on your farm? Or worse still, only daughters? Personally, I fail to understand why anyone would desire children unless one could send them away to be civilized until they are of age. . . . Well, that is neither here nor there. Consider yourself lucky to be rid of the obligation, man."

For the first time Cooper's steady gaze wavered, and the vicar thought he had seen reason. But finally the farmer shook his head.

"A bargain is a bargain," he said slowly. "If a man can't stand by his handshake, he ain't no man."

It was a speech of epic proportions for Cooper, and one that carried his vilest insult. But the vicar controlled himself through sheer will. The thought of the countess's money and what it would buy also helped his restraint.

All his instincts cried to throw the fellow unceremoniously out the door. But Will Cooper had something Markham wanted. He tried another tack.

"I see how you could feel cheated," he began slyly. "But let me tell you that you are being cheated far worse by another."

Scowling dangerously, Cooper mumbled, "Who?"

"John Fairhope."

Cooper blinked. "How so?"

"He wants the small cottage that borders on his land, for his bailiff, am I correct? He offered you fifty pounds, to be paid before the end of the month, did he not? Ah, do not bother to deny it. Well you know that a secret lasts but ten minutes in this town. Am I correct or not?"

Reluctantly, Cooper nodded.

"Well, then," Markham said, heartily rubbing his hands together, "I shall offer you the fair price for that land. Seventy-five pounds."

The true value actually was far higher, but at last he had provoked a response in the farmer. Cooper's mouth dropped open and a glimmer of light appeared in his bland gaze.

The vicar suppressed a smug smile. The farmer's slowness was no match for his own agile wit. It had not occurred to the man that Fairhope would ever covet that land, offering, besides the cottage, a forest full of game and a splendid fishing stream. Markham could rent the property to Fairhope, recovering his investment in five years and adding to his nest egg for the rest of his life. Along with Lady Garwin's "donations," he would spend the remainder of his days quite comfortably.

"I will give you the money before the week is out," he offered, appealing to the man's avarice. Surely Cooper possessed a hefty dose of greed. All men did. "A bird in the hand, so to speak. What do you say?"

Cooper took his time, but finally gave a brief nod. "The money before the end of the week. In full."

Bounding to his feet, Markham grinned. "Done. I must say, you are quite the shrewd businessman, Will."

Turning toward the door, Cooper made to leave. But at the threshold, he stopped and peered at Markham over his shoulder. "This don't change things. I still got cheated of a wife."

The vicar waved his hand expansively. "We shall find you another. One far more suitable. You will bless the day that piece of fluff called Emmaline decided to stay in London."

Shaking his head, unconvinced, Will Cooper trudged out the door.

In London, Emmaline had finished her bath, immune to Floss' steady spate of downstairs gossip. She still brooded on her forced confinement in a situation that was becoming increasingly less tolerable.

"And Nan was ever so cross when that one kept her all afternoon trying on ball gowns," Floss was saying as she dressed Emmaline's hair. "She's sweet on a fellow who drives an 'ackney. Arthur, 'is name is. Ain't that a grand name? 'Is stand is just down on the corner, and—promise you won't tell 'er ladyship, Miss Em—when Nan has a few minutes, she sneaks down to see 'im. Ain't that the most romantical story you ever 'eard? Oh, not like your opera, to be sure. But still . . ."

Through Emmaline's haze, a piece of Floss' chatter penetrated. For fully a minute, she did not grasp the significance of the statement. But when she did, she sat up straight, her eyes agleam.

" 'Old still, Miss Em. I nearly dropped all the pins."

"Floss," Emmaline said, careful to keep her tone casual, "I shall most like go visiting with Lady Minerva later, and I do not wish to have to change clothing. I shall wear a carriage dress. The fawn-colored sarcenet, I think."

Floss shrugged, accustomed to the inexplicable whims of the gentry. She helped Emmaline into the dress and tied a cream straw bonnet over her curls.

Glancing out her window, Emmaline noted that the rain had ceased, a good omen for her bold plan. She smiled secretly to herself.

"Thank you, Floss. You may go now."

Impatiently, Emmaline dawdled at her dressing table until the girl had picked up the breakfast tray and departed. Then she scooped up her reticule, hearing the reassuring jingle of coins inside. Pulling on her gloves, she peeked into the hallway, finding it deserted. As quickly as she dared, she flew down the stairs and out the front door.

The hackney stand, Floss had said, was on the next corner.

From a vantage point across the street, a pair of dark Spanish eyes followed her progress. This young lady must be the stranger of whom his spy had spoken. An alluring little thing, with spirit in her step. Guillermo frowned thoughtfully. It was supposed that the cousin, appallingly named Cecil, was taken with her. But as he noted her graceful walk, her appealing figure, he decided that she might indeed interest Ransom. And whoever interested Ransom absolutely fascinated Guillermo.

A slow grin inched across his face. With a glance to his left and to his right, he sauntered out to the street. After that, his gaze stayed trained on the quick-moving figure in front of him.

11

The simple act of walking unaccompanied down the street filled Emmaline with a renewing exhilaration. The morning drizzle had ceased entirely, leaving the trees over her head glistening with emerald leaves, and the pavement under her feet clean and shining. She inhaled the rain-fresh air, a smile dimpling her cheeks. For the first time in weeks, she felt truly unfettered.

Her step quickened as she espied a hackney at rest at the corner. Yet, drawing nearer, she realized that the cab was but one of several, their drivers patiently awaiting fares. Her need for rebellion had emboldened her to venture out alone. But no fool she, Emmaline determined to engage a driver whom she knew at least by reputation.

"I beg your pardon," she said politely to the cabmen grouped about a lamppost, "but may I ask if one of you might be Arthur?"

Ignoring their curious gazes, she waited patiently until a lanky, youngish man tipped his hat to her. "Aye, that's me name."

"How do you do? I should like to engage your services."

With a flourish, he escorted her to his vehicle and opened the carriage door. "Aye, miss. Where'd ye care to go?"

Emmaline stepped up into the hackney, then spilled her cache of coins into her palm for him to see. "As far about London as this will take me and bring me back again."

Arthur rubbed his jaw thoughtfully, but craft

gleamed in his eye. "Won't be far, miss. 'Yde Park, per'aps is all."

Regarding him shrewdly, Emmaline said, "How disappointing. I had hoped to drive to Westminster, and Parliament, and St. Paul's. When I mentioned my desire to Nan—"

"Nan?" He frowned mightily. "Ain't be named Miss Verity, are ye?"

"No," Emmaline averred, "I decidedly am not. But I am staying at the Garwin house. And should I be disappointed in my outing today, I shall no doubt develop a case of the vapors, which will require the week-long, undivided attention of two maids, one of them sure to be Nan."

A light seemed to break over Arthur's face. "Ye've two 'ours of me time, miss, an' anywhere ye care to go."

Emmaline smiled. "Splendid. Shall we begin with Westminster?"

In a trice Arthur had closed the carriage door and climbed upon his perch. With a smart crack of his whip, he urged his horse into the milling traffic.

Neither Arthur nor Emmaline noticed that another of the cabmen had also taken on a fare. And naturally they could not hear the terse orders given by the dark-complexioned Spaniard engaging him: "Follow the hackney ahead."

With one hand clutching the door, Guillermo peered out the side of the cab.

"Keep them in sight," he snapped at the driver. When the man merely grunted in reply, Guillermo added, "Double your fare if you do. And nothing in payment if you do not."

His teeth were on edge, his focus concentrated. After weeks of frustration, hope that his plan might take the solid form of reality glimmered.

The ruin of Nicolas Ransom had fired his mind, waking and sleeping, until Guillermo was nearly consumed by the heat of his lust for revenge. And until now, the perfect opportunity had eluded his grasp, as if he were trying to clutch a handful of the detestable English fog. Had he chosen merely to waylay Ransom, the cur's blood would have run in the streets long ago. That the man had come through the Peninsular War unscathed disgusted Guillermo, for Ransom had no head whatever for tactics or strategy. He ventured out blithely on his morning rides at the same hour each day, with no thought to the weakness on his flanks. No groom rode alongside, rendering him an easy target, should an enemy wish to strike. Even now Guillermo's lip curled in contempt at the man's foolhardiness.

But however tempted Guillermo was to plunge a dagger into the blackguard's heart and find the peace of justice, he disciplined himself. Death would pain Ransom but for a moment, or at the most, considering Guillermo's vast talents for the art, a few excruciating days. The Spaniard's honor demanded that Ransom suffer the tortures of the damned for years, decades, the rest of his natural life. And Guillermo knew well that the instrument for Ransom's lifelong agony was a beloved of his. That beloved must suffer ignominious degradation and death.

As Guillermo's beloved had.

Abruptly, he rapped on the carriage roof with his walking stick. "Turn to the left. At the square."

"Aye, guv. I sees 'em," the driver growled.

In the beginning, Guillermo had considered an abduction. But his spy had informed him that the doors and windows were religiously locked and that the male servants had been chosen carefully for their strength and familiarity with various weapons. Thus, there was no assailing the Garwin house, itself a veritable fortress. Guillermo was left with one option: to seize a member of the family on an outing. But before now, the pompous aunt and the doltish cousin had not left the house without an entourage of burly footmen. In the evening, Ransom himself rode along with the guards to every social affair.

And now, at last, the golden favor of chance had shone upon Guillermo. Centuries of noble Spanish cunning, concentrated in one man, was pitted against an innocent bit of fluff and a slightly built hackney driver. True, the young lady was not a relative of Ransom's. But she might well act as the bait to lure the cousin or the aunt into Guillermo's trap.

He salivated with the possibilities.

"Good day, madam," Nicolas said, strolling into his aunt's sitting room. "Are you recovered from last evening's opera?"

Lady Minerva, resting on her chaise lounge, put down the latest edition of her gossip sheet and sniffed.

"All that nonsense of exchanging identities and swearing undying love. And in a language unfit for understanding, sung by temperamental foreigners unfit for social reception. I vow 'tis the last such trial to which I shall submit myself."

Nicolas suppressed a smile. "But think of how devastated you would be not to read your name in the columns the next morning. And you would be reduced to hearing the latest *on-dits* from your friends instead of passing them on."

Her mouth twitching, Lady Minerva smirked. "You know my foibles too well, Nephew. And you have the cheek to call me on them. Ah, much of my family's blood runs in you."

"Quite so. Have you an interesting day planned, Aunt?"

"Certainly. After suffering through Herr Mozart's farce, do you suppose I shall not take advantage of the one saving grace of the evening? I shall pay calls upon several ladies of my acquaintance, where we may share tittle-tattle to our hearts' content. I merely await Cecil's and Emmaline's presence to go on about my pleasure. And if they do not show their faces soon, Verity will rouse herself and I shall be saddled with her on my calls."

Cecil was always tardy, Nicolas well knew. But Emmaline was almost faultless in her appointments. "Where is Emmaline?" he asked casually.

The countess shot him a keen glance, but kept her voice even. "Most likely she is stilll in her room. I myself prefer the comfort of a dressing robe until I am forced to attire myself to go abroad for the day. Pray, do stay and keep me company, Nicolas, while I wait."

For the next half-hour, she entertained him with tidbits gleaned from the gossip sheet, adding her own trenchant comments, chuckling at his responses. When at last Cecil breezed in, sprinkling his usual apologies before him, Lady Minerva frowned at the timepiece on the mantelshelf.

"Where is Emmaline? Unlike you, Cecil, she is generally quite punctual. Ring for Andrews and tell her to fetch the girl."

When Andrews, Lady Minerva's maid, reported what Floss had told her, that Emmaline had left her room dressed for paying calls near two hours previously, Lady Minerva's frown of annoyance turned to puzzlement. "Where might she have gone?"

Further inquiries of the servants revealed that no one had seen Miss Emmaline in the nonce. The countess received the news with unusual quiet. When she glanced at her great-nephew, her eyes were wide with consternation. Nicolas, whose uneasiness had progressed steadily to alarm, attempted to reassure her with a nonchalant smile.

"Do not vex yourself, Auntie. Go about your toilette. I shall find the illusive Miss Hazlett and send her up posthaste." He wheeled and forced himself not to hurry out of Lady Minerva's room.

Cecil dogged his heels into the hallway.

"My bride-to-be has misplaced herself," he cried, the back of his hand pressed dramatically to his brow. "I must find the poor lost lamb."

Abruptly, Nicolas halted and turned, causing Cecil to almost barrel into him. "Cecil," Nicolas said tightly, "your cravat is creased."

"No!" Cecil gasped and bolted toward his room, calling epithets down upon his valet even as he ran.

Nicolas spared but a moment in regretting the lie. Fear was clutching at him, and he could not be hindered by Cecil's histrionic excess.

"Rink," he shouted to the first footman. "Summon the staff, everyone, from the scullery maids to the grooms. I want to see them in the foyer. Immediately!"

His darkened expression told of his urgency even more than his command. Rink hastened to obey while Nicolas' voice still rang in the stairway.

In less than five minutes' time, which to Nicolas seemed an eternity, the servants were assembled and peering at him with a mix of curiosity and trepidation.

With massive effort, Nicolas tempered his voice.

"I want the house searched, from attics to cellars. Do not disturb his lordship or her ladyship in their rooms, but look everywhere else. Including the stables and the grounds. It is imperative," he said slowly, staring at each of them in turn, "that Miss Emmaline be found at once. Go!"

As they scurried off, Nicolas heard a low chuckle from the top of the stairs. He glanced up sharply to see Verity leaning on the banister.

"Well, Nicolas, it seems your Miss Hazlett has managed to get herself lost. Poor dear, we scarcely can blame her. A London town house undoubtedly has more rooms than her entire village. Not to worry, she also will manage to be found."

His face suffused with a dangerous glow, Nicolas glared at her. "Madam, can you possibly be as stupid as you pretend? Are you so dim-witted as to be completely unaware of the treachery that threatens this family? Oh, I forgot. You were a part of that treachery, were you not?"

Verity blanched but recovered quickly. "You forced me into such a position, Nicolas. And well you know that I long since have renounced my role in that business. I loved you. I sought only to win your heart."

Nicolas' smile was chilling. "Then you sought a bad bargain, madam. For my heart was once yours for the taking. 'Twas you who put a price upon it. Now if you will excuse me . . ."

As he turned his back to Verity, Nicolas saw a maidservant peering uncertainly from behind the parlor door.

"Well, what is it?" he asked impatiently. "Have you seen Miss Hazlett? Come here, speak up."

The girl moved forward in hesitation, and Nicolas sensed her uneasiness.

"I should not have barked at you," he said more gently. "But I am concerned. You are . . . ?"

"She is my maid," Verity called down the stairs. "Nan, why are you skulking about? Come help me into my bonnet. I shall not stay here to be insulted—"

"Be silent," Nicolas roared at her. Then to the girl, "Have you seen Miss Emmaline? Please tell me, for the matter is most urgent."

The girl stared miserably from him to her mistress and back again. "I . . . I did, sir," she mumbled.

Hardly able to control his excitement, Nicolas said, "Where? When?"

"Nearly two hours ago. She was goin' down the street—"

"In which direction?" Nicolas asked eagerly, wanting to shake the story from her.

"Toward . . . toward the 'ackney stand, sir."

Verity hooted. "Balderdash! You are telling tales

again, Nan. You cannot see that part of the street from any window in this house."

Nan shifted uncomfortably, her expression the picture of misery. "Well, I wa'n't lookin' out no window."

"Where were you, then, you little chit? I vow, I shall have you dismissed—"

Nicolas silenced Verity with the blackest look he had ever given. "If you say another word," he promised with a deadly calm, "I shall mount those stairs and wring your neck."

For once, Verity believed him.

After Nan had burst into tears, Nicolas spent precious minutes vowing that she would not be dismissed no matter her infraction. At last, she relented and the story poured out. She had come from a rendezvous with her friend Arthur, ducking into a hedge when she spotted Miss Emmaline coming toward her, fearing a scolding or worse. From her vantage point, she had seen Miss Emmaline get into Arthur's hackney and drive off.

Nicolas professed his gratitude hastily and added, "You shall have a bonus for speaking the truth. Now, hurry out to the stable and tell Merkle to prepare my horse."

He never heard Nan's relieved reply, for he was running to the library to fetch and load a pistol.

12

Emmaline, standing before the imposing edifice of Westminster Abbey, sighed happily. Her outing had proved most enjoyable, satisfying both her boundless curiosity about London and her restless need for rebellion against the confines of the Garwin town house. She had viewed the city from the proper perspective, strolling in the streets and lanes, always careful to keep in Arthur's sight. Yet a small sense of guilt tinged her mood, for she knew she was behaving most improperly, venturing out unchaperoned.

It was a guilt she could ignore, though, for the spirit of the day exonerated her conscience.

As the sonorous bell chimed the hour, Emmaline realized with a start that her allotted time was almost gone. On this occasion, her sigh was more regretful, and she began to make her way back to Arthur.

Approaching the hackney, she noticed a man pacing in agitation, blocking her path. She slowed her step, and as he saw her, he stopped, removing his tall hat with a sweep.

"I beg your indulgence, miss," he said urgently.

Alarmed, Emmaline turned her head, appealing with a glance to Arthur. But the cabman appeared to be dozing on his perch and offered no assistance.

"Do forgive me," the man urged apologetically. "I am not in the habit of accosting ladies of quality on the street. But I am a stranger in your land and my sister is ill in the coach. I desperately need help."

Emmaline hesitated, gazing more closely at him.

He was obviously a gentleman, dressed in an elegant, almost dapper manner. His dark complexion and perfect but slightly accented English gave witness to his claim of being a visitor.

"The best course," she murmured somewhat stiffly, "would be to return her to your lodgings. Or to summon a doctor."

He gave a ragged smile, the picture of a flustered brother. "I agree entirely. But she insists that the motion of the carriage will but make her more ill. She is feeling faint, a ladies' complaint of which I am woefully ignorant. Dare I presume . . . Might I ask if you have a spirit bottle with you?"

As she regarded him, in his abject helplessness over female vagaries, Emmaline's manner softened. She reached into her reticule and handed him her spirit bottle. "Wave this under your sister's nose. 'Twill restore her quite quickly."

Gazing at her offering doubtfully, the man asked, "Shall I do her harm should I give too potent a dose? I am sorry to say, I am unaccustomed . . ."

Emmaline smiled. "Show me to your carriage, sir. I shall be happy to help the young lady."

The man's teeth gleamed white beneath a thin mustache. For a moment, Emmaline thought she detected a flash in his gaze, but she owned she must be mistaken, for when she glanced at him again, his dark eyes were focused blandly on her.

"Many thanks, miss," he murmured, lightly taking her arm. "You have no idea how gratified I am."

He escorted her to a hackney much like Arthur's. Opening the door, he stepped back. Emmaline poked her head inside, only to frown curiously. The hackney was empty.

"Sir, your sister—"

She turned to speak, but the man, standing beside her only seconds before, had vanished.

"What in the world . . ." Emmaline muttered, and at that moment, a strong hand clamped upon her shoulder, startling her half out of her wits.

She gasped as the hand swung her around.

"Nicolas!"

"Emmaline, thank God!"

He was breathing heavily, his face flushed deep red, his eyes glowering and intense.

"Are you injured?" he demanded urgently. "Did that cur harm you?"

"Certainly not," Emmaline muttered, rubbing her shoulder. "But you may well have, with your unwarranted assault."

"Assault!" Nicolas glared at her. "My assault might well have saved your ungrateful life. Why ever did you allow him to lure you?"

Shrugging uncomfortably, Emmaline replied, "He told me that his sister was faint and requested the use of my spirit bottle."

He peered at her incredulously. "You little fool. You are deuced fortunate that this wretched adventure of yours did not end in your murder."

Emmaline blanched as the harsh word rang in her ears. "Murder? Whatever makes you think such a horrid thing?"

His jaw tightened in exasperation. "Have you no notion of his scheme? He invented a nonexistent sister to lure you to this cab. When I came bounding on the scene, he was poised to shove you inside and whisk you away to . . . I shudder to imagine what fate he had in mind for you. The man is truly unnatural, for he sensed my approach before he saw me and scurried like a waterfront rat into the crowd. In another minute . . ."

Nicolas paused, staring at her intently as if to assure himself that she was indeed unharmed. Suddenly he drew her to him, wrapping her in his arms, nearly crushing her with the vehemence of his embrace.

"Oh, Emmaline," he murmured, his voice ragged with the force of emotion. "Thank God I arrived in time."

Her anger melted in the warmth of his embrace but raised her confusion to new heights. When he relaxed his hold long enough for her to breathe, Emmaline peered at him, bewildered.

"And how did you find me?"

"The cabmen on the street corner overheard your destination. Judging by the time that had elapsed, I concluded that you must be nearing the end of your folly. I only prayed that I might reach you before the worst happened."

"I understand nothing of this. Please explain to me what is happening."

Nicolas stepped back. "You are safe," he said grimly. "But you must never, ever go abroad alone again. Never. That is all you need to understand."

Emmaline lifted her eyebrows, her vexation surging once more and finally spilling over. "Indeed, sir? Well, pardon my impertinence, but I have had quite enough of your explanations that serve more to cloud the issue than to shed light upon it. Since the day I arrived in your household, I have been aware of currents running beneath conversations, sentences left unfinished in my presence, situations that all save I comprehend. I refuse to live in a fog one more day. Either you tell me this instant what is happening, Nicolas Ransom, or I pack my bags immediately when I return to Garwin House."

She halted her impassioned speech abruptly, challenging him with her resolute gaze. Nicolas' mouth, set in a rigid line, finally softened and he nodded.

"You acted irresponsibly, Emmaline, but I accept your rebuke. You shall know the truth, mostly because knowing may well save your life." Before she could reply, Nicolas turned toward the teeming street and gave a short, piercing whistle. His big gray gelding obediently trotted over and Nicolas took the reins. "Now where is the hackney you engaged?"

Emmaline gestured speechlessly to the cab where Arthur still dozed, despite the commotion.

Following her gaze, Nicolas frowned, then hurried to the cab. He shook Arthur, whose head lolled forward. "Pass me your spirit bottle," Nicolas muttered, abruptly dropping the reins to his horse. "This fellow has more need of it than the phantom sister had."

"What do you mean? Has Arthur taken ill?"

Nicolas fixed her with a piercing gaze. "No, what Arthur has taken is a nasty chop to the head. Undoubtedly, your needy friend thought to put him out of the way so there would be no one to come to your rescue."

As Nicolas waved the bottle under the cabman's nose, Emmaline felt a distinct chill. The potential hazard of her situation began to sink into her mind. The swirl of people on the streets went on about them undisturbed, yet the crowds no longer seemed an exuberant part of her adventure, but a swelling mass that could hold a dangerous man. She felt exposed and vulnerable. The seclusion of Garwin House suddenly appealed to her.

Arthur moaned and stirred. "W—wot goes 'ere?"

"You have had a crack on the head," Nicolas informed him. "How are you feeling?"

Wincing, Arthur touched a spot over his left ear. "Never saw the blow comin', worse luck. 'Ere, was Miss Emmaline 'armed?"

"No. I arrived just in time. Are you up to driving us home?"

"Aye, sir, that I am." He peered at Nicolas sheepishly. "I was watchin' 'er right careful all day, sir. Don't know 'ow I got coshed."

Nicolas smiled briefly. "You did well. You shall have a bonus for driving us home quickly." He helped Emmaline into the hackney, then tied his horse behind the cab and joined her inside.

"Now tell me what this is about," she said.

Nicolas stared straight ahead. "When we are home."

From a vantage point at the corner of the abbey, obscured by the massive stone of the building, the Spaniard witnessed the entire scene. The sudden appearance of Ransom, bounding toward him, his face that of an enraged tiger, had startled and infuriated Guillermo. With the quick responses learned in childhood, he had taken off like a pocket thief, darting through the crowd with lightning speed. When his instincts told him that Ransom had not given chase, Guillermo had doubled back.

His fists had clenched when he thought how close he had come to victory, only to be foiled at the last possible moment by that uncannily fortunate blackguard. Guillermo stood in impotent fury, gnashing his teeth at his bad luck.

And then his fists loosened and he bared his teeth in a wily smile. He had seen the emotion that Ransom could not hide when he found the chit. The crude embrace was but confirmation of his suspicions. Ransom was in love with the girl.

A pleasant warmth suffused Guillermo, exciting his purpose anew. He could add another pawn to the game, another expendable piece to go with the aunt and the cousin. The bit of fluff with the cool blue eyes could be the perfect instrument of Ransom's torture.

Guillermo chuckled as the hackney departed and he began a leisurely stroll back to his lodgings. When he thought of the girl's milky skin and graceful figure, he laughed aloud, startling passersby. He had just realized that he might well enjoy himself into the bargain.

13

Nicolas spoke nary a word until they reached Garwin House. Once inside, he gave a curt order to the first footman, telling him to inform Lady Minerva of Miss Hazlett's safe return. Then, without a word, he escorted Emmaline into the library and closed the door firmly.

Gesturing for her to be seated, he strode to a side table, poured a splash of brandy into a glass, and downed it in one long gulp. Then he peered at Emmaline for long seconds.

"Would you care for a sherry?" he asked at last.

She shook her head and then removed her bonnet carefully, waiting for him to speak.

"You showed abominable judgment today, Emmaline," he began slowly. "Venturing out without a protector is bad enough. But accompanying a stranger in a closed hackney is just short of insanity."

Emmaline shifted guiltily. "He seemed so distraught over his sister's illness and I had no reason to doubt his word." Her stubborn chin tilted. "And he looked the perfect gentleman."

Nicolas gave a snort of disgust. "In this case, looks are shockingly deceiving. The man is a villainous snake."

Looking askance, Emmaline murmured, "Surely you exaggerate."

Nicolas set his brandy down carefully. "On the contrary. He is the very embodiment of evil."

Despite her doubt, Emmaline felt a shiver run through her as she gazed at Nicolas and saw that he was quite serious. "Who is he?" she asked.

With a deep sigh, Nicolas sat opposite her, leaning forward, regarding her intently. "His name is Guillermo Rescate. Do you know Spanish?"

"I regret not."

"He prefers the Spanish version of his English surname. Rescate translates to Ransom. He is my half-brother."

Blinking, Emmaline stared at him wordlessly. Upon reflection, she recalled a slight, although distorted resemblance. Guillermo had the same penetrating eyes, the same strong nose. But he was far smaller in stature than Nicolas, seeming a wizened, shrunken version of his half-brother. Remembering further, Emmaline realized that he had none of Nicolas' warmth. She had not detected a coldness in the man, but the absence of vibrancy that resonated through Nicolas. The "embodiment of evil!"

"How could two men from the same parent be so different?"

When Nicolas shook his head, she became aware that she had spoken her last question aloud.

" 'Tis a long tale. But to understand Guillermo now, one must understand the past, and it begins with my father."

Nicolas sat back and his gaze shifted, seeing images, Emmaline knew, created long ago.

"My father was an adventuresome man, a big, good-natured fellow who took a small inheritance and bought a sailing ship. He traveled around the Iberian Peninsula, settling in Barcelona, where he befriended Don Pedro Arbuguel, a small landowner. Together they formed a partnership, exporting fine lace and *indianas*, the printed cottons, as well as olives and nuts. The business prospered beyond their dreams, and eventually my father married Don Pedro's daughter, Luisa. My mother."

Nicolas' expression softened. "She was a beautiful, gentle woman and my father adored her. The pearls you wore were his marriage gift to her, especially matched and ordered from the Orient and set by the finest Catalan craftsman. She was wearing them when she died."

Once again, the pain at this recollection flickered across Nicolas' face. Emmaline silently touched his hand, and he smiled slightly in acknowledgment before his frown deepened once more.

"And here is where the tale turns ugly. My mother had been ill for a number of years, and in excruciating pain. In the end, so racked was she with this illness, she appeared to be a living corpse. I was five years old when she died." Nicolas paused for a moment, then finished simply, "I thought my heart would break."

Emmaline could find no adequate words, but her own heart ached in sympathy with a little boy of years ago.

"In his grief," Nicolas continued, "my father was remarried to Consuelo, a distant cousin of the Arbuguels who had come to visit and stayed to attend to my mother all through her illness. For a while, it seemed we might put our lives back together. But there was one flaw: Consuelo was slightly mad.

"Don Pedro felt bound by honor not to mention this small problem, as it reflected disgracefully on his family. And I think he convinced himself that Consuelo might be cured by marriage to a good man. What he never supposed, and what I found out only years later when a dying duenna wanted to clear her conscience, was that Consuelo wanted my father from the moment she saw him. And that she poisoned my mother to get him."

Emmaline gasped. For a moment, she thought to question Nicolas' bald statement. But gazing at him, seeing the absolute certainty in his brooding eyes, she could not but believe his claim.

"How awful!"

Nicolas nodded sharply. "Yes. At the time, of course, none of us had any idea why my mother had been failing so steadily. Consuelo was with her near every moment. 'Twas a simple matter to add the poison gradually to her food. No one suspected that the eccentric but undoubtedly devoted cousin, who never left my mother's side, had anything but Doña Luisa's well-being at heart.

"When she died, I only knew that my beloved mama was gone. I had never felt any warmth from Consuelo, but at my father's urging I promised to give her a chance as my stepmother."

Running his fingers through his black hair, Nicolas paused, the force of harsh memory lining his face.

"Consuelo was difficult to love. One moment she was smothering in her affection, the next she turned cold and shrewish. I quickly learned to hold my thoughts and feelings to myself, and not to place any faith in absolutes.

"When she bore my father a son, I was delighted, envisioning a future ally to ward off my loneliness, but Consuelo had plans for her son to replace me in my father's affections. She saw to it that I was shipped off to school in England when I was barely seven. I believe that is when she began her campaign of lies."

Emmaline ached for the pain still gnawing at Nicolas, the effects of which showed plainly in his haunted eyes. Impulsively, she thought to beg him to cease speaking, hoping to spare him additional agony. But Nicolas scarcely seemed to remember her presence. Once unleashed his words flowed in a torrent. Emmaline realized that she could not stop them if she tried. She kept her peace.

"Guillermo was always a strange lad," Nicolas mused aloud. "Consuelo filled his ears with insidious slander about me and my mother from the moment he could hear her voice. Her falsehoods warped Guillermo. Her bitter madness infected him. Although he blatantly adored his disturbed mama, he was near barbarically cruel to others.

There was about him a belligerent air. He needed to challenge anyone who crossed his path, especially me. When I would return on school holidays, he competed constantly for Father's attention. He went on rampages, then blamed me for his bad behavior, and Consuelo backed his claims to Father. As a result, to my eternal regret, my father and I grew distant. Yet I did not comprehend the extent of Guillermo's hatred for me until he tried to kill me."

Emmaline blanched, her hand clutching her throat. "Oh, no."

" 'Twas made to look like an accidental firing of his pistol, but at that moment, when the shot grazed my side, I saw Guillermo's expression. There was triumph and loathing, and a sheen of madness in his eyes. My blood chilled. My brother was all of eleven years old."

Abruptly, Nicolas rose and refilled his glass, taking a long swallow of brandy before resuming.

"My father died in the guerrilla action against Napoleon's troops. Sadly, we had not reconciled before his death. He could not see the evil in his second son, or he chose not to see, out of shame or love. I shall never know. But when my father's last will and testament was read, he left all his holdings to me. 'Twas a mixed blessing, for it fanned Guillermo's hatred hotter."

"And Consuelo?" Emmaline asked softly.

"A little more than a year ago, I heard of the duenna's confession from a loyal servant. My anger was so intense, I returned to Barcelona for the first time since my father's death and confronted her."

He frowned. "I am ashamed to own that I said very many horrid things to her. Ashamed, not because she did not deserve confrontation, but because in her madness, Consuelo was near the edge of insanity. I fear that my accusations may have pushed her over that edge. She took her own life not long after I left."

Closing her eyes, shaking her head, Emmaline could offer no words to express adequately her shock at Nicolas' revelations. She had lived a sheltered and uneventful life compared to him.

"Guillermo went into a rage of grief and anger," Nicolas said, shrugging in resignation. "He blamed me for the tragic ending of his mother's life. Possibly he blamed me with good cause. I cannot think rationally on the subject, so filled with festering emotions where he is concerned am I. But since that time, he has openly vowed to see me ruined. And since he is clever and cunning in his hatred, I fear that he shall try to accomplish his aims not by harming me but by attacking those for whom I care. As, in his twisted mind, he thinks I attacked the only person for whom he cared."

Pausing, Nicolas peered at Emmaline. "Now do you understand why you were in grave danger today?"

Emmaline was torn between conflicting emotions. On one hand, she shuddered in horror at the thought of Guillermo's treachery. On the other, a warm happiness suffused her when she realized that Nicolas had included her in the category of those for whom he cared.

"I have noted," she replied softly at last, "that the footmen and coachmen are unusually powerful for their posts, and that you accompany us whenever possible. I had not dreamed, however, that such a frightening reason prompted this attention. Do Cecil and Lady Minerva know of the danger to them?"

Nicolas allowed himself a brief smile. "Danger is comprehensible to Cecil only in terms of social acceptance. Were he threatened with ostracism by the *ton*, he would take precautions. Ordinary danger to his life and limb, he would blithely dismiss as unimaginable. I have not told him, for he would make romantic nonsense of the matter and try to reunite us, because feuding half-brothers are 'bad form.' I am fond of Cecil, but he needs looking after."

Emmaline nodded in understanding. "And Lady Minerva?"

"I have never told her in so many words, but my great-aunt is a wise and perceptive woman. She is well aware of Guillermo's propensity to violence. I believe she senses my worry."

Sighing, Emmaline said, "Lady Minerva is so dear to me. I cannot bear to think how distressed she would be by this threat."

"Aunt Minerva is as strong of backbone as she is of will," Nicolas commented with a trace of pride. "She is the youngest of my grandmother's sisters, and she tells me that all the women in the family are, in her words, 'sturdy old hens.' She imagines herself unassailable, yet she has one tremendous fear: that Cecil will die young, as do many of the men in the line, without leaving an heir. There is even a danger that, should Guillermo manage to kill both Cecil and me, he will inherit the family fortune. To Aunt Minerva, such a prospect is unthinkable."

Once again, but this time more forcefully, Emmaline shivered. If Guillermo had made an attempt at age eleven on Nicolas' life, what was to prevent him from accomplishing the nefarious deed now?

"Nicolas . . ." she said with a shade of nervousness.

"I wish to God he would try," Nicolas muttered fiercely, surprising Emmaline with his vehemence. "Each day I ride out in the morning alone, taking the same path, hoping to tempt him into attack. Perhaps I could beat some sense into him, to convince him that we are, after all, brothers. We have something in common: we both lost our mothers, we both loved our father. We share his blood. I would gladly share his estate, were I certain that Guillermo would cease this skulking mission of revenge. We shall never be friends, but we need not be open enemies. If only I could make him believe that and settle the matter once and for all!"

Draining the last of his brandy, Nicolas placed the glass carefully on the side table and returned to sit opposite Emmaline. Gently, he took her hand, rubbing his thumb across the flesh of her palm.

"You see why I was so frantic today. Were you to be harmed, my dear Emmaline, I should never forgive myself. I . . . the entire household has grown fond of you. Promise me that you will never take such risks again."

His touch set off a tingle inside her. "I promise."

As he removed his hand from hers, Emmaline gazed fretfully at the snapping fire on the hearth. She could only pray that the matter would be settled between the half-brothers without a fiery clash.

14

Outside the library doors, Verity paced restlessly. Nicolas had been inside with Emmaline for nearly an hour's time. Although Verity could hear the murmur of voices, she could not make out the content of their conversation. And the long silences had her more worried than she cared to own.

Enticing Nicolas had seemed such a simple matter to her when first the plan was unfolded. To her chagrin, he was being extraordinarily resistant to her charms, and Verity suspected with vast annoyance that the Hazlett person was the cause. What Nicolas found appealing in Emmaline was beyond Verity's comprehension. Still, the thought that another woman was standing in the way of her revenge rankled.

Now Verity was forced to fall back upon her alternate option: to aid Guillermo in effecting Nicolas' ruination. She was not certain of his precise plan, but knowing the male of the species as she did, Verity surmised that puncturing Nicolas' pride and fortune would quench Guillermo's thirst for revenge quite nicely. And into the bargain, she could be content with the outcome, if not completely satisfied.

Stopping just short of pressing her ear to the door, Verity was interrupted by a tentative cough. She turned to see the creaky majordomo gazing discreetly at the ceiling.

"Yes, what is it, Humble?"

"Message for you, milady," he replied in his rheumy voice.

"Thank you, Humble," Verity muttered, snatching the missive from his hand. Quickly, she scanned the crabbed handwriting: "Urgent I speak to you. Go now to visit Lady Atherby for tea. Stay exactly twenty minutes, then depart through the servants' entrance to the mews. A hired carriage will be waiting for you. G."

Verity grimaced. How very like Guillermo to order her around like some lowly scullery maid.

"Who delivered this note, Humble?"

"A hired messenger, milady. Will you require a runner for a reply?"

"No, indeed. I will require a carriage, though. I am visiting Lady Atherby for tea."

Humble frowned and cocked his inoperative ear at her. "For-ty what, milady?"

Verity sniffed in vexation. "Never mind, you fool. Just order the carriage brought 'round."

"The carriage. Very good, milady."

With a last piercing glance at the library doors, Verity rang for Nan to fetch her bonnet and gloves, still miffed at Guillermo's curt summons. Reluctantly, she knew she must own that he was clever. Lady Atherby was an elderly romantic. Should Verity blush daintily and beg to take her leave by the servants' entrance, the whimsical old bird undoubtedly would believe that Verity was off to some clandestine meeting with a dashing lover. Furthermore, without Verity having to request her compliance, Lady Atherby would swear to anyone who asked that Verity was with her at tea for as many hours as the assignation required.

Yes, Guillermo was undeniably ingenious. Personally, Verity never had found him fascinating but rather slightly repulsive, although she could not say exactly why. Suddenly, she chuckled to herself. Plotting did indeed make for strange bedfellows, albeit in Guillermo's case, merely figurative ones. Her annoyance became tempered pleasantly by anticipation. Perhaps Guillermo would have at last, composed the final act, and she would be satisfied with her revenge.

She was smiling prettily as she stepped into the waiting carriage.

"You are late," Guillermo snapped as Verity joined him some time later in the hired hack.

Verity sniffed. "The blame is not with me. Lady Atherby prodded relentlessly to learn the name of my mysterious lover. She would not allow me my leave until I had fed her the proper hints and innuendos."

With a smirk, Guillermo rapped on the carriage wall and the vehicle began to roll. "And you could not resist the opportunity to enhance your reputation by dishing up outrageous lies pointing to Ransom."

Before she could protest, Guillermo silenced her with an uplifted hand. "Spare me your denials, madam. I know you much too well."

Disdainfully, Verity peered down her nose at him. "If you sent such an abrupt summons merely to insult me, you are squandering my time as well as yours."

"I am well done with squandered time," Guillermo muttered with such deadly vehemence that Verity glanced at him. "The moment for action is near."

Anticipation quivered through Verity. "You have decided upon a plan?"

"Perhaps. But first I must know the household's social calendar for the next weeks. What functions will they attend?"

Exasperated, Verity shrugged. "I do not keep such a schedule in my head. I should have to consult Lady Minerva's engagement book."

"Then do so," Guillermo commanded. "I shall send a messenger on the morrow. Give the list to him."

As strongly as Verity disliked being ordered

about, she nodded silently. She had decided some time ago to abide Guillermo's distasteful ways for the greater goal of revenge. To be sure, she had given Nicolas numerous opportunities to tumble into her beguiling trap, but he continued to reject her open invitations. Any pain inflicted on Nicolas would be caused by his own stubbornness, clearing her own conscience.

"One final item," Guillermo was saying, "tell me about the woman called Emmaline."

Startled, Verity gazed at him. "Why are you suddenly interested in that chit?"

"Because, my fine coquette, it appears that she offers more charm to Ransom than you. You have failed miserably in your attempt to lure Ransom into your bed. Correct me if I am wrong, madam, but 'twould be most difficult to humiliate the man by rejecting him when he has not the slightest interest in you at all."

Stung, Verity pouted. "I see no need for sarcasm, Guillermo. Nicolas obviously is blind if he prefers her to me. At any rate, I do not wish to discuss the matter further. The thought of her makes me ill. And besides, she is not that much of an influence in his life. She is my vexation, and none of your affair."

With surprising swiftness, Guillermo leaned close to her. "Should you attempt to foil me, I should be forced to consider you my enemy. A designation that I assure you, madam, is not a pleasant one."

Against her will, Verity shivered, yet her voice remained strong. "I am your ally, Guillermo. Well you know that."

"Then never, I repeat never, tell me what is or is not my affair. Do you understand?"

For a long moment, their gazes locked in silent combat. Guillermo's force bore through his dark eyes with a dangerous intensity that chilled Verity to the marrow. Finally it was she who broke the contact.

"Emmaline Hazlett has, by wiles incomprehensible to me, wormed her way into the Garwins' good graces. They are all so taken by her as to be revolting. She is either the world's mewling fool or the most clever of opportunists. I tend to credit the former, for she seems far too fluff-headed to conceive a plan to fleece the Garwins, and far too mousy to carry out such a scheme even if she should think of one."

Guillermo gestured impatiently. "I care nothing about her motives. What is Ransom's interest in her?"

"Why do you assume that Nicolas has any interest in her whatever?" Verity asked coolly, secretly annoyed.

With a cruel smile, Guillermo said, "Do I detect the green of jealousy in your tone, Lady Lockridge? Not that I blame you. Emmaline Hazlett is far more delectable than you care to admit. Her skin is smooth and unwrinkled. But then, she is quite a bit younger than you, is she not? And still trim, she is, but I would assume that she, unlike you, is more discriminating about her pleasures. You might watch the number of sweetmeats you gobble, madam. Your excess is beginning to show."

Her eyes blazed momentarily. Then Verity smiled with feline smugness. "My dear Guillermo, I have never in my life heard a complaint from any man I have chosen to favor. I have turned down more invitations to share a bed in one week than you shall ever receive in your entire existence."

She had aimed her arrow deliberately, well aware that long ago his invitation had been one she had rejected summarily. For a brief moment, she enjoyed the triumph of seeing his mouth twitch in remembrance. Then Guillermo's hand closed tightly about her throat, stifling her gasp of alarm.

"Do not taunt me, madam. Should I so desire, I could take you at any time, in any way I chose."

Verity instantly regretted her words. For all that

Guillermo was a useful ally in that they shared the same thirst for revenge, she scarcely had to be reminded that he was also a dangerous foe. She bowed her head meekly and nodded, knowing that no other response would remove that clutching hand from her throat.

"We understand each other," Guillermo said easily, as if the frightening moment had not occurred. "So the estimable Miss Emmaline is a modest, pliable creature, not a hoyden like you. She would most likely faint in a crisis and not fight."

Mollified, Verity confirmed his analysis. Without further comment, Guillermo gave orders to the driver to return to Lady Atherby's mews, and then sank deep into thought. Verity also remained silent, noting the cruel set of his mouth and the feverish potency of his gaze, her throat still aching from his grip. Just as she was about to leave the carriage, she hesitated.

"Guillermo . . ." she began tentatively. "We are agreed that Nicolas should merely be humiliated the way he humiliated us, are we not? You do not intend to harm him, do you?"

The Spaniard smiled blandly. "Well you know that I am an aficionado of the rapier, not the bludgeon. I shall be content to make him a laughing-stock before all his high-toned friends. A fatal blow through his . . . pride shall suffice for my revenge."

Relieved, Verity departed, never dreaming that in his own mind, Guillermo substituted the word "heart" for "pride."

During the journey home, Verity squirmed with an uneasiness she did not understand. As the carriage deposited her at the Garwins' door, she had decided that the feeling stemmed from her vexation at failing to entice Nicolas. She had to make one last, forceful thrust through his defenses.

Leaving her bonnet and gloves with a maidservant, Verity listened carefully at the library door. Utter silence greeted her.

Boldly, she pushed her way through the door and strode into Nicolas' inner sanctum. He stood by the hearth, with one hand resting on the mantelpiece, staring with brooding concentration into the fire.

As she called his name, he looked up in anticipation, only to resume his frown when he recognized her.

"I have asked not to be disturbed in this room, Verity. Have the common decency to abide by my wishes, will you?"

His tone was devoid of emotion. Not even the fiery anger with which he had spoken to her of late was present. His animosity had encouraged her. The heat of apparent hatred could be turned so deftly to the heat of passion, but stony indifference . . . Verity, planning a bombast of epic proportions, felt an uncharacteristic deflation.

Slowly, she walked over to the hearth, holding out her hands to the warmth.

"Ah, Nicolas. 'Tis a sad state of affairs when lifelong friends cannot speak civilly to one another. Once we could laugh and enjoy life together. Now, we can scarcely be in the same room without unpleasant words bounding between us."

She felt Nicolas' gaze upon her and looked up to find him silently searching her face.

"Remember the times in Spain, when we were so young and unsullied by life?" she asked softly. "You loved me, Nicolas. And with you, all emotions that you own to are intense and serious. Love of that proportion cannot die."

He considered for a moment, then replied evenly, "Perhaps not. But it can be killed."

Verity flinched. "Your stubbornness required that you slay the very love that might have made our lives glorious."

A bitter smile pulled at his mouth. " 'Twas not I who was the killer of that love, Verity."

"Oh," she replied haughtily. "You imply that I was?"

Nicolas sighed deeply. "I must own that many years have passed. But my memory is that ultimately you led me to believe that you had betrayed me with my brother. I still consider that to be an effective means to murder a love."

"But I never betrayed you, with Guillermo or anyone!"

"Quite correct. You merely said you did. The results were the same, even though you lied to me."

"You are not being fair," Verity said sulkily. "I was a child of fifteen, and near ecstatic with joy at the thought that you were near to offering for me. Then, you told me that you were leaving on some fool's mission . . ."

"I would scarce call it that. Napoleon's troops were invading our adopted country, if you recall."

"Oh, posh. The Spaniards could have fared quite well without the addition of one more man."

"Perhaps," he agreed softly. "But I could not have lived with myself had I avoided the fight. Do you understand nothing of duty and honor, Verity?"

She shook her head stubbornly. "I understand that you had a duty to me. You might as well have told me that I was of little importance to you. How would any woman react?"

Suddenly Nicolas laughed gently. "Ah, Verity, you were an endearingly greedy child, so eager and enthusiastic when you had your way, so vexed when you did not. I did not understand you then, but I do now. And the time has long past come for you to leave your childish ways behind."

With an arch to her brows, Verity regarded him. "So you understand me now. And what, pray tell, sir, do you understand?"

"You were a lonely child," Nicolas said softly. "Your mother dead, your father seldom home. You were a flower that craved the sunlight of attention, and you were denied. Until you found the power to create your own light, until you bloomed and men began to notice you."

Verity fidgeted at the truth in his statement. Yet a smile curled her lips. "You cannot imagine the feeling, Nicolas. To be powerless all one's life and suddenly to find the power in a wave of the fan, a flutter of the lashes. 'Tis a heady feeling—much, I assume, like the feeling you men have when you outwit a fellow in a fencing match or triumph in battle. We of the fairer sex are denied such games of power. We take our victories where we can, in smaller, more subtle doses."

Nicolas gazed at her in surprise. "Verity, that is the most profound observation I ever have heard from you."

"Hmph. Now you mock me."

"No. But all games of power are dangerous when one is unconcerned with the potential damage."

"What damage can be wrought with a flutter of lashes?"

Nicolas paused, serious once again. "One has only to look at Freddy's life."

Stung, Verity tossed her head. "I freely own to you that I married poor Freddy because you had rejected me. But I made him happy."

Nicolas snorted in disbelief, prompting a knowing smile from Verity.

"Freddy knew that he was a weak man. He allowed me to tread upon him, which was not to either of our credit. But I did make him happy, Nicolas, in ways that were worth any amount of treading upon. In ways that even you should understand, after last year."

Abruptly, Nicolas strode to the side table and splashed brandy into a glass. Swirling the liquid absently, he stared piercingly at Verity and then gulped the brandy in one swallow.

"Our encounter in Spain was a mistake, one for which I take full blame. You must understand my state of mind, Verity. I had just discovered the truth of my mother's murder. My confrontation of Consuelo had perhaps pushed her to take her own life. Guillermo, the only member of my family remaining, had sworn vengeance upon me. 'Twas the lowest ebb of my life and I was vulnerable, I must own, to your charms."

"Ah, yes," Verity murmured, moving slowly toward him. "You were enthusiastic. Our love rekindled."

Nicolas shook his head emphatically. "Not love. Need."

"Very well," Verity agreed. "Perhaps need is accurate. And sufficient. You need me now, too; I can sense it. And I need a strong man, Nicolas, one who refuses to abide my nonsense, one whom I cannot tread upon. I can make that man incredibly happy."

She reached out to place her hands on his shoulders. Her heart beat rapidly and she exulted that her last stab at enticing him was near to succeeding. Now her only dilemma was choosing the precise moment to toss him aside as he had so callously rejected her. She knew that he would always own a small corner of her heart. But Verity was too long a player in the games of power. She knew that being vulnerable was the swiftest path to becoming powerless, a state to which she had sworn never to succumb. Her hands moved sinuously about his neck.

Nicolas sighed as she tilted her head to rest her cheek against his.

"Verity, you do need a strong man. But I am not the one. I . . . I love another."

Her breath caught in her throat as Verity saw her triumph crashing into defeat. Her eyes blazing, she stared at him for a moment, then crushed her mouth against his, taking Nicolas completely by surprise. He stood stiff and unyielding for a moment, and Verity knew she had stunned him by her passion. He merely did not know that the passion was revenge, not love.

Locked in their private drama, neither of them saw the figure frozen at the open library door. Even the rustle of Emmaline's skirts as she fled away did not intrude upon their world.

Emmaline slammed the door of her bedchamber and leaned against it, breathing heavily. She closed her eyes and a tear squeezed out and rolled slowly down her cheek. Furiously, she wiped the tear away.

What a fool she had been! To think that Nicolas might love her, that he might care for her in any other manner than that of a gentleman's concern for his great-aunt's companion. His true feelings were apparent now. Verity had wended her way into his heart. Perhaps she had never left.

Even through closed eyes, Emmaline could see the heat of their embrace. There was no mistaking the significance. Verity's was no maidenly kiss, but one that intimated a history.

For a brief moment, Emmaline was stirred to fight, to win Nicolas away from that scheming coquette. But her combativeness swiftly ebbed when she owned that she was but an inexperienced foot soldier in the war of feminine wiles, and Verity was a marshal of Napoleonic stature.

And ultimately, what had she to fight for? If Nicolas preferred Verity, the battle was lost before it was fought.

She thought to summon Floss, to plead a headache that would excuse her from the ordeal of a family dinner. But just as her hand reached for the bellpull, she stayed the motion. She would have to face the two lovers eventually, and as fortune would have it, a rare night without a social affair stretched before her. If she could simply last through the meal, the headache, surely coming, would spare her the remainder of the evening.

Deliberately, Emmaline went to the basin and sponged away the traces of her tears. The face confronting her in her hand mirror bore the effects of shattered hopes and pride, and just as deliberately, she removed them, too, forcing her expression into undisturbed lines.

Her head erect, Emmaline proceeded calmly downstairs.

Moments after she was seated in the dining room, next to Nicolas, across from Verity, Emmaline knew she had made a mistake in coming down. Nicolas was preoccupied to the point of distraction, and Verity alternated between smiling coyly at him and smirking meanly at Emmaline. Lady Minerva frowned continuously, annoyed at all of them for their failure to follow the course of her conversation; only Cecil seemed oblivious to the tension tightening around the table.

Emmaline's emotions, which she had thought contained, shivered on the edge of spilling over, and in her fragile state, Cecil's cheerful, innocuous patter seemed like a steadying force. She found herself encouraging the gossip that usually bored her, clutching at neutral, unvolatile topics.

"So what did you tell Rosetta, Cecil?" she asked, focusing intently upon him.

Cecil beamed. "I counseled her to invite both ladies in question, and to let the earl deal with the consequences. After all, 'tis hardly good form to embroil dear Rosetta in his mishandling of the affair."

"Oh, Cecil," Emmaline replied, knowing her smile was far too bright, her tone far too brittle, "how devilish of you."

Gazing at her with the eagerness of a spaniel puppy, Cecil asked, "You truly think me devilish,

Emmaline? I say, I consider that a compliment. In truth, I do."

This time Emmaline's smile was more sincere. 'Twas difficult to sustain impatience with Cecil. His world was simple, drawn in distinct lines of what was socially acceptable and what was not. There was no artifice in the man, no complicated emotions roiled beneath his surface. Indeed, every thought that passed his mind flashed clearly and distinctly upon his face. On this night, Emmaline found that trait refreshing and reassuring.

"And what morsels did you learn upon your ride in Hyde Park this afternoon?" she asked.

"Well," Cecil began, forking up his crab mousseline with gusto, "a certain lady, whose name delicacy forbids my mentioning, has treated her dressmaker so abysmally that the woman decided to revenge herself in a most unconventional manner. Let me simply say that you might be alert at the next ball. Someone might lift her delicate arms to dance one time too many and find that her gown has split down the sides."

Emmaline's laugh was genuine. "Cecil, how appalling! And however do you gain these confidences? I can think of several ladies who fit the description. Which is it?"

Shaking his finger playfully, Cecil said, "I am sworn to secrecy. However, you should ask me questions where I may answer yes or no, not mentioning names, and perhaps you might discover the identity of Madame X by yourself."

Emmaline pondered. "Has she a repulsive little dog who nips at heels indiscriminately?"

"No," Cecil replied emphatically. "The woman in question should surely gain pleasure by kicking defenseless dogs."

Cecil would never know, Emmaline mused, how grateful she was for his banter. Her mind thus occupied, she could for the moment erase the image of Nicolas and Verity together. Cecil amused her, and he was so eager in his desire to please her, her fondness for him grew. She gave herself to the game wholeheartedly.

Nicolas' mind was too heavily weighted to pay heed to their talk. And in truth, he was mortally sick of games. He had tried to neutralize Verity's exasperating version with a dose of honesty, hoping that she would give up her single-minded quest to conquer. Unfortunately, she had caught him at a moment when his mind was centered on a larger, more dire threat. He might have known Verity could not recognize honesty should it hit her in the face. Once again, and for the last time, she had attacked him in a vulnerable state.

Her talk of love did not deceive him. Well he knew that she was merely vexed, a child who was denied the latest toy of her fancy. But the problem of Verity did not disturb him one fraction as much as the problem of Emmaline.

Words could not convey the depth of his fear for her. If Guillermo even suspected that Nicolas cared for her, that he was on the verge of falling in love with her, if indeed he had not already, her very life was in peril. Guillermo would stop at nothing to wreak his vengeance. Emmaline would be mere a pawn in his deadly game.

Gazing at her, so young, so innocent, Nicolas felt a leadenness in his heart. His protectiveness surged more powerfully than his desire for her. He knew that he could not subject her to such terrible danger.

And so he must harden his heart against her. The very idea filled him with despair, such a bitter contrast to her sparkling laugh, her intoxicating smile. The thought almost made him ill, but he knew what he must do.

The meal ended with little of his food touched. But as the others made their way to the music room, he pulled Lady Minerva aside.

"Please excuse me, Auntie," he murmured tightly, unable to disguise his melancholy. "I have an engagement tonight."

Lady Minerva observed him shrewdly. "Your dear late great-uncle upon occasion bore that same expression. It presaged a night of prodigious losses at the gaming tables and even more prodigious ingestion of whiskey. May I ask what calamity prompts this prospect?"

"Business," Nicolas mumbled vaguely. "Properly boring to you, but highly annoying to me."

Lady Minerva sniffed. "Indeed. I have never seen you more highly annoyed. And being the understanding auntie that I am, I shall refrain from pressing you on the subject. Please have the good sense to take a groom to drive you and keep track of your whereabouts. I should be highly annoyed should I be forced to have you fished from the river in the morning."

Nicolas smiled bleakly. "I thank you, madam, for your concern." He planted a brief kiss on her brow and started to leave. At the last moment, he turned once more to her. "And Auntie. Consider this and, if you agree, pass it along to Cecil. I believe the time has come for him to offer for Emmaline. They should be wed as soon as possible."

Before Lady Minerva could close her astonished mouth, Nicolas was gone.

15

"Emmaline," Cecil said eagerly, "do sit down."

They had been strolling in the rose garden, amid the bushes with their soft green leaves and buds. Cecil stopped abruptly at a stone bench situated under a flowering apple tree at the edge of the garden. The spring breeze gently stirred the blossoms, sending forth a slow-drifting shower of white petals.

"Please, Emmaline," Cecil implored once again, brushing the petals from the bench. "I must speak to you about a vital matter."

With a flourish, he placed his handkerchief over the stone and gestured for her to be seated. In good nature, Emmaline complied. But as Cecil dropped down beside her and opened his mouth to speak, he suddenly froze. Even a rather rude clearing of his throat did not facilitate his words.

"What is it, Cecil?" Emmaline asked encouragingly.

Gulping, Cecil tugged at his cravat, which signified the serious nature of his coming speech, for Cecil never disturbed his appearance once it was perfectly set. He did not take lightly the efforts of two hours of his valet's time.

Emmaline stifled a smile. Cecil was such a boy in so many ways. His primary concerns ran day to day; secure in his heritage, he gave little passing thought to the morrow. And yet his very simplicity of motives had proven attractive to Emmaline in the past five days.

The image of Nicolas and Verity embracing

would not fade in her memory. Like a deep woodcut engraving, the lines distinct and harsh, the picture remained, embedded in her mind. Remembering brought fresh pain, and so Emmaline, too, concentrated on the immediate, the day to day.

Cecil provided welcome distraction. In contrast to her inner gloom, he exuded a bubbling excitement that caught Emmaline in its froth. The secret, she had realized, was constantly to keep moving, from visits and teas to crushes and routs; to chatter about inconsequentials, to find humor in the obvious, and to dance into exhaustion. Only then was she assured a dreamless sleep.

Now Cecil hinted at a most uncustomary mood. He threatened to become serious.

"Cecil, I vow that the fish from luncheon has disagreed with you," she said lightly.

"No, no," he murmured, decidedly ill-at-ease if not at stomach. "I, er . . . Well, the truth of the matter is that I have been anticipating this moment for aeons, and yet now that it has arrived . . ."

Emmaline laughed softly. "Ah, Cecil. We have become dear friends of late. Surely you know that we can speak upon any subject. What is it? Has your valet been spirited away by another gentleman? Have you not been invited to the ball of the Season?"

Cecil drew himself up in a huff. "Certainly not, on both counts. No, Emmaline, the event I have anticipated is assuredly a joyful one, and yet I wonder if you will look favorably—"

"Cecil," Emmaline said, lightly patting his hand. "Well you know that I should look favorably upon any matter that is of such importance to you."

Swiftly, his mood reverted and he was the eager, happy Cecil of old. Inwardly, Emmaline sighed in relief. Until this moment, she had not understood how much she depended upon Cecil's lightheartedness.

"By Jupiter, Emmaline, I always knew that you were a splendid woman. And so it gives me great pleasure, tremendous joy, to ask for your hand in marriage."

For a moment, Emmaline considered a suitable riposte. Cecil delighted in amusing her with jests, and her first reaction was that he was up to his antics once more. But a quick perusal of his expression, open and earnest, shed an astounding light on his interpretation.

"Cecil," she near gasped, "you are not joking."

"Well, certainly I am not. 'Tis hardly a joking matter for the ninth Earl of Langdon to offer for his bride. Emmaline Countess of Langdon . . . Is it not the most exciting of ideas?"

"Overwhelming," Emmaline murmured, her thoughts whirling.

"Emmaline, dear . . . I may call you 'dear' now, may I not? The proper form is for you to accept graciously."

"Oh, Cecil." Emmaline, lost for words, fell back on a threadbare but decidedly truthful response: "This is so sudden."

"Sudden?" Cecil laughed happily. "On the contrary, I have been at my wits' end trying to control my eagerness for the match. Oh, we shall be ecstatic together. We do get on quite well, do we not?"

"Y-yes, indeed," Emmaline stammered, frantically searching for soft words that would do no harm to his feelings. "But am I truly suited to be a countess? Surely there are far more eligible candidates—"

"Oh, no. From the very day I first set eyes upon you, there has never been a doubt. I merely patiently awaited our destiny. I knew that you were perfect for me, indeed a paragon among potential brides."

Emmaline pressed her hand to her temple. "But,

Cecil, would not a marriage between us be in bad form? After all, I am Lady Minerva's hired companion."

"Silly girl," Cecil said, patting her arm. "You fear Grandmama's disapproval. Well, you may rest your fears. 'Twas Grandmama's idea from the start. 'Twas she who first espied you, a gentle dove with cherries on your bonnet. She saw the sign in the tea leaves, Emmaline. Our destiny was sealed from that moment. Is that not the most splendid of fates?"

As his revelation penetrated her mind, Emmaline stared at him, stunned. Suddenly, all her knotted questions of the last weeks broke loose, like a tangled rope suddenly shaken straight. She finally understood why Lady Minerva had suffered her boorish guardian, why she had been offered the position of companion and then presented to the *ton* as a guest. For an instant, she supposed she should be flattered. And then her anger surged.

'Twas but another exasperating example of her fate being decided without the slightest consideration of her wishes. And this case was far worse, for the people whom she thought had cared for her had deliberately deceived her for their own ends—including, most devastating of all, Nicolas.

He must have known of Lady Minerva's plans, for she confided all matters of importance to him. In a flash, Emmaline remembered the puzzling conversation on the night when first they met, when Nicolas and Lady Minerva engaged in a spirited debate concerning a horse race. Reddening in indignation, she realized that the "filly" in question had been she herself. She was nothing more to him than an interesting wager. The idea cut her to her soul.

Yet her anger remained, and frustrated in her attempt to focus it at Nicolas, she lit upon the next-best target, Lady Minerva. Abruptly she stood and hurried as quickly as she could manage back to the house.

"Emmaline!"

"I shall speak to you later, Cecil," she snapped over her shoulder.

"Certainly, dearest," he called after her. "Well I know the female need to avoid the suggestion of overeagerness. I shall await your acceptance this evening. *À bientôt*, my dove!"

Emmaline found the dowager countess exactly where she had expected, in her chamber, sitting down to tea.

"Emmaline, what a pleasant surprise. Come join me, will you? Cook has presented the most delicious cream cakes and . . . Whatever is troubling you, my dear?"

With effort, Emmaline controlled her voice. "Cecil has just spoken to me. Imagine my stunned reaction when he informed me that I have been chosen as the paragon bride."

Lady Minerva grimaced as she spilled a drop of the tea she was pouring. "Confound that headstrong lad. I told him to wait until we had an opportunity to discuss the actual wording of his declaration to you."

"I cannot fathom what difference it would make," Emmaline replied with some heat. "His declaration was merely a matter of good form, my acceptance obviously having been purchased from my guardian and assumed by you long ago."

With a keen glance at her, Lady Minerva set down the teapot. "Come and sit, Emmaline. You are distraught."

"Indeed I am! I have been the victim of a gross deception, I have been played for a fluff-headed fool, and I believe I have every right to be distraught."

"Yes, you do," Lady Minerva agreed, diffusing some of Emmaline's ire. "Please allow me to explain."

The countess had no ability to speak humbly, so her words sounded more the command than the entreaty. And yet, in her eyes Emmaline read a tinge of compassion and indeed of slight regret. Slowly she sat down across the tea table.

"I assume," Lady Minerva began, "that Cecil has told you that I read of you in the tea leaves. I own that the prediction formed the initial impetus. But credit me with some brains, Emmaline. Had you proven unsuitable for Cecil, I should have paid you generously and dismissed you long before any marriage was mentioned."

"I have no quarrel with your intelligence, Lady Minerva," Emmaline said more quietly. "I do strongly object to the deception involved."

"And what if I had been candid with you from the start? You should have run to bury yourself in that dreadful village with that dreadful guardian of yours. What other choice would a lady of honor have? I immediately sensed that you were no fortune-seeker. The only manner in which you might agree to marry Cecil was if you became well-acquainted with him. My grandson is impetuous, a trait he inherited from his father. But he is a dear lad, and one cannot know him well and not be inordinately fond of him, do you not agree?"

Relenting a bit, Emmaline nodded. "I own that I have grown fond of him. But I do not love him. And marriage is another matter entirely."

With a deep sigh that caused her bosom to rise and fall impressively, Lady Minerva peered at Emmaline. "My dear, I am about to impart a great truth to you, one that is the distillation of all the wisdom I have garnered in my years.

"At this gaming table we call life, the men presume they hold all the cards. They control the wealth, they make the major decisions, they formulate the rules. Up to a certain point, they are correct. We must comply with their game until one certain card is played. After that, women, who in truth hold the stronger suits of brains and cleverness, can trounce them soundly, and with such finesse that they smile and beg to play on. Do you know what that vital, fateful card is?"

Intrigued despite herself, Emmaline shook her head.

"That card is marriage, my dear. We must marry to gain stakes in the game. The secret is knowing when to play the card and whom to challenge by throwing it down."

The countess smiled in a near conspiratorial manner. "If one chooses the correct player, the power shifts. 'Tis an ironic truth, but only by tying herself to a husband can a woman find freedom. Think upon it, my dear."

Rubbing at the beginnings of a headache, Emmaline frowned. "But love—"

"—develops over time," Lady Minerva interjected. "One must be intelligent enough to choose wisely from the start. Not all women are. In fact, most are not. But you are, Emmaline. Cecil is young, but he is good-hearted and comes from solid stock. You will complement each other quite well, I think. And he will demand very little and offer a great deal. Your life will be most pleasant. In essence, you will be free to do exactly as you choose."

Emmaline had not thought of the prospect in quite this manner. She imagined running her own household, choosing to spend her time exactly as she pleased, answering only to a man who, she realized, would be only too willing to grant her every whim. In a strange way, Lady Minerva had spoken a great truth: Emmaline at last could control her own life.

But where did love enter? Emmaline had tasted the intoxicating brew and grown heady with her deep feelings for Nicolas. Cecil could never make her heart soar . . .

Nor, she reminded herself, could he cause it to crash to the ground like a pheasant shot out of the sky.

Perhaps the pain of love was too great. Too well she knew that sharp pang. The very thought of Nicolas brought it plunging into her heart once more.

Oh, the treachery of the man, allowing her to fall in love with him when all the while he had designated her as his cousin's bride! Emmaline tightened her fists in fury and then, just as abruptly, allowed her hands to fall limp in her lap. Nicolas had only shown the fondness of a man for a future relative by marriage. Never had he proclaimed, nor even subtly hinted, that he might love her himself. It was a love born in her heart alone, solitary and doomed from inception.

"I shall consider Cecil's offer," she said slowly at last.

Lady Minerva rubbed her hands together. "Splendid. I think that when you do, you will see that this is the best choice for you. All women of determination and intelligence must marry eventually, Emmaline. Cecil is certainly a far finer alternative than that sheep farmer—what was his name?—to whom you were promised."

"Will Cooper," Emmaline answered distractedly.

"Indeed. The very thought of Bevindale and sheep makes me ill. You deserve far better."

Emmaline knew that marrying Cecil would keep her safe from Bevindale forever. For that fact alone, she should be overjoyed.

So why, she wondered, did she feel so hollow inside?

As Lady Minerva poured tea for Emmaline, Verity tiptoed away from the door. Sheer curiosity had prompted her to follow Emmaline as she had stormed her way to the countess's chamber. And sheer good fortune, courtesy of Emmaline's anger, had left the door ajar, almost begging Verity to have a listen. The results were intriguing, to say the least.

On one hand, Verity exulted that the country

mouse would never land in Nicolas' arms. How perfectly fitting, she thought smugly, that he should find his heart broken as he had so cavalierly tried to break her own. In a vulnerable state, as all men were when rejected, Nicolas would surely turn to solace his pride with the first comely woman available. Verity would be certain to stand at the head of the line.

Yet, on the other hand, it did not seem fair that Emmaline, who had caused so much vexation for Verity, should end up a countess, with the Garwin fortune and a fine twit of a husband at her disposal. Far more seemly would be an alliance between the country mouse and the sheep farmer . . . Who was he? Ah, yes, a certain Will Cooper of Bevindale.

In either case, Emmaline would be effectively out of Nicolas' reach. But how much more satisfying if the mouse should end up back in her dreary village, where she no doubt belonged.

Slowly, Verity's green eyes lit with a mischievous sparkle. To those who knew her well, the look warned of a vixenish plan that boded no good for anyone involved.

16

The flowers that had budded on the day of Cecil's proposal were unfolding their crimson petals as summer bloomed. Rosetta Cavendish gazed out the windows of the Garwin music room at the splendid show, wondering why the sight did not overwhelm her with the customary happiness. But, then, little filled her with pleasure these days. She had acquired an unusual case of ennui, which had chased her normal contentedness away.

"Ah, dear Rosetta," Cecil enthused, bounding into the room. "How lovely of you to call. But did Humble neglect to tell you that Grandmama is not receiving?"

She turned and raised her cheek for his proferred kiss. As she gazed upon his cheerful face, a small pocket of warmth glowed inside her. "Hello, Cecil. Humble did inform me, much to my concern. In all the years I have known Lady Minerva, she has never missed a Thursday at home unless dire circumstances prevailed. I pray she is not ill?"

"Oh, no, nothing of the sort," Cecil hastened to assure her. "With all the festivities of the upcoming wedding, she claims that the whirl has quite exhausted her."

The warmth slowly chilled. No matter that Rosetta had convinced herself that Cecil's happiness was of utmost importance to her. No matter that she saw the logic of his marriage to Emmaline. She could not summon a particle of joy at the thought of the wedding a mere two days hence.

Still, generations of good breeding promised that

not one line of sadness creased her brow. She remained composed.

Cecil, naturally, saw nothing of the mixed feelings she suppressed. "I suppose 'tis no small wonder that Grandmama is indisposed. I trust I am not imparting any secret when I say that she is rather frail of health."

Suppressing a smile, Rosetta refrained from comment.

Suddenly Cecil clapped a hand to his brow. "Oh, where are my manners! Please do be seated, Rosetta dear, and I shall ring for tea."

"Do not bother," Rosetta said, sitting on the chair he offered. "Although I am always glad to pay a call on Lady Minerva, in truth I have come to see how you are faring."

Preening in delight, Cecil pulled his own chair up to hers. "Splendid! No doubt you wish to hear all the details of last evening's ball, which I am so sorry you missed. Well! Lady Melton, you will be fascinated to hear, was the talk of the *ton*. Imagine! Introducing as her intended a lad one-third her age, and if you listen to Grandmama, that carefully guarded number is impressive indeed. No wonder, now that she has employed such a skillful modiste to lure the poor lad with promises she cannot keep. The late Lord Melton surely will come back to haunt her, what?"

Rosetta chuckled in appreciation as she was meant to while Cecil related all the newest bits of gossip to her. When he paused for breath, she turned a gentle gaze upon him.

"Cecil, how are you faring? Truly."

He made to offer a light reply when his happy expression abruptly melted. "Ah, Rosetta dear, you know me too well. I cannot hide from you. In truth, I am perplexed."

"But why?"

Bounding to his feet, Cecil began to pace restlessly. "I vow that I shall never understand the fairer sex. Delightful creatures that they are, they do indeed confound one with their whims. 'Tis enough to drive a man mad."

"Have I done aught to concern you, Cecil?" she asked, leaning forward.

He peered at her in surprise. "You? Oh, no. You are ever steady, Rosetta, and not given to whims. Why would you entertain such a notion?"

Fidgeting with her fan, Rosetta replied evenly, "Must I remind you, dear Cecil, that I too belong to the fairer sex that so perplexes you? 'Tis not the far side of ridiculous to suppose that I may have caused you some distress."

Frowning in irritation, Cecil paused in his pacing. "Certainly you are a woman, Rosetta. But you are different. I know I may always depend upon you to understand what is done and what is not. Unfortunately, this is not true of all those of your sex."

"You are referring to Emmaline?"

"Certainly Emmaline." Resuming his restless prowl, Cecil waved his hands in agitation. "I assumed that she should enjoy a long period of betrothal, with the wedding taking place next spring. How else to accept all the balls to be given in our honor? How else to plan a trousseau and all the fine details of a grand wedding celebration that our place in society demands? Imagine my astonishment when she announced that she preferred to be wed in near scandalous haste, a mere four weeks from my proposal."

Rosetta fanned herself slowly. "I imagine that she has her reasons. Emmaline is a sensible girl."

"Sensible? Sensible?" At last Cecil dropped down in his chair, spreading his arms as if to lay out his case before her. "If she is sensible, why does she insist upon such haste? Why does she plague me with questions about how and where we shall live, what duties might be expected of her? She should know these things, Rosetta. You would."

Hiding her sharp intake of breath behind her fan,

Rosetta considered. Indeed, she would know, for she knew Cecil's mind as she knew the colors of sunrise, the scent of a forest glade. He was her dear friend, and her happiest days were spent delighting in his *joie de vivre*. She was proud to be his confidante. No one realized his tenderness of heart as she did, for in her patience she had come to know the man inside the boy. A slight annoyance left her wishing that Emmaline would take the time to learn to please her intended. Yet Rosetta offered no comment and Cecil did not seem to notice her bemusement.

"I cannot be concerned with such . . . trivialities," he muttered. " 'Tis the important matters of life that concern a man of my position. What should happen if I did not keep up with the latest style of dress, or the tidbits of gossip upon which the *ton* revolves? Or if I did not know whose note to honor at White's and whose to refuse? I say, Rosetta, the very foundations of this family would falter."

He spoke in all sincerity, and Rosetta smiled fondly at him. "I do understand you, Cecil."

"And deuced glad I am that you do. At least one person can sympathize with my plight."

Nodding his head, satisfied that she had validated his grievances, Cecil sat back in silence.

Rosetta felt emboldened to ask the question that had been plaguing her mind ever since she had heard of the proposal. "Cecil, are you certain that you want this match?"

"Well, naturally I do," Cecil said petulantly. "Rosetta, I am deeply wounded that you think me a man who does not know his own mind. I am confident that Emmaline will improve her outlook once we are wed. I am capable of patience, you know. Besides, Grandmama has read my destiny in the tea leaves. If Emmaline is the paragon of brides, then all will be well, you will see." Suddenly cocking his head to the side, Cecil considered as if hearing the echo of his declaration. Then just as abruptly, he beamed. "I say, Rosetta, I am confident. Why, I feel ever so much better now. And I have a splendid idea. Come with me for a jaunt in Hyde Park. I am dying to see if Lady Melton appears with her betrothed, and I have a new coat to wear."

Hesitating, Rosetta finally said, "But perhaps 'tis Emmaline who should accompany you."

Cecil shook his head and then raised his eyebrow significantly. "Emmaline insists that she is a terrible horsewoman and never rides. Can you credit such a claim from a woman who shall be my wife?"

"But, Cecil," Rosetta replied more tartly than was her custom, "we shall cause a scandal, with your wedding day so near."

Laughing, Cecil slapped a hand on his knee. "Ah, Rosetta, only you can amuse me so thoroughly with your jests. Everyone knows that there could not possibly be any scandal with you and me. Come, I shall ring for two splendid mounts and accompany you home so that you may change into your riding habit. We shall have a glorious time."

She stood to follow him and paused to peer out the window once more. Her question had been duly answered: Cecil was keen for the match. He thought of Emmaline as his one and only bride, and of Rosetta herself as a genderless, if agreeable companion. She sighed in deep resignation.

The roses still lifted their magnificent blooms to the pale afternoon sun, and the sight still filled her with abject sadness.

Had Rosetta remained at the window a few moments longer, she would have seen a figure moving slowly about the paths in the garden.

Emmaline adjusted her parasol to shade herself. Although for Lady Minerva's sake she regretted the indisposal that caused the countess to withdraw to her chambers, Emmaline herself felt a vast relief

to be excused from the strain of receiving a stream
of callers.

The solitude and fresh air were meant to revive
her. For the past weeks it had seemed as though
there was not a waking moment when she was not
expected to chatter in excitement, accepting good
wishes under the curious eyes of the *ton*. She could
understand their eagerness to probe her background, the necessity of trotting out her pedigree
for the approval of all and sundry. It was a require-
ment for admittance in the *ton*, and if she wished
to be Cecil's wife, she must play by their rules.

Lady Minerva's "great truth" kept her going.
Knowing that the guidance of her own destiny
would be assured once she was wed, Emmaline
could withstand the onslaught of near rude
questions, the miles of receiving lines, the rush
from one grand house to the next, and night after
night of forced gaiety.

What did concern her was her impatience with
the intended groom himself. A few moments of his
gossip amused her. But when the tales dragged on
for hours, she had to fight yawns of boredom.
Surely there were more scintillating topics to
discuss than who wore the most outrageous jewels
or whose fortune was in danger of depletion. But
Cecil merely gazed at her in perplexion when she
attempted to raise other subjects.

She paused at the shaded bench where he had
made his proposal some time ago, considering if she
regretted her acceptance. No, she told herself
firmly, snapping her parasol shut. It was the correct
decision to make.

"For God's sake, Emmaline! Why are you out
here unaccompanied?"

She whirled around. Nicolas stood before her, his
face dark with annoyance.

Against her will, to her utter consternation, her
heart fluttered. The mere fact of being in his

presence, regardless of his black mood, affected her profoundly.

She swallowed the lump that rose to her throat before replying coolly, "Good afternoon, Nicolas."

He took a deep breath and relaxed his frown. "Emmaline," he said reasonably, "I thought we had discussed the need for caution. You should have had one of the grooms accompany you on your stroll."

"I am in the garden of a veritable fortress," she replied just as reasonably, "with a thick wall surrounding the grounds. I presumed I should be safe."

"No, you did not. You merely did not think upon the subject of your safety at all."

Emmaline avoided his direct gaze, for indeed he spoke the truth.

"I should appreciate," he continued evenly, "your returning to the house."

"Thank you, no," she said in a stiff tone. "I have not had a moment to myself for so long, I had near forgotten what silence and solitude are. So you will forgive me if I wished to spend a quarter-hour strolling in the garden in peace." Gazing at him pointedly, Emmaline stood her ground.

No opportunity to speak privately with him had arisen since that fateful day she had seen him with Verity. In truth, Emmaline was grateful for that. Were she to have any hope of expunging him from her heart, she knew she must not spend any time alone with him. His nearness wove a spell about her that misted her mind and clouded her resolve.

As he peered at her now, his mouth drew in a tight line.

"Why must you be so stubborn?" he asked in exasperation. "Have I not explained the danger of my situation? Use your wit. I thought you an intelligent woman, Emmaline. I thought you understood that I cannot afford additional worries about you."

Stung, she threw her folded parasol to the

ground. "Oh, yes, well I know your worries about me from the start. Are they any cause for you to speak so hatefully to me?"

"How else may I make you understand? And what do you mean, 'from the start'?"

She had vowed never to speak of his role in the Garwin deception. She had promised herself to carry her awareness of his treachery to the grave. But all her intentions melted in the heat of her repressed anger, and the accusations came flooding out.

"You were part and parcel of the master plan, Nicolas. And did you have hearty laughs at my expense? I vow that you did. The innocent country maid, a mere pawn in the Garwins' plotting. Did you win your wager on the horse race, Nicolas? Did the filly in question content you with her pace?"

He had the grace to blanch, although his jaw clenched and his eyes never lost their scowl.

Emmaline smiled grimly. "Yes, I am an intelligent woman, Nicolas—intelligent enough to see how you used me. How my susceptibility to a charming dance and a few tender words aided you in your plot. You softened me, pretended to care for me, so I would be amenable to any plans the Garwins had. I own to being a fool, Nicolas, but do not think for a moment that I am not aware of your deception. You cared only for the security of the Garwin line."

"That is a ridiculous claim," he muttered, his voice rasping. " 'Tis my nearly mad half-brother who concerns me, not the family succession."

"Truly? How many times in the past weeks, do you suppose, have I heard Lady Minerva rhapsodizing upon that very subject? I shall bear sons, she tells me, the tea leaves having assured her. And once Cecil has a son, the Garwin inheritance is safe from your half-brother. You see, Nicolas? This intelligent woman has figured that possibility, too. The earldom will stay in direct succession, all safe and secure. You are always concerned with safety, are you not? The idea should send you into ecstasy also."

Abruptly he grasped her shoulders, and his dark eyes bore into her more startlingly than his fingers. "Yes, safety! From Guillermo. Have you any idea of what atrocities he is capable of, should he get his demented hands upon you? Even marrying Cecil will not protect you should Guillermo even suspect that I care for you—"

"You care naught for me," Emmaline cried, struggling in his grasp.

He refused to release her. "Care naught?" he roared. "You little fool, you are in my head constantly. I cannot eat for the pain that tightens my stomach at the thought of harm coming to you. I cannot sleep for the fear that I have not foreseen all possibilities and protected you. I rail at the grooms to keep you always in their vision on your outings. I search your face for the slightest hint of distress. I drive myself to the edge of madness with imaginings of the evil that could befall you."

She could feel his intensity as palpable as his hands upon her. All her retorts withered in her throat. She felt the guards about her heart weakening, threatening to leave her vulnerable to the pain of loving him again.

Then Emmaline struggled in earnest against him. Her heart pounded inside her, a wild creature fighting to break free of the restraints of her control. As she tossed her head from side to side, denying the mighty pull of her feelings, her hair tumbled from its loose knot and spilled a molten gold down her back.

"Emmaline, Emmaline," Nicolas shouted, grasping her all the tighter. "For God's sake, I—"

For a piercing moment, they both froze, their hearts pounding as one. And then his arms clasped her in an encompassing embrace and her lips strained hungrily for his. His kiss burned through her, searing into her a truth she could not deny. His strength flowed into her, forging the bond that had ever existed between them with iron enforcement.

Entwining his fingers in her hair, Nicolas pulled her even closer, until she grew dizzy from his power. The scent of roses and sunlight and crisp linen blended in an almost unbearable beauty, heightening all her senses. His mouth moved fervently on hers, and Emmaline thought she would surely faint from his ardor.

Abruptly, he drew his head back, his muscled chest rising and falling rapidly. Only his strong arms kept Emmaline upright.

"Oh, dear God," he whispered. "What have I done?"

His final words blew over her like an arctic wind, extinguishing the flames of her feelings. Slowly, he released her from his clasp. Realizing the import of her surrender to his embrace, Emmaline wobbled. He set her carefully on the stone bench and then stood rigidly before her.

"I beg your forgiveness," he murmured, his voice uneven. "I never should have . . . I have no excuse."

"You need not ask my pardon," she said softly, surprised that she could speak at all. "I am as much to blame."

"Oh, no. I am appalled with myself. I cannot fathom what came over me."

Breathing deeply, still shaking inside, Emmaline could not summon any words at all.

He had set his expression in stiff, uncompromising lines. For a moment, the resolution in his gaze faltered and he looked away. Then, as if drawing upon a reserve, he inhaled sharply and blew out a deep breath.

"The best course would be for both of us to forget the past few minutes ever occurred."

Emmaline nodded. "We must." She risked a glance at him and her heart lurched. "But however can we?"

Nicolas' intent seemed to strengthen in proportion to her doubt. "You are betrothed to Cecil. You will marry in two days. This indiscretion should not have occurred and I should confess my dishonor to him, but I cannot do that without compromising you. Therefore, I believe it best to forget the entire incident. I shall have to live with my dishonor."

Emmaline gazed beseechingly at him. "And what of the feelings involved?"

" 'Twas anger," he said slowly, intently, "and it led me onto a path that should never have been taken. In the moment's heat, I forgot my place. You must put this incident completely out of your mind. You were not in any way responsible. I merely lost my head."

She bit her lip to keep from blurting out that her heart told a far different tale. In the space of a few moments, in the intense heat of a kiss, she had thrown herself headlong into the truth: her love could never belong to anyone but Nicolas. And for all his denial, she had tasted his true feelings for her.

"You have accepted Cecil's offer. Furthermore, marrying Cecil is the right course for you to take. No mention of this afternoon will ever be made."

At last, Emmaline saw the bleak reality of his insistence. She could not deny her heart. At the same time, she must fulfill her promise to Cecil, even at the expense of fulfilling her love.

Bowing formally, Nicolas said, "I am terribly sorry I took such abominable advantage of you. Please find it in your heart to forgive me. Good day, Emmaline."

Before she could reply, he wheeled and marched down the path toward the house. Emmaline stared after him until her tears blurred his image.

In the safe harbor of the library, Nicolas downed two brandies and was gulping the third before his hand ceased its shaking. As the spirits spread warmth and relative calm through him, he breathed heavily twice, thrice, and then in a fury hurled the glass to smash into the fireplace.

He cursed himself from every direction. How could he have been so stupid, how could he have allowed his guard to drop? He knew how susceptible he was to Emmaline's presence. Daily he posted sentries about his feelings when she was near him, even distantly. Her very life depended upon his staunch defense against her.

It was her loosened hair that had triggered his feelings. So innocent a release . . . and so intimate. Watching it tumble down her back, smelling the sweet softness of violets released in the flow, he had clearly lost his mind. Secret passions he had guarded as vigilantly as the rarest of gems spilled out almost against his will. And in a moment of weakness, he had nearly destroyed all that he had so painstakingly built.

Now he had the additional, almost unbearable burden of knowing that she had responded eagerly, openly to him, too. For a wild, brief moment, his heart had threatened to soar with joy. And when reality weighed heavily, he knew despair at his loss.

Suddenly a vast weariness overtook him. He dropped disconsolately into his leather chair, staring numbly at the shards of glass on the hearth.

17

Lady Minerva, alone in her rooms, sat back on her chaise longue, frowning. Teatime was usually the pivot of her day, more often than not spent *en chambre* with her family, a refreshing interlude between the meat of managing her household and the dessert of social outings. A bracing pot of tea, sipped in pleasant and devoted company, provided a sense of equilibrium.

Yet that sense had been missing of late. Of all the situations that caused her annoyance—and there were a considerable number—nothing vexed her more than a feeling of unbalance.

A shadow caught her eye, and she realized that her maid had slipped into the room.

"What is it, Andrews?"

"Your gown for this evening," Andrews replied in her usual taciturn manner.

Lady Minerva, annoyed at the distraction to her fit of pique, grimaced. "Must you prepare it now?"

"Yes," Andrews replied curtly. Forty years of patient service, in her opinion, had given her the privilege to be abrupt, a view her mistress did not dispute.

The countess ruled her domain as a benevolent despot, as was her right and, indeed, her duty. The ship of her state was meant to sail smoothly, with hearty winds and minimum turbulence. In her vision, ambitious men governed the kingdoms of landholdings and politics, and strong women reigned over the rest of the world, a far more interesting and important realm at any rate. And just as small, seemingly insignificant rumblings might presage the beginnings of wars or financial collapse in the men's world, whispers of discontent and unbalance threatened hers.

There was nothing to which she could point a finger and declare the source of her worries. To be sure, orchestrating a wedding of *le beau monde* proportions in a mere four weeks' time would tax the balance of even so tightly run a household as hers. But the challenge, not to mention the prospect of stirring the gossip pot of the *ton*, invigorated her. She secretly enjoyed being the focus of speculation, so long as she controlled the outcome. The tactical problem of such a social production was a minor nuisance.

For a while, she had surmised that the happy couple themselves caused the tremors of instability. Cecil was acting more witless than usual, his never-concealed emotions running the gamut from stormy lows to sunny highs. But most men in imminent danger of leg-shackling behaved similarly, as if marriage were not the redemption of their existence. And Emmaline's nervous distraction also seemed appropriate to her position as bride- and countess-to-be.

Next, Lady Minerva had been near to blaming Verity for her sense of uneasiness. The minx's tirades actually had decreased in number and intensity, and at times she put on a most pleasant face. This lack of petulance caused Lady Minerva no end of suspicion, for undoubtedly Verity plotted some mischief. Yet even realizing that Verity might be the cause of unbalance did not satisfy.

"Andrews, what is the gossip belowstairs?"

The maid, laying out a flame-colored satin gown, shrugged. "Same rubbish as always."

"No, I am referring to the upcoming wedding."

"Lord Cecil's valet whines. Floss jabbers romantic nonsense. A wedding abovestairs just means double the work belowstairs."

"Well, certainly, but the staff shares in the glory, also."

Andrews paused in her work to pass a jaded glance in her mistress's direction, but she said nothing. Even forty years of service did not give passage over certain boundaries.

"What of Mr. Nicolas' valet?" Lady Minerva persisted.

Rolling her eyes, Andrews replied grimly, "Humble has had to lock up the cooking sherry."

The countess nodded in understanding, not surprised to learn that the man felt beleaguered in regard to Nicolas, for she shared the feeling. It was Nicolas who disturbed Lady Minerva most these days. His brow constantly furrowed, his mood unrelentingly black, he hardly spoke a civil word even to her. Before this, when Nicolas tendered signs of disturbance, she always had adopted a quietly watchful stance. She thought that she understood him, supposing that his temperament was the masculine equivalent to her own. When his particular world teetered, he gathered his considerable concentration and power to set the situation aright. Lady Minerva merely awaited this turn of events.

Now her low tolerance for patience had ebbed away entirely, for his mood showed no signs of lifting. She thought to confront him, to seek admittance to that masculine world that usually bored her. If circumstances left Nicolas so negatively affected, she should be aware of them. Disturbances of such magnitude would shake her world also. Yet she hesitated to intrude. Nicolas had demonstrated a firm capability in the past. Surely he would again, would he not?

Still debating thus, Lady Minerva roused herself to drain the last of her tea. Pausing a moment, she swirled the dregs and inverted the fine porcelain cup upon its saucer. Then, with the intensity of a field marshal viewing the scene of a battle, she turned the cup upright and peered at the tea leaves' pattern.

Her frown deepened. Opposing forces. Cross-purposes. Turmoil. Certainly not the most auspicious reading for two days before a wedding. In vain, she searched for a sign of good fortune, one small omen to counteract the bad. Then she noted a symbol that could be interpreted as a knife, an irrefutable sign of imminent danger.

Shaken, she set the cup down firmly, not noticing Andrews' scowl of disapproval as she cracked the delicate porcelain. The situation had gone too far. Still clad in her rose brocade dressing gown, mindless of the fact that she never emerged from her rooms in such a state of dishabille, Lady Minerva proceeded in a direct and determined line to the library.

Andrews shook her head in disgust. "Quality folk," she sniffed, and returned to her chores.

"Lubbock, you worthless scut," Nicolas growled in repugnance. "You shall receive not a penny more from me. Get out."

The crusty sailor scuffled his grimy boots on the priceless library Aubusson.

"Jest give a listen, sir," Lubbock wheedled. "I got good information this time."

Nicolas deliberately allowed his silence to hang in the still air. He stood with his feet firmly planted, his forearms crossed over his chest. The only sound in the room emanated from the steadily ticking mantel clock.

"Lubbock," he said finally, slowly, "should you try to sell me some useless tripe again . . ."

"Nay," the sailor answered eagerly, "this is quality news, sir. You'll bless me for certain."

Glaring in suspicion, Nicolas nonetheless nodded for the man to proceed.

"Tomorrow night," Lubbock began, his words nearly tripping over his tongue in his eagerness to prove his worth. "The Spaniard told me to be at the ready, 'e did. Says I might be needed. That shows 'e's up ter no good, eh, guv'nor?"

Nicolas shrugged, careful to keep his expression bland. But inwardly his sense for treachery prickled. Tomorrow night. As a final prewedding celebration, his great-aunt had planned a grand party at Vauxhall Gardens. Although torches would light the main walks and the concert area, there were numerous paths among the trees and bushes where darkness would reign. Guillermo would find the setting perfect for hatching any nefarious plot.

Turning his back on the sailor, pretending to consider the worth of his information, Nicolas cursed under his breath. The potential for peril worried him; his own lack of foresight chilled him to the bone.

He should have seen the danger from the first mention of an outdoor celebration, immediately dissuading his great-aunt from this folly. He had allowed his mind to wander the maze of his conflicting emotions, distracting him from the constant vigilance so imperative to the safety of those he loved.

"Well, sir, ain't that good information?"

Straightening his spine, Nicolas strode to his desk, reaching into a lockbox in the drawer.

"How much will the Spaniard pay you for aiding in his filthy plans tomorrow?" he asked brusquely.

The sailor's rheumy eyes narrowed as he swiftly calculated. "Well, guv'nor a princely amount, to be sure. Lubbock's services don't come cheap. As for the exact price—"

"Never mind," Nicolas snapped. "That tongue of yours has never tasted the truth." Then he regarded the sailor shrewdly. "But I am willing to wager that a few pints of gin might roll over it quite smoothly."

Grinning sheepishly, Lubbock nodded. "Aye, you pegged me, guv'nor. Me and the Blue Ruin is good chums."

"Very well." Nicolas selected a handful of coins and shoved them into Lubbock's eager hand. "This is five times any 'princely amount' the Spaniard would offer you. See to it that you and your chum meet up early tomorrow afternoon. By nightfall, I want you snoring under a tavern table, of no use to anyone but pickpockets. Do you understand?"

"Aye, sir, I do indeed," Lubbock answered cheerfully, pocketing the coins lest Nicolas change his mind. "Not to worry. By sundown, old Lubbock will be snockered good and proper. And thankee, guv'nor. I'm right pleasured to be at your service."

Nicolas grunted. "Just be certain—"

The doorknob rattled, interrupting his warning. Nicolas froze, thankful that he had turned the key in the lock when Lubbock had made his appearance.

Raising his voice, Nicolas barked, "Go away!" in tones designed to daunt even the most dull-witted servant. But the imperious knock that followed could not have been delivered by any servant.

"Nicolas," came the muffled but unmistakable voice of Lady Minerva, "I wish to speak to you."

With a fierce wave of his hand, Nicolas commanded Lubbock to leave by the terrace door. The sailor moved quickly but halted after a peek through the glass.

"There be a lady outside," he whispered loudly.

Nicolas hurried to see for himself. Verity had chosen to take her tea al fresco and sat not thirty feet away, sipping from her cup and scolding her maid.

"Nicolas," Lady Minerva called from the hall, obviously annoyed to be kept waiting.

Swiftly, Nicolas shoved the sailor behind the heavy draperies that lined the wall. "Do not move," he ordered harshly, "or I cut your fee in half."

Before Lubbock was settled in the folds, Nicolas rushed to the door. With one quick backward glance, he turned the key.

"Please forgive me, Aunt," he murmured,

blocking the passage as Lady Minerva peered into the library. "I was in the midst of sorting through some papers. Actually, I am quite occupied. Perhaps later—"

She gave a regal wave of her hand and Nicolas reluctantly stepped back. As she swept into the library, he inhaled deeply, darting a furtive glance at the unmoving draperies.

Lady Minerva regarded the stacks of books and piles of papers on his massive desk, and the open crate on the floor beside it. Raising an eyebrow, she said, "I daresay, Nicolas, that you were in the midst of packing."

Her gaze held his immobile.

Finally he broke the contact. "Would you care to discuss this at a later time?"

"No, Nicolas," Lady Minerva replied calmly, lowering herself into one of the leather chairs flanking the hearth. "What I would like is an explanation."

Running his fingers swiftly through his dark hair, Nicolas paused, then came to sit opposite her. "I intended to tell you after all the fuss of Cecil's wedding was over," he began slowly. "I did not wish to add to the turmoil in this house."

She sat in queenlike dignity, her shoulders straight, her chin royally steady. But a small quiver at the corners of her mouth betrayed Lady Minerva's poise. "Why?" she asked simply.

"I am returning to Spain," he replied, more woodenly than he planned. "My father's estates sorely need my attention and I have tarried overlong in London."

"Forgive me, Nephew. I did not realize we were keeping you from your duties."

The irony in her tone was not lost on Nicolas. He rubbed a tired hand across his brow. "Oh, Auntie. This business with Guillermo—"

Suddenly he curbed his tongue, mindful of

Lubbock's presence behind the draperies. Once again, his guard had been in danger of faltering, of letting slip some vital information that could well cost the safety of those for whom he cared. Nicolas had no illusions about the greedy sailor. Well he knew that the man was a rank opportunist, with his news for sale to the highest bidder. He had never entertained a doubt that every word he said to Lubbock was faithfully reported to Guillermo. In fact, he had used the man as a conduit all along, and perhaps, he thought as a possibility of advantage occurred to him, he could use Lubbock once more.

Stiffening, Nicolas rose, his face an impenetrable mask. "I sail for Spain the day after the wedding. I am sorry to give you such short notice, Auntie. But I must leave immediately."

Lady Minerva, peering shrewdly at him, nodded. "To oversee your father's estates. Not to recover from a loss."

Nicolas blinked in surprise. "What do you mean?"

Drawing a deep breath, Lady Minerva sighed, as if about to plunge into murky waters.

"Nicolas, your mood these days has been as black as a highwayman's heart, and twice as cold. You rumble fiercely about, shooting looks at the servants that leave them cowering in the corners. You mutter curses in your sleep. Your food goes untouched, your brandy disappears at an alarming rate, and even your favorite horse turns skittish when you approach. Oh, do dispense with that suspicious expression, dear Nephew. No one spies upon you. 'Tis my duty to know the innermost workings of this household, and what I know disturbs me profoundly."

Nicolas had no reply.

"I had thought," Lady Minerva continued evenly, "that the direst of peril endangered this household, prompting your mood. But upon reflection, I own that another motive may be driving you. In my vast experience, I have found that the same symptoms that are caused by anger and worry may be caused by an unfulfilled passion."

Despite his considerable skill at masking his expression, Nicolas blinked in astonishment. With all his painstaking effort to disguise his love for Emmaline, had Lady Minerva seen through him so easily? Again his mind flew to Lubbock, to the juicy tale he could offer Guillermo if this conversation continued. He knew it was vital to guide their talk upon a diversionary path, to give the sailor, and thus Guillermo, a new trail to explore, one that led firmly away from his feelings for Emmaline. Silently praying his great-aunt would forgive him eventually, he proceeded to do what he had never done before: he turned harshly, cruelly, on Lady Minerva.

"Madam, you are spinning intrigues where none exist," he snapped. "I have no passion save for my father's holdings in Spain. I have played nursemaid to this household overlong, and to be frank, I am sick unto death of the role. In Spain, I shall once again be my own man, as my father wished me to be, expanding his bequest to me. Now, if you will excuse me, I must attend to my packing. Good day, madam."

He strode to the door, holding it open for her, staring straight ahead and avoiding her eyes.

Lady Minerva hesitated but a moment before rising. As she passed him, she paused. Although he towered over, her stance was far from intimidated. Indeed, at that moment she seemed the taller.

"You are, by far," she said softly, "the most honorable man of my acquaintance. You have always chosen the right course, considering the best interests of all involved. I have every confidence that you will not disappoint me now."

Daring to glance down at her, misery at his

cruelty cutting at his heart, Nicolas was astounded
by the expression on his great-aunt's face. She was
smiling broadly, and the most amazing flicker of
anticipation gleamed in her sagacious eyes.

Far away in Bevindale, another pair of eyes
glinted in anticipation. The Reverend Mr. Markham
surveyed his new equipage, a sleek two-wheeled
carriage and a high-stepping bay gelding, with
unconcealed pleasure. Let the small-minded
villagers grumble about ostentation; he cared not
a fig for their opinions, knowing in his heart that
God would approve of his good use for the
countess's monthly stipends.

"When will ye return?" asked his housekeeper,
standing in the vicarage garden behind him.

"Perhaps a week's time," he answered vaguely.
"Perhaps longer. The dowager countess no doubt
will require that I prolong my visit. She may be in
need of solace from the rigors of the wedding."

The housekeeper snorted and headed off to her
kitchen, but the vicar's mood was such that he paid
her no mind.

When the invitation had arrived three weeks
before, Markham's first reaction had been one of
astonishment. Imagine the little mouse Emmaline
evolving into such a minx as to snare Lord Garwin
as a husband! Then, realizing that no request to
officiate at the nuptials was forthcoming, his mood
had turned to resentment. But finally, seeing the
advantage of being owed one's due rather than of
casually being given such, he relaxed and let his
mind wander to more practical objectives.

Surely the dowager countess could not afford the
social embarrassment of an impoverished relative
by marriage. And if the thought did not occur to her
naturally, the vicar had no qualms about subtle
reminders that his recently elevated status as
guardian to the new Countess Emmaline deserved

a far more generous settlement. Lady Minerva was a woman of high moral principles; she would demand that propriety be served, and her purse strings would open like a rain cloud in May.

His thin mouth quirked in what was for him a jovial expression.

"Good day, Reverend," piped a small voice, and the vicar glanced down to see a young lad staring in admiration at the gelding. "Fine horse you got there."

Scowling, Markham shooed him away from the carriage. "Here, now! You are splashing mud on the wheels. Have you nothing better to do? Idle hands are the devil's workshop. Off with you!"

As the boy made a face and skittered away, the vicar mumbled to himself. Parents of these times taught their offspring no respect.

Straightening the sleeves of his new coat, tailored in London, he stepped into the carriage and hefted the reins. Just as he would take his leave, a tall form on a black horse loomed beside him.

"Vicar," Will Cooper said urgently, dismounting.

Sighing, Markham turned to look pointedly at the sheep farmer. "I am in somewhat of a hurry, Cooper."

"I'll take but a minute of your time."

The vicar groaned, well aware of how long a villager's minute could last. "Well, get on with it, man."

Angrily, Will thrust forward a folded note penned on pale-blue paper. "This came to me by post from London."

When it became apparent that the man would not budge until he had read the letter, the vicar impatiently snatched it from Cooper's massive fist. He glanced over the words, obviously written in a feminine hand:

Dearest Will:

Perhaps you have heard that I am betrothed to marry Lord Garwin this Saturday coming. Although, when he declared for me, I in my haste accepted, I now find myself beset with second thoughts. I ever think of you fondly, dearest Will, and beg your assurance that I made the best choice. Events might be quite different, had you held to your promise . . .

I often find myself longing for dear Bevindale and the quiet country life. Perhaps I shall never see my lovely home again. But whatever you advise, I shall abide by your judgment.

Fondly, E.

Roughly, the vicar shoved the letter back at Cooper. "This is nonsense. Believe not a word of it."

Will glared belligerently. "Is it Miss Emmaline's hand?"

"Certainly not, it could not be. My ward is delighted to be marrying Lord Garwin. This is an obvious forgery."

"Is it?" Will said bluntly, the muscles in his jaw working. "Who else would write such words?"

Fumbling for a possible perpetrator, the vicar sputtered, "How should I know? A mischief-maker, no doubt. Throw it away. It has no worth."

His expression hardening, Cooper said, "I knew all along that 'tweren't proper, her going off to London like that when she was betrothed to me. But I let her go, even though you broke your word and did me a dishonor. Now—"

"Now you will disregard this preposterous forgery and get on with your business," Markham snapped, "as you permit me to get on with mine."

Snapping the reins, the vicar set off, leaving Will

to stare after him. But before the fancy carriage was fifty yards down the road, Will determinedly mounted his horse, never letting the carriage out of his sight.

18

Emmaline watched in the hand mirror as Floss gathered wheat-colored ringlets atop her head and entwined a woven string of tiny bluebells through the curls.

"Oh, Miss Em, what a night this will be," Floss babbled excitedly. "The Pleasure Gardens twinklin' with a thousand lamps, more p'r'aps, and the music playin', and everyone ever so gay. 'Er ladyship made special arrangements, says Cook, for the staff to bring a supper over. And she invited us to stay, she did, for the Chinese fire."

Attempting to stir up a breath of enthusiasm, Emmaline smiled briefly. Vauxhall Gardens was an enchanting site, with the splendor of lamplit trees and fountains. Lady Minerva had been quite pleased with herself for choosing that location for a last celebration with close family and friends before the wedding. And the promise of her first view of the renowned fireworks display might have fanned Emmaline's interest. Yet she felt curiously unmoved by the prospect.

Since her encounter with Nicolas in the garden the day before, Emmaline had had the eerie sense of dream-walking through her own life. Detachment had stepped in and claimed her, and in her mind she had stood aside and watched the outwardly composed Emmaline gently sipping champagne, gracefully dancing at the final prewedding ball, responding politely to conversation. She was two people, the visible person a forgivably nervous but placid bride-to-be, the inner, a mass of conflicting emotions. It was as if her spirit refused to occupy her body, for the pain inside was too acute to bear.

"Come, now, Miss Em. You mustn't dawdle. Let me 'elp you into yer gown. And a fine gown it is, p'r'aps yer loveliest yet."

Emmaline supposed that Floss spoke the truth. Fashioned of an ethereal blue silk, with edging of creamy lace, the dress had brought a solitary smile when the modiste had presented it that morning. Yet when Floss carefully draped and fastened the gown, Emmaline could but stare into the pier glass and notice how dull her eyes looked.

After a soft knock at the door, the parlormaid stuck her head inside Emmaline's room.

"Pardon me, Miss Emmaline. Lady Cavendish is 'ere and asks if she might see you for a moment."

Emmaline brightened a bit. "Yes, certainly. Please show her into the music room. I shall be down shortly." Where Floss' excitement merely emphasized the bleakness of Emmaline's feelings, Rosetta's serenity always contributed a soothing balm to her mood.

"Will that be all, Miss Em?" Floss asked hopefully as the parlormaid departed. " 'Er ladyship has said the staff might take a free night, to celebrate belowstairs before we bring the supper to the gardens. Even said 'Umble might open the wine cellar so's we might drink a toast to the 'appy couple."

"Yes, thank you, Floss. Enjoy your celebration."

Emmaline attempted to erase the irony from her tone. With grim certainty, she knew that her abigail's evening would be far more pleasurable than her own. After one last, disinterested glance in the mirror, Emmaline left her room.

She found Rosetta standing by the pianoforte, gazing with a strange sadness at the bowl of glorious crimson roses that sat proudly upon the lid of the instrument.

"Rosetta, dear," Emmaline said fondly, extending her hands in greeting.

With a start, Rosetta turned toward her, replacing the sadness with a weak smile.

"Oh, Emmaline." She sighed. "You look enchanting."

They embraced briefly. Emmaline had found a true friend in Lady Cavendish, one blessedly devoid of the frivolity of most of her acquaintances in the *beau monde*. Through their frequent contact at social events, and more so, through regular weekly visits, Emmaline had grown to trust and respect Rosetta. On the surface, they had little in common. And by nature, Rosetta was far more inclined to accept life's tribulations than Emmaline. Yet their dissimilar temperaments complemented and made them compatible.

Even so, Emmaline had refrained from confiding her most intimate yearnings and troubles to Rosetta. Keeping silent, she had never revealed her feelings for Nicolas, nor the duplicity of the Garwins' plans to make her Cecil's bride. She did not understand her restraint completely, for she had no doubt that Rosetta would prove a sympathetic listener. Perhaps, Emmaline mused, her reticence stemmed from her solitary childhood, when she had been forced to depend solely upon her own inner strength. The habit was long ingrained.

Now, as Emmaline gazed into her friend's gentle eyes, she longed to spill the secrets of her heart. Still, reluctantly, she refrained. Her destiny was forged; unloading the burdens of her soul would not change it.

When they were seated side by side on the settee, Emmaline smiled. "What a pleasant surprise to see you. But I hope this does not mean you will not be joining us this evening at Vauxhall."

Rosetta's eyes shifted slightly. "Oh, no, I never would disappoint Cecil. Or Lady Minerva. Although

I may be forced to take my leave early, which is why I wished to see you now. I may not have the opportunity to speak with you privately later."

Emmaline gazed at her friend more carefully. Rosetta always presented a youthful appearance, yet this night Emmaline noticed tiny lines accentuating the corners of her eyes, the traces of strain evident in the slight wrinkling of her brow.

"Dear Rosetta, are you troubled?" she asked softly.

Brushing her question lightly aside, Rosetta shrugged. "No more so than any woman with too many households to manage. The bailiff at my country home has been plagued overmuch with poachers this year. I find I may have to repair to the estate before I had planned."

"Certainly not before the morrow," Emmaline said, alarmed.

"No. No, I shall be at your wedding. But the next day, I am departing."

Maybe it was the fact that Emmaline, divorced through self-preservation from her own feelings, was able to read Rosetta's more clearly. Maybe Rosetta had never allowed her expression to reveal so much. Nonetheless, Emmaline detected a pronounced disturbance in her friend, bearing strong resemblance to abject misery.

"Rosetta, as much as the country matter may be bothersome, I sense that a far deeper problem plagues you."

Before she could answer, Lady Minerva sailed into the music room.

"There you are, Emmaline. By Jupiter, I have been chasing all over the house for you. Hello, Rosetta. Are you going to Vauxhall in our carriage? A splendid idea, one I should have thought of myself."

All through her hurried speech, Lady Minerva had been advancing toward them. Now she stopped before Emmaline and thrust a velvet case at her.

"A gift for you, my dear. The last six countesses of Langford have worn them on their wedding days. Go on with you, open the case."

Emmaline complied and gasped at the splendor before her. The glow of topaz met her eyes: necklace, earbobs, tiara, bracelet, each crowned by a jewel the size of a plover egg.

"Well, what do you think?"

"They are magnificent, Lady Minerva. I shall be honored to wear them."

"Certainly you will," the dowager countess replied complacently. "Now if you are ready to depart for Vauxhall—"

The remainder of her statement was interrupted by a groan of disgust as Verity entered the room.

"Lady Minerva, I really must insist that you dismiss that insufferable abigail you assigned to me," she said hotly. "Just look what she has done to me."

Having heard this particular protest many times upon other occasions, Emmaline regarded Verity with little interest. Her flame-colored gown revealed a bit too much décolletage for good taste, and her lips looked suspiciously red. Otherwise, Emmaline was forced to own, Verity was as always a thoroughly beautiful woman, discounting her vile temperament.

"I fail to see," Lady Minerva said archly, "any difference. As usual, you present the appearance of a vixen, and woe betide any man in your path. But I always assumed this was your intent."

Verity pouted. " 'Twill avail neither of us to make snide comments, Lady Minerva. Look what that Nan has done to my hair. She has fried it."

In evidence, Verity offered one curl among the many, with the ends frizzed.

"*Quelle catastrophe*," Lady Minerva murmured dryly, and Emmaline hid a smile. "I can remedy this disaster with one snip. Bring me my shears."

Yelping in protest, Verity clutched her head

protectively. "You may take the situation lightly, but I certainly do not. I may be forced into remaining at home tonight, if—"

Suddenly she espied the open jewel case on Emmaline's lap. Her hands dropped and her green eyes gleamed covetously.

"The Langford topaz set," Verity sniffed with forced nonchalance. "How unfortunate that Cecil's intended is a blonde. A brunette would set them off to perfection. I do hope they do not make you look pale, Emmaline."

"I do so worry about that," Emmaline replied solemnly. "Maybe you would lend me some of the cosmetics that so disguise your pallor."

Verity regarded her haughtily. "I would not presume to enhance what nature has so bountifully bestowed. However, perhaps you might borrow from some much older ladies of my acquaintance—"

"I being one of them," Lady Minerva interjected tartly, and Verity had the grace to desist. "I feel it a woman's duty to make restitution to time. A duty you will find thrust upon you ere long, Verity."

As Emmaline and Rosetta hid smiles, Verity opened her mouth to protest. What might have been a rousing debate was short-lived, as the head footman announced another visitor.

"The Reverend Mr. Markham, your ladyship."

Emmaline stifled a groan. She had all but forgotten the invitation sent weeks earlier, a distasteful but necessary obligation. Her guardian entered, his saturnine face reddened from the journey, or more likely from the anticipation of proximity to Lady Minerva's wealth. He surprised her with a dry-as-ashes kiss upon her cheek, and Emmaline found herself hard-pressed not to recoil. She still resented his role in the deception, his eagerness to sell her to the highest bidder.

Following the introductions to Verity and Rosetta, the vicar virtually ignored them all to claim Lady Minerva's attention.

"Ah, Countess, you have no idea how grateful I am to have arrived in a decent home. The situation in the streets of London has deteriorated shamefully since my last visit. Drivers were unbearably rude, peddlers hawked wares in my face, and worst of all, a gang of street urchins beset my carriage, begging for coins. And not a humble request, I might add, but the most impudent demand! Worthless little guttersnipes, all of them should be locked in prison."

Lady Minerva pursed her lips. "Indeed. Then at least they would have a place to sleep."

Realizing a potential faux-pas, Markham quirked his mouth in a caricature of a smile. "Forgive my vehemence, Countess. Believe me when I say that I have naught but charity in my heart for the unfortunate. Well you know my concern with pitiful orphans, my care for Emmaline being the perfect example."

Emmaline could take no more. She stood abruptly, nearly upending the jewel case. "If you will excuse me, Lady Minerva, I should like to take these to my room before we leave."

The vicar's eyes widened at the sight of the gems.

Lady Minerva smiled slyly. "You find the Langford topazes interesting, Vicar?"

"Oh, they are incredibly beautiful. One never sees such magnificence, such quality outside of London. But, of course," he hastened to add, "we are more practical in the country, more concerned with adorning our roofs with thatch to keep out the rain."

"Apparently," the countess mused, "Bevindale is not so prosperous as I had assumed."

"No, I regret that we are hardly a wealthy village," Markham said modestly. "I do hope that

I shall not embarrass your renowned family by association."

Emmaline cringed in shame for him. But she noted that Lady Minerva's eyes suddenly lit with a twinkle.

"Vicar, I feel I must help your situation. If the rest of you will excuse me . . ."

Verity, thoroughly bored at the turn of conversation, which did not center upon herself, hurried off mumbling about skinning Nan alive.

Emmaline closed the jewel case and turned to Rosetta. "Will you come with me?" she asked, and her friend nodded in relief.

Safe in her room, she faced Rosetta with an apologetic laugh. "My guardian is neither the most subtle nor the most gracious of men."

With a wave, Rosetta dismissed him. "The only question is how you developed such levelheadedness in his household. However did you manage?"

Pausing a moment, regarding Rosetta, Emmaline said softly, "He is unimportant now. I want to talk about you."

Surprise registered in Rosetta's eyes. "Me? Why?"

"Because I never have seen you upset, and although you try to hide it, you definitely are disturbed."

Refusing to meet her gaze, Rosetta remained silent.

Emmaline took her hand. "I consider you to be my friend. I do not wish to pry into your heart, but I cannot abide the prospect that you may be hurting and I may be able to help."

Suddenly, Rosetta burst into tears. So astonished was she by the flow, Emmaline stared for a moment before rushing to fetch a handkerchief. Then, gently, she eased Rosetta into a slipper chair and pulled a stool up beside her to pat her friend's arm until the tears subsided.

"You may confide in me, Rosetta. I will keep your secrets to the grave, and I am guilty of too many sins of my own to be judgmental. What is it? You may tell me."

Shaking her head, Rosetta murmured, "Oh, I cannot. You of all people."

Emmaline searched for enlightenment. "Because you do not wish to distress me on the eve of my wedding? I assure you that I am quite composed. Cecil is the addled one."

At the mention of his name, Rosetta paled in guilty misery.

"You are distressed about Cecil?" Emmaline prodded gently. "He has perhaps offended you?"

"Oh, no! Cecil never could do that. I have too much understanding of him. He is ever the gentleman, ever . . ."

Her voice trailed off wistfully, and she dropped her forlorn gaze. But not before Emmaline had peered into the mirror of her heart and recognized a yearning she knew too well.

"Oh," she said, astonished, her mouth rounding in comprehension. "Oh, dear heavens! Rosetta, you are in love with Cecil."

"Do not even speak such words," Rosetta pleaded, covering her ears. "I am so ashamed of my dishonor. He is your intended, and I swear to you I never thought for a moment to act upon my feelings. I never meant for you even to know." Abruptly, she jumped up. "I told you I was leaving for the country. But I neglected to tell you that I am staying permanently. I promise, Emmaline, I shall never see Cecil again, in any capacity."

Emmaline laughed, startling them both. "Forgive me, Rosetta. I am by no means making light of your concerns. I merely had not the foggiest notion that you love Cecil."

"You have said it again. Please, have mercy on me." Rosetta's tears descended once more.

"Oh, dear," Emmaline sighed. "Wait right here. Lady Minerva hides a bottle of sherry in her bureau drawer. I shall be back in a moment. Promise me you will not move."

Rosetta nodded through her sobs and Emmaline hastened to collect the wine and glasses. She hastened back to her room as quickly as possible.

"Drink this," she commanded, and as Rosetta meekly complied, Emmaline poured a glass for herself.

Now that Rosetta's confession was out, Emmaline ruefully marveled that she had not suspected such before. When she paused to think, she could remember numerous instances when Rosetta's feelings were transparent, if one only bothered to look. There were no dramatic moments of revelation, but subtle flashes of the truth: the crinkle of Rosetta's smile and the warmth in her eyes when Cecil was present; a tender hand laid across his arm; a youthful blush when they danced. None of the clues had made an impression on Emmaline until now.

The sherry had restored Rosetta's color and her composure. "Please try not to hate me," she begged.

"Hate you? Never," Emmaline said, positively beaming.

Rosetta frowned. "Indeed, you seem uncommonly cheerful, having just been given such news. Do you, like Cecil, suppose me so genderless as to be no threat to you?"

"Oh, no," Emmaline said intently, serious once more. "But you are correct. I am feeling more cheerful than I have in weeks. And that alone should tell you that I am not the one who should be marrying Cecil."

They both stopped short at Emmaline's words, and who was more astonished, Rosetta or Emmaline, neither could tell.

Raising her hand to her cheek, Emmaline

pondered aloud. "Oh, Rosetta. There was never a doubt that I am fond of Cecil, but neither was it in dispute that I did not love him. We all—Cecil, Lady Minerva, and I—assumed that fondness was enough. Many have wed contentedly on the basis of far less. But now . . ."

Her mind whirled, and with it her emotions spun dizzily out of their discordant opposition, meshing neatly into place. Emmaline felt whole again; her detachment having vanished, she embraced her feelings.

"Oh, Rosetta"—she laughed—"how misguided we both have been! Each of us feeling honor-bound and resigned to accept a wedding we each deplored. Each of us miserable and determined to make the best of a situation we could not change. We were wrong on both counts."

Bewildered, Rosetta stared at her. "Emmaline, I do not understand."

"Listen," she said, grabbing her friend's hands eagerly. "There is no honor in abiding by a decision that will make all parties to it miserable for the rest of their lives. There is honor in truth. And the truth is, you love Cecil, and whether he knows it or not, he loves you."

"No," Rosetta said numbly. "His romantic words are always of you."

Emmaline gave a most Lady Minerva-like snort. "Only because he is predisposed to think of me as the paragon bride."

Briefly, and with more ease than she imagined, Emmaline related the story of their "destiny" being foretold in the tea leaves. Such was her mood that for the first time, she found the story more amusing and whimsical than hurtful.

"That is not romance," Emmaline concluded. "It is the power of suggestion. But in his actions, Cecil's true feelings emerge. Who does he turn to when his world crumbles, as it does thrice weekly? Who does he seek first to tell his beloved gossip, first to ask for advice on any purchase of note? And who does he admire more than anyone, even himself? You, of course."

Rosetta shrugged. "Even supposing you are correct, nothing changes. You will wed Cecil on the morrow."

"Everything changes," Emmaline declared forcefully. "You will wed Cecil, as is honorable and true. Perhaps not on the morrow, but soon."

"Impossible."

"Only if you wait for Cecil to come to his senses instead of forcing him."

Suddenly Emmaline ran to her writing table and began scribbling away. After a few moments, she blotted the letter and handed it to Rosetta.

"Give this to Cecil. In essence, I have told him all that I have told you, releasing him from his offer for me. And then, Rosetta, you must tell him how you feel—and how he feels, also, for he has no notion. And finally, you must—must, I repeat— clasp him to you and kiss him as though your very life depended upon it, for it does."

"Emmaline," Rosetta gasped, blushing.

Emmaline smiled wryly. "Subtlety is entirely lost upon that man. A wagonload of paving blocks must be dumped upon his head, and you must supply the stones."

For the first time, Rosetta laughed and looked youthful once more. "Indeed, Emmaline, with that statement you sounded the twin of Lady Minerva."

"I consider that a high compliment. She is without a doubt one of the wisest ladies on earth."

Suddenly Rosetta's expression sobered. "Poor Lady Minerva! What will she think if you cancel the wedding? What of the scandal?"

"She will adore it," Emmaline said, relishing the certainty. "It will make her the talk of *le beau monde* for years to come."

Still, Rosetta hesitated. "I do not know, Emmaline."

"Look upon it in this manner: the topazes suit a brunette far more agreeably than a pale blonde."

Rosetta chuckled and then bit her lip, considering. She glanced reflectively at the letter for Cecil and slowly smiled. "What is this reference to 'the tea-leaves reading signified the dove gray of Rosetta's eyes and the cherry-red of her lips'?"

"Cecil will understand. But he will still need to be hit with the paving blocks. Now you send your coachman home and go on to Vauxhall with them. I shall make an excuse to delay, to come later, to give you time to speak to Cecil."

Anticipation lit Rosetta's face, yet she gazed in concern at Emmaline. "And what of you? What shall you do if you do not marry Cecil?"

Emmaline shrugged. "I may remain Lady Minerva's companion, if she would have me. I could be content in her house and her company. But I am hoping that a different fate awaits me. You see, I have someone I must speak to myself." When Rosetta regarded her curiously, Emmaline said softly, "Nicolas. As you love Cecil, I love Nicolas."

"Oh, but he is perfect for you," Rosetta enthused. "Why did I not think of it myself? And now that you mention him, I do recall your first waltz together, at my ball. You both had the look . . . How blind I was!"

"No more than I."

"But why did you agree to marry Cecil, then?"

Emmaline sighed. " 'Tis a long story, one I shall tell you someday when we are both bouncing our children upon our knees. Suffice it to say that I thought to solve the problems of love by denying it. What I have learned, Rosetta, what I hope I shall never forget, is that the problems one solves by denying love are more disastrous by a hundredfold than those one inherits by accepting love."

She gazed off into the distance, as if peering into the future. "I know that he loves me, too. And I shall not rest until he is mine."

As Emmaline and Rosetta made hasty plans, a silent figure tiptoed away from Emmaline's door. Verity waited until she reached her own chamber before hurling a vase and her fury against the silk-lined walls.

The nerve of that sly minx! Just when Verity was set to savor the smallest victory, she had to try to snatch it away. Verity could accept losing Nicolas herself, so long as Emmaline would not have him either. But now the country mouse had declared herself, thrown down the gauntlet in front of Verity, although with Verity hiding behind the door she had left ajar, Emmaline had no notion of that fact. Still, while there was a breath left in her, Verity could suppose that there was a chance Nicolas would, in his temporary and misguided disappointment at losing Emmaline, turn to his childhood friend for solace. Now that last hope was dashed, and Emmaline was the cause.

Impotent in her fury, Verity paced like a caged lion, pausing only to emit roars of anger that went unheeded. For once her mind, an ever-fertile source of schemes, produced nothing. Guillermo would sneer at her . . .

Guillermo! Suddenly Verity ceased her pacing, a feral smile curving her lips. She remembered too well Nicolas' distaste when he thought that she had given herself to Guillermo. Not that the Spaniard actually had to ravage Emmaline. Although at this point, Verity felt a vast indifference as to whether he would or not. Just the suggestion would be enough to spoil Emmaline's appeal in Nicolas' eyes. A mere hint had certainly spoiled her own.

A scheme burst full-blown into her mind, and Verity relaxed, feeling herself set to rights once more. She, too, would make her excuses to Lady

Minerva, promising to accompany Emmaline later to Vauxhall. But she had a stop to make first.

As a bonus, she realized that Guillermo should pay her quite handsomely for this new information. She laughed aloud, anticipating the finest revenge of all.

19

Nicolas guided his gray gelding through the horse paths surrounding Vauxhall Gardens, his uneasiness growing. A series of worries, one chaining into the other, occupied his thoughts. So many factors seemed to weigh heavily against him. Even the weather did not favor his aims.

He glanced up with growing tenseness through the canopy of trees at the evening sky. The mists of the day had cleared, swept away by a soft breeze, but the night promised the obscurity of clouds. With no moon to shed light upon treachery, the advantage went to those who plotted evil.

He had spent the past hours wandering through the gardens, and with every minute, his concern grew. There were countless points perfect for ambush throughout the darkened paths. Even without the help of the doltish Lubbock, his half-brother would have a dozen black opportunities to wreak his particular havoc.

Nicolas felt his blood racing with the scent of danger. Although he had tried zealously to hide his feelings for Emmaline, a slim chance remained that Guillermo, with his skill at intrigue, had found out. For any man other than his half-brother, the prospect of Nicolas losing the woman he loved would be revenge and enough. But not for Guillermo. Never for Guillermo.

And given the state of the man's surely un-balanced mind, who was to say that he would stop, even once Emmaline was wed? For all Nicolas knew, Guillermo might well plot Cecil's demise as well as Nicolas'. With no other male heirs in line, Guillermo had a legitimate claim on the Langford fortunes as well.

Nonetheless, Guillermo might well make a devastating move before this night was over. The elements of darkness, subterfuge, and intrigue would appeal powerfully to him. On one hand, Nicolas nearly relished the thought, for until Guillermo came out with an open threat, Nicolas could not defeat him. But on the other, the potential risk, the mere possibility that his mad half-brother might succeed, filled Nicolas with the most fearsome dread.

He emerged from the gardens and headed toward home to change his clothing. Impatient, hot with frustration, Nicolas kicked his heels into the horse's flanks, and the animal obediently speeded up his pace. The wind cooled his feverish face, but his internal fire blazed more angrily. When would this agonizing situation end? He had tried every way he could think of to diffuse Guillermo's volatile obsession with his ruination. Signing over the Ransom fortune would accomplish nothing; Guillermo demanded vengeance. Attempting to lure his half-brother into a confrontation had been unfruitful, for the man was too wily, too bent upon scurrilous destruction of a more notorious sort. For a heady moment, Nicolas let his mind wander into extreme territory. When pressed, he could think of a most effective way to stop Guillermo. A bullet in the blackguard's heart would end his threat for all time.

Wearily, Nicolas pulled on the horse's reins, slowing him to a less-harried pace. He knew in his heart that he could not kill deliberately. No matter Guillermo's own murderous obsessions, their father's blood coursed through them both. And who was not to say that Nicolas' own deed, maybe pushing Consuelo over the edge into suicide, was not the true cause of Guillermo's own mind warping? He had no right, or stomach, to take his half-brother's life.

And besides, nothing would change for him personally. Honor decreed that he could never possess a woman promised to Cecil. Without Emmaline, Nicolas had lost the taste for a peaceful life, at any rate.

Now, all he could do was protect her, see her securely wed, and return to Spain, luring Guillermo to follow. His half-brother's interests lay mainly in that country; he had always detested chilly England, the fiery sun of Spain igniting his passions. The two of them would be locked in deadly combat until one or the other emerged victorious. But Emmaline would be forever safe.

His jaw clenched in determination. Yet his eyes bore the haunting of abysmal loss.

While Nicolas roamed the paths of Vauxhall, Lady Minerva, Cecil, Rosetta, and the vicar were climbing into the Garwin coach.

Once seated, Lady Minerva grumbled. "I do wish I had not allowed Emmaline to dissuade me. We should all arrive at Vauxhall together."

"I agree," Cecil said, frowning. "Bad form for her to arrive late."

"Not to worry, Lady Minerva," Rosetta said brightly. "Her abigail will fix up the tear in her hem, and she will be ready before the coach returns for her."

Lady Minerva snorted in annoyance. "Fancy, catching the lace of her gown in her shoe just before we left. I have ever known Emmaline to be a graceful girl, and at the most inconvenient moment, she turns clumsy."

Markham sighed portentously. "I fear that she has some bad qualities that need correcting, undependability being one of them. You must take a firm hand with her, Lord Garwin."

"Whatever will our guests think?" Cecil demanded hotly. " 'Tis scandalous that she should arrive alone."

"Verity will be with her," Rosetta reminded him. "She too was delayed, in her hairdress, which was no more her fault than Emmaline's torn hem was hers. These accidents happen, especially upon important occasions when everyone is anxious. I think that you are all making a to-do about a small mishap. Let us all relax. There is no harm done."

Rosetta patted Lady Minerva's arm encouragingly, and the dowager regarded her askance. Even in the darkness, her eyes gleamed with anticipation, and when Rosetta glanced at her grandson, the excitement glittered the stronger. Weighing Emmaline's uncharacteristic clumsiness with Rosetta's uncommon animation, Lady Minerva found her never-failing instincts deducing that a plot was afoot. And she even had an inkling of where the trail of intrigue would lead. But while she had no objection to and even delighted in such schemings, she was quite put out that she was not privy to the particulars.

"We should have waited," Lady Minerva declared.

"And leave your guests unattended at Vauxhall?" Rosetta asked reasonably. "You are much too diligent a hostess."

And you too quick with answers, the dowager countess thought, holding her tongue.

Rosetta, unusually verbal this night, went on. "All will be well," she said confidently. "I know you will appreciate the time to introduce the vicar to your guests, and Cecil and I shall be happy to see that all the arrangements are taken care of. Will we not, Cecil?"

As her grandson uncertainly muttered assent, Lady Minerva narrowed her eyes. Ah, yes, the path of the scheme was unwinding.

"Perhaps," the countess said with her most

ingenuous smile, "Emmaline should wait for
Nicolas. He could escort her to the gardens."

"Splendid idea," Rosetta enthused. "You should
tell the footman to inform her."

"Indeed," Lady Minerva murmured, leaning back
against the cushions of the carriage in satisfaction.
There was Verity to contend with, a minor tangle
in the skein of the plot, but the countess had every
confidence in Emmaline's ability to dispatch the
minx. And she did not for a moment doubt that it
was Emmaline herself who had set this scheme
aspinning.

Her only regret was that she had not invited more
of the *haut ton* to witness what was sure to be a
most enjoyably scandalous evening.

Verity waited only until the Garwin coach was
out of sight before summoning her maid.

"There you are at last," she said irritably. "I rang
for you near a quarter-hour ago. Where have you
been, you lazy creature?"

Nan, as well aware as her mistress that the time
had been exaggerated tenfold, pursed her lips. " 'Er
ladyship said that we might 'ave a celebration in the
servants' parlor," she murmured, not quite successfully hiding her resentment.

"Hmph. Now I know why you deliberately fried
my hair, in your haste to carouse with the rest of
them. Well, now that you are finally here, listen
well. I want you to go down to the hackney stand
and fetch that fellow of yours for me."

Nan's eyes widened. "Fellow?"

"Do not play the innocent with me. You forget
that I learned all about your hackney driver, and
how you sneak off to meet him when you should be
at your tasks. Now fetch him quickly, or I shall tell
Lady Minerva about him and you will be dismissed
on the morrow."

"But, madam, what if 'e's not there?"

Verity's brows arched slyly. "I am certain that

by now you know many of his fraternity. Fetch me the most reliable one."

Nan wrung her apron in her hands. "But the staff is all set to leave for Vauxhall, madam. We're bringin' the supper and we're to see the Chinese fire. 'Umble is packin' up at this very moment."

Verity turned her back to peer into the mirror as she arranged her bonnet. "Then," she said sweetly, "you had better stop wasting time and hurry down to the corner, had you not?"

Across the street from the Garwin house, hidden in the shadow of another grand house, Guillermo watched the maid as she ran down the street. Muttering curses, he frowned. He had no reason to doubt Verity's information about the proposed gathering at Vauxhall. Yet, when the household had climbed into the carriage, Emmaline was not among them. Why? his scheming mind asked over and over, and with each unanswered question, his frustration grew.

His fists clenched and unclenched rhythmically, remembering the elation he had felt when he realized that Vauxhall Gardens offered him a golden opportunity. The darkened paths, the spectacle of the fireworks as a diversion, even the moonless night itself . . . all lucky omens. It would be a simple matter to carry out his plan to kidnap the girl.

Even the defection of that stupid Lubbock, incoherently drunk and useless to Guillermo, had not deflated his excitement. But now, the idea that his plans might be foiled by some flit's whim filled him with almost uncontrollable rage.

Moments later, while he still fumed inwardly, a hackney pulled up to the house, and Guillermo's eyes narrowed as the maid stepped out. She began to speak animatedly to the driver, and Guillermo strained to listen. Fortune returned to smile upon him once again; with the cloudy night, with her agitation, her words carried clearly.

"Arthur, what if that one keeps you all hours?" she fretted. "You promised to meet me at the gardens, to watch the Chinese fire with me."

"I'll be there," the fellow called Arthur insisted. "I'll drop her off, make an excuse if I must. I wouldn't miss this night, Nan, me girl." He drew her into a swift embrace, from which Nan quickly disengaged.

"If that one sees us, she'll 'ave me 'ide. I must go, Arthur. The staff is all waiting for me. We must take the supper over to Vauxhall."

Even from his vantage point, Guillermo could see Arthur's playful grin.

"So everyone will be gone, gentry and staff, eh? P'r'aps we should sneak back 'ere, to 'ave all the 'ouse to ourselves."

Nan giggled, but shook her head. "Meet me at Vauxhall, Arthur. I've a special kiss waitin' for you."

With that she turned and ran up the steps to the house. A moment later, Verity emerged, half-hidden under a voluminous cloak and a wide bonnet. She hurriedly murmured to Arthur and climbed into the coach. Arthur flicked his reins and the hackney clattered off into the night.

Guillermo hunched to the ground and allowed himself a delicious smile. So the servants were all leaving. He himself had scouted the stables earlier, noticing that Nicolas' steed was absent. With Verity's departure, Emmaline was all alone in the house.

All alone, unprotected. A luscious pear ripe for the plucking. His smile widened to diabolical proportions.

Thus savoring his uncommon good luck, Guillermo failed to notice a solitary horseman stopped in the shadows farther down the street. As the hackney rolled away, the horseman, one Will

Cooper of Bevindale, feeling slightly confused and totally out of his element, spurred his horse to follow.

He had seen the woman entering the hackney, and the elegant clothing had almost fooled him. But the faint light from the open door had glinted in her blond hair, and Will knew that, elegant clothing or not, he gazed upon Miss Emmaline Hazlett—the woman promised to him, not to some fancy earl.

His confusion vanished. At last he was about to right a terrible wrong. Determined, he set off after her.

20

Verity clung to the hand strap as the hackney swung through the streets. Arthur had been as good as his word, delivering haste after she had promised him double his fare. Maybe that worthless Nan was proving she had use, after all, for no doubt the man feared Verity's wrath upon the maid, should he fail to speed her to her destination.

And Verity knew well that her wrath was evident upon her face and in her voice. She still burned to see Emmaline punished for her duplicity. And only the thought that Guillermo would be her instrument for revenge tempered her distaste at traveling through the seediest sections of London.

The cabman slowed his horse as the streets narrowed into lanes. Verity tried to curb her impatience. She knew she had a good chance to catch Guillermo, for he had developed into a night creature, more comfortable in the shadows. She also knew that he would delay his journey to Vauxhall because, when she had told him of the Garwins' plans for the evening, the fireworks display had interested him most. She prided herself on having learned to read him so clearly.

But why Guillermo still insisted on residing incognito in such surroundings escaped her. Shuddering, she drew the curtains on either side to shut out the disgusting filth of the streets.

Suddenly, she heard a shouted curse, and the hackney halted so abruptly, she was thrown off-balance. Righting herself, Verity angrily opened the cab door.

"What is the meaning—"

Her outrage proceeded no further, for as she was speaking, she saw Arthur topple from his perch to land unconscious in a heap on the cobbled lane. Without thinking, she jumped from the hackney and rushed over to him.

"Arthur! Are you—"

In a nonce, she was seized from behind, so forcefully that her bonnet fell off. In quick succession, a foul-smelling rag was stuffed into her mouth and a tattered horse blanket thrown over her head.

Truly frightened, Verity struggled, flailing and kicking at her assailant. One powerful, muscular arm held her hands tightly behind her while the other wrapped a rope around her, securing both her arms under the blanket. Shoving her back into the hackney, he then captured her wildly thrashing feet and bound them, too.

"This be for your own good," a deep voice murmured calmly, frightening Verity all the more. "I'm righting a terrible wrong. Now rest easy."

The door slammed, and after a few moments the hackney began to roll again. Verity, crouched on the floor of the cab, tried to swallow her rising panic.

After a few attempts, she was able to sit up. With all her might she kicked at the carriage doors, but when they each refused to budge, she realized the man had tied them shut. She let out a scream stifled by the vile rag, and her fear heated into a brew of frustration and anger.

Thank God she had not worn the Lockridge rubies. He could steal only a small amount of money and a replaceable woven gold necklace from her. A small satisfaction gave way to the chill of dread, for she then realized that the man had made no attempt to rob her. He obviously had more nefarious plans in mind.

Well, just let him try, she thought, furious. She well knew that most vulnerable portion of a man's anatomy, and she had no qualms about delivering a blow that he would only wish was fatal. She gathered her wits, storing her strength for the battle.

The journey seemed interminable. From the lack of city noise and the jouncing of the hackney, Verity eventually realized that they had left London and were traveling some rural road. After what seemed hours, she almost wished the man would get on with his foul deed, just to stop the bouncing of the hackney. Her head throbbed from being knocked against the seat, her bones ached from her cramped position, and her hands and feet were numb.

At last, the carriage halted. Verity held her breath when she heard the hackney creak as the man descended from the driver's perch. After a long silence, a whisper of sound indicated the ropes being released from the door. Then her assailant pulled her out of the hackney.

She stood unsteadily on her bound feet, pain shooting up her limbs. The man held her firmly by her shoulders, and Verity tried to twist away.

"Calm yourself. We'll rest for the night now and be on our way, come the dawn." The deep voice turned apologetic. "I'm right sorry we cannot stop at a proper inn. Those people you were staying with might find us. But we'll be comfortable here."

Her mouth so dry she could not summon a scream, Verity nonetheless flung herself violently away from the man, landing on the hard ground. Her breath taken, she tried to gasp for air. Suddenly she found herself scooped up effortlessly into the man's arms.

She had not the strength to struggle further. He was tall and exceedingly powerful, and Verity felt a thrill of apprehension. This man would not be easily dispatched.

His long strides brought them to a creaking door. Once inside, from the sweet smell of hay and the distant lowing of cattle, Verity knew they were in a barn. After some maneuvering, the man lay her down upon another blanket in the hay and unbound her feet.

She waited until her feet were free and then she kicked out at him with all her might. He must have jumped back, for she found nothing but air.

"There's no cause for that," he said patiently. "I know you may be a bit angry that I didn't claim my right before now. It might have taken me too long, but Will Cooper stands by his word."

At the mention of his name, Verity froze in stunned surprise.

"See? I knew you'd be pleased, Miss Emmaline. I saved you from the dishonor of wedding that fancy earl. And I have a plan that will make you mine, as was meant to be."

Verity heard a rustling and knew that he knelt beside her.

"I intend to make you mine this night, Miss Emmaline. Then none can dispute my rights."

As the import of his words sank in, Verity tried to scream her fury through the gag, kicking wildly for emphasis. But maddeningly, the man—Will Cooper, for the love of heaven, brought to London by Verity's own false letter!—merely chuckled.

"Oh, now I understand. And right you are, Miss Emmaline. Wouldn't be honorable for you, before we're proper wed, to give yourself to me willing. If I forced you, you could tell those fancy city folk that you had no choice. Good thought. Then no hard feelings anywhere."

Verity's fears had dissipated altogether and she now neared the point of self-immolation, so hot was her anger. As he lay down, stretching out his strong, muscled body beside her, she vowed with every fiber of her being that when this was over, she'd skin Will Cooper alive.

As she so fumed, Will gingerly rolled her over, and Verity realized that he was unfastening her bonds. She reached under the blanket to release the vile gag and lay quite still until he lifted the horse blanket from over her head. Then, with lightning speed, she aimed a furious punch to his nether regions.

Will howled in pain, bending double. Jumping to her feet, gloating with satisfaction, Verity unleashed a string of curses that the crudest of sailors would have admired greatly. She ended with a smug "That will teach you to molest a lady of quality."

Stomping indignantly toward the barn door, she suddenly felt herself grabbed by the ankles and toppled into the hay.

"Where," Will gasped, straining to catch his breath after her blow, "did you hear such language, Miss Emmaline?"

Despite Verity's struggles, he held her immobile until he had crawled up to face her. His eyes bulged. "You ain't Miss Emmaline."

"How very brilliant of you," Verity said scathingly. "Now unhand me, you peasant."

"It were an honest mistake," Will declared stubbornly. "No cause for you to take on like that."

Staring at him, Verity sputtered. "You have the cheek, the unmitigated gall, to suggest that . . . Oh, you are mad!"

Still, he refused to budge and Verity glared malevolently at him. To her secret relief, he appeared not to be the cretin villager of her imaginings. Indeed, his jaw was firm, his hair threaded now with hay but full and thick. Altogether, he actually was not an unpleasant-looking man. But his unrepenting stubbornness quite infuriated her. The trait was too much one that she possessed.

"Take me back to London immediately," she demanded.

Will shook his head. "Sorry, ma'am, can't. The horse was nearly dead from the journey. He'll need a night's rest. And this barn's been abandoned. There's nary a house for miles."

Pondering the import of his statement, Verity said slowly, coldly, "Do you mean that I shall be forced to share this . . . this hovel with you for the entire night?"

Will shrugged. "Afraid so, ma'am."

Verity closed her eyes and silently swallowed her ire. "If you dare to come near me," she said at last, "I shall not rest until I have tracked you down and cut out your heart."

Will backed off and Verity took a deep breath, clenching her fists. Will Cooper was not the only target of a revenge too terrible to mention. Someday she would, with the greatest of pleasure, tear out every hair on the head of Miss Emmaline Horrid Hazlett.

Emmaline had seen Verity leave with Arthur and heaved a sigh of relief. Fate had removed a last obstacle from her path, confirming in her mind that her plan was favored. Now she must merely await Nicolas' return.

Her azure eyes sparkled with anticipation and her spirits soared. Nicolas could deny his love for her all he pleased. She knew better. And with Cecil releasing her from their betrothal, as he certainly would once Rosetta convinced him of his true love, there would be no impediment blocking their way to happiness.

Their kiss had not lied. Nor had the quiet moments they had spent together. She always felt alive and vital in his presence. The mere sight of him righted any imbalance in her world. She loved him so deeply, the very thought filled her with awe and joy.

With swift fingers, Emmaline finished repairing her deliberately ripped hem. Then she hurried down to the foyer. She did not intend to waste one moment when Nicolas walked through the door.

Silence filled the Garwin house, a friendly,

peaceful sound. Emmaline sat on a brocade-covered bench, perched to fly into Nicolas' arms.

A polite cough behind her brought Emmaline out of her reverie.

"Oh, 'tis you, Humble. You startled me."

"Stars, Miss Emmaline?" The old majordomo pondered. "I doubt very much, ma'am. While loading the wagon with the supper baskets, I noticed that there appear to be clouds in the sky."

Smiling, Emmaline shook her head. "No, Humble, I said . . . Well, never mind." She raised her voice perceptibly. "What is it?"

"The coach has returned, ma'am, to fetch you to the gardens. He claims her ladyship said to tell you—"

Emmaline waved her hand breezily. "Humble, my good man, you may inform the coachman and footmen that I shall have no further use for them tonight."

The majordomo had ceased being surprised at the quirks of the gentry forty years ago. Furthermore, he was too well-trained to question her instructions. "Very well, Miss Emmaline. If you are in need of anything, please ring."

"I thought the staff had left for Vauxhall."

"They have, ma'am." Humble drew himself up importantly, as far as his rounded shoulders would allow. "I remained behind. Her ladyship would not wish the house left unattended."

Emmaline nodded solemnly. "You are a loyal retainer, Humble. Please do not bother yourself about me. What I need, I shall secure all on my own."

He glanced at her a bit oddly as he left, but Emmaline barely noticed.

She stretched her arms, reveling in anticipation, fully confident. Never again would she be buffeted by random winds. She was standing at the rudder of her own life, and exhilaration washed through her. Oh, the sheer exuberance of deciding one's own fate! She laughed aloud at the thought and set the force of her will to bring Nicolas home the sooner.

At last the knob rattled in the door and then swung open slowly, tentatively. Emmaline jumped up, her feet near flying toward him.

But it was not Nicolas who stood before her.

Emmaline halted abruptly and gaped. "You are . . ."

"Guillermo Rescate, at your service, madam." He bowed urbanely, but with a dangerous smile. "I must ask you to accompany me."

Her eyes wide with alarm, Emmaline turned to shout for help.

"I fear you call to no avail," Guillermo said smoothly. "The servants all have left some time ago. Shall we depart?"

Her pulse pounded, and Emmaline fought to regain her wits. Apparently, the Spaniard was not aware that Humble remained.

"Leave this house," she said through a tight throat, praying that Humble might be nearby. Swallowing, she repeated more forcefully, "Leave this house immediately."

Guillermo merely laughed softly. "I intend to, but only with you. I have the urge for the company of a beautiful woman this night. And I must reluctantly own that my despicable half-brother has a Spanish eye for beauty."

Frantically, Emmaline groped for a manner of dissuading him. A scream would be of no use, for Humble's hearing was minimal even at close range. Delay was her sole ally, for perhaps Nicolas would arrive to foil Guillermo's plans.

"I fail to understand," she said coldly, stifling the tremor in her voice, "what grudge you hold against Nicolas. Do enlighten me."

"It shall be my pleasure," Guillermo said agreeably. "But not here. I grow impatient, madam. I wish to go. Now."

His lethal tone brooked no dissent. Emmaline

stared at him, the cruel resemblance to Nicolas in his face distorted by evil motives. Sighing in annoyance, he slowly began to advance toward her, and her hands began to shake.

Suddenly she realized that she still held her needle case, gripped tightly in her fingers. Keeping her terrified gaze locked onto his, Emmaline slowly withdrew a needle.

As Guillermo's hand reached out, she plunged the instrument into the flesh of his palm. Guillermo howled and slapped the needle and its case from her hands. The rage in his eyes chilled her to the bone. She tried to flee, only to be yanked from behind by her hair. Stifling her groan of pain, she stood shaking, immobile, frightened.

Guillermo sighed. "I anticipated your resistance. I regret that this is necessary."

Before Emmaline could react, he drew a strong-smelling cloth to her mouth. She writhed against it, but Guillermo held her tight.

"Sweet dreams, *querida*," he murmured.

Emmaline struggled in panic, but the Spaniard clutched her tightly. Nicolas, her heart cried wildly. Her foot crunched on the needle case, and the last, drug-induced thought Emmaline had was that he would find it lying on the floor and somehow know she needed him.

The foyer began to swirl in her vision. Then all went black.

Frowning uncertainly, Humble peeked into the foyer. He had been set to enjoy a blissful night of peace, with a cozy fire on the grate in the servants' parlor and a glass of the late Earl of Langdon's best port at his side. Near half a century's service brought privilege of which he was glad to partake.

A vague disturbance had roused him, more a vibration than a sound. Although he would never own to the rest of the staff, he knew that his hearing failed him occasionally. Still, he had put on his coat and trudged up the stairs for a look.

The foyer was empty. Miss Emmaline must have retired to her rooms. Shrugging, he turned to leave when a strange smell assaulted him. He frowned in earnest. The roses on the foyer table must be souring.

Grumbling at being forced to perform a parlor-maid's chores, Humble retrieved the flowers, and as he did, he noticed Miss Emmaline's needle case lying on the floor. Sighing, his aged bones creaking, he picked up the case and hesitated. He knew he should return it to her now, but the cheerful fire and the splendid port beckoned. He slipped the case into his pocket and went to answer the call.

As he left, he smirked a bit. Say what they might about his hearing, there was nothing wrong with his sight.

Nicolas tethered his gelding to the hitching post and climbed the steps to the Garwin house wearily. Once inside, something odd distracted him. Then he shrugged, thinking that his sense of oddity came because no servant was there to welcome him. The staff was at Vauxhall, too, the burly footmen earlier having been given strict orders not to let Emmaline out of their sight there until he arrived. He glanced at the hall clock, noting that he was dreadfully late.

Quickly he went to his rooms, stripping down to wash his face and arms, dressing swiftly in evening clothes. Feeling slightly refreshed, he descended to the foyer.

To his surprise, he found one of the footmen placing a bowl of fresh scarlet roses on the center table.

"Calley, what are you doing here?" Nicolas asked sharply. "I told you to stay with Miss Emmaline until I arrived at Vauxhall."

"She is not there, sir."

Alarm creased Nicolas' brow. "What do you mean? Where is she?"

"Upstairs in her rooms, I believe, sir. Mr. Humble told us she said she wouldn't need us."

Before Calley had finished speaking, Nicolas was bounding up the staircase. He paused to rap at her door, and when there was no reply, he pushed through the door.

The room was empty. His worry growing steadily, he ran through the halls, urgently calling her name, to be answered only by deep silence. Swallowing his fear, Nicolas raced back down to the foyer.

"Calley, who saw her last?"

"Mr. Humble, I suppose, sir."

"Get him up here. Now!"

While the footman rushed to comply, Nicolas ran his fingers through his dark hair, thinking rapidly. Where could she have gone? Surely she had not blithely traipsed off on another of her adventures.

"Yes, sir?" Humble said.

"Miss Emmaline," Nicolas said quickly. "Where and when did you see her last?"

Humble peered at the hall clock for a maddeningly long moment.

"About half an hour ago. Right here in the foyer, she was. In fact . . ." He reached into his pocket. "She left her needle case."

Snatching it from his hand, Nicolas opened the case and found all the needles broken. He stared at them, frustrated at his failure to comprehend the significance.

"Calley," Humble was reproaching the footman, "I removed those flowers because they needed replacing. That smell . . ."

"I did replace them, Mr. Humble. These are fresh from the conservatory."

Nicolas looked up sharply. Now that his senses were alert, he too sniffed a cloying scent lingering faintly in the air. He had been through a military hospital in Spain and he knew that smell.

" 'Tis not the flowers," he said in a hushed voice, cold fear chilling his words. "That is ether."

Humble and Calley gazed at him curiously, but Nicolas' thoughts raced elsewhere. There was but one reason to explain the odor: someone had had to be immobilized in order to be abducted. Nicolas gasped as a cold fist seemed to slam into his heart.

His fear nearly exploding, he ran to the library to fetch and load his pistol, willing his trembling fingers to be calm. When the weapon was ready, he heard through the open library door the sound of knocking.

For a moment he froze. Then Nicolas drew a deep breath and raced back, stepping in front of Calley to answer the door.

A hackney driver stood uncertainly before him, recoiling at Nicolas' fierce scowl.

"Message for Mr. Nicolas Ransom."

"I am he," Nicolas muttered, grabbing the note. "Where did you get this?"

The fellow shrugged. "Bloke stopped at the stand and paid me to deliver this in an 'alf hour's time."

Muttering curses, Nicolas flung a few coins at the boy and slammed the door. His heart pounded as he read the words that he had fearfully expected:

"The stakes in our game have risen, dear brother. And I seem to hold the trump card—the Queen of Hearts. If you wish to fold your hand, I shall gladly return the fair Emmaline to you, not too much worse for the wear."

The note ended with an address: "Quillbottom Lane. Five doors down from The Blue Gander. Upstairs."

Guillermo, in his arrogance, had known that no signature was necessary.

21

"The demented swine!" Nicolas crumpled the note in impotent fury.

"Calley," he snapped, "prepare horses for yourself and whoever is left in the stables. Make it quick, unless you want to spend your life scouring pots in the scullery."

"Yes, sir!" The footman turned to go.

"No, wait," Nicolas dully called him back, shaking his head futilely. "Never mind."

An army of footmen would be of no avail to him, not while Guillermo held Emmaline hostage. Her life hung in the balance, and if that blackguard felt threatened . . . Nicolas shuddered to think of the consequences. Thundering force would not win this deadly game his half-brother had chosen; Nicolas' sole chance was to hope to outwit Guillermo, his one advantage the possibility of appearing suddenly and catching Guillermo off-guard.

Peering squarely into Calley's eyes, he said, "If I have not returned by dawn, send the authorities to this location."

He smoothed out the penciled note and handed it to the footman. "Tell them Guillermo Rescate is responsible for whatever they find."

Nicolas tucked his pistol into his waistband and strode purposefully through the door, leaving Humble and Calley to stare apprehensively at each other in his wake.

His gelding had barely cooled from his earlier ride, but Nicolas mounted and spurred the horse relentlessly. The image of Emmaline's lovely face swam before him, urging him on. He ached to think of her fear, her vulnerable delicacy. He could not bear even to imagine Guillermo's vile hands upon her.

In the caldron of his anguish and rage, all his thoughts distilled into elemental clarity. How trivial his grand gesture of honor seemed now. Of what importance was honor should the very embodiment of his love be in peril? What an utter fool he had been to deny his feelings for Emmaline. All else paled into insignificance beside his love for her. And how ironic was his reluctance to end this dangerous feud with his half-brother in the only manner by which Guillermo could be stopped. Insane obsession knew no boundaries of conscience. He could not fight against madness while confined by the rules of reluctance.

As Nicolas neared the docks, he slowed his horse and tempered his intensity. Knowing that a clear head demanded a certain detachment, he deliberately blanked his mind and threw an iron guard about his heart. When the cool force of reason chased all other thoughts from his head, he breathed deeply, storing his courage. He silently blessed the experience he had gained fighting with the guerrillas in Spain. Although at a fierce disadvantage, they had dealt the stunning blows that had defeated the monster Napoleon. Now Nicolas could but hope that one judicious strike could vanquish the monster who was his half-brother.

After a few twists and turns, he found a sign marking Quillbottom Lane, a street lively with carousing sailors and taverns standing shoulder to shoulder. Turning away, Nicolas sought the alley behind the lane and slowly made his way through. A menacing darkness cloaked the alley, with only an occasional lamp throwing queasy light onto the filthy passage. It was the domain of thieves and cutthroats, doxies and sots, all hidden in the shadows, calling tauntingly at him. Nicolas grimaced. It did not surprise him that Guillermo would feel quite at home with them.

Deliberately, he drew his pistol and pointed it upward. The taunts melted into jeers, but no one approached him. When he espied a livery barn, half tumbling down, Nicolas dismounted and led his gelding inside.

A half-dozen weary steeds stood in stalls, guarded by a massive one-eyed man.

"How much will you give me for this horse?" Nicolas asked bluntly, making a great show of replacing his pistol in his waistband.

The man grunted. "Five pounds."

A cold smile touched Nicolas' mouth. "You can command more than that from these stolen nags. I shall give you thrice that amount if you keep him safe from the thieves for a few hours."

The man's good eye regarded him unflinchingly. "Done."

"Good. Now, where is The Blue Gander?"

Given curt directions, Nicolas set off on foot. But he kept to the alley. No doubt Guillermo would be watching Quillbottom Lane. Blending into the shadows himself, Nicolas at last reached the rear of the tavern. He stood back to look upward. Iron railings encircled the windows, ledges, and tops. By boosting himself up, he could reach the higher floors.

Slowly, with painstaking effort to create no disturbance, he grabbed the railings and climbed to the top floor. Edging sideways on the ledge, he finally found a window ajar. Quickly scanning the dingy rooms, lit by one flickering candle, he saw only a blowsy woman stretched out on a cot. Taking a deep breath, he swung the window open on its hinges.

"Eh! 'Oo's that?" a woman's voice, thick with gin, demanded.

"Father Christmas," Nicolas said dryly as he entered through the window.

"Blimey," she chortled. "A bit late, ain't ye? Brung me a present, 'ave ye, ducks?"

Nicolas flipped a bright shilling through the air and the woman caught it with surprising dexterity.

"Thanks, ducks."

"You are quite welcome. What is your name?"

"Call me Sal."

"An honor to make your acquaintance, Sal. Who else lives on this floor?"

The woman tucked the shilling inside her half-open bodice and grinned toothlessly until Nicolas tossed her another coin.

"Elsie, across the hall. Old Grelch next to me. Then a strange bird at the front, don't see 'im much, mean-lookin' 'e is. And Dorrie across from him. Then there's Patch—"

"Thank you. Now, there are three more bob for you if you might do me a small service . . ."

Swiftly, Nicolas explained his request. Sal nodded her assent, and after a cautious glance out the door Nicolas slipped into the hallway. He waited a few moments until his eyes became accustomed to the darkness, then motioned for her to precede him.

Stopping before Guillermo's door, Sal gave Nicolas a wink and then boldly knocked. When after a few moments there was no reply, she knocked again, harder.

" 'Ere, ducks," she called loudly, "I knows yer in there. I can see the light under yer door. 'Ere now, open up."

After a long pause, they both heard a low, intense voice. "Go away."

Nicolas felt his blood begin to pulse. Deliberately, he willed himself to regain his calm.

"Aw, 'ave a 'eart, ducks," Sal whined. "Me candle

burned down to a puddle, it did, and I need another."

"I have no candles. Now go away."

Sal grinned, pounding now with her fist. " 'Ere now, I can see that you do. Be a sport. 'Ave pity on a poor, 'ardworking gel. 'Ow am I to pretty meself up for the night with no candle to see by? Eh, ducks?"

Nicolas heard a brief, fierce growl and, after a pause, the sound of a bolt sliding back. Quickly, he shoved Sal toward her room and she scurried away agilely. Nicolas drew his pistol and pressed his back against the wall.

Slowly, the door opened. Nicolas held his breath, straining to control himself and wait for the precise moment when he could surprise Guillermo.

He saw the shadow clearly outlined on the floor as Guillermo warily glanced out the door. A few seconds longer . . .

But just then a muffled cry echoed from inside the room. Emmaline, Nicolas' heart cried, and his instincts overrode his control. He stepped into the doorway a moment too soon. Guillermo knocked the pistol from his hand and emerged from behind the door, with one arm around Emmaline's neck and the other pointing a gleaming knife at her chin.

"Make one sudden movement, dear brother," Guillermo said smoothly, "and I shall cut her throat."

Nicolas froze, his hands upraised, his gaze focused tightly on Emmaline. The monster had bound her hands behind her back and tied a scarf over her mouth. Her elegant gown was rumpled and soiled, and her loosened hair disheveled. The ether had left her slightly groggy, but her wide blue eyes pleaded eloquently with Nicolas. His first thought was a prayer of gratitude that she was alive. Yet his heart lurched, for the agony in her eyes did not tell him whether or not she was unharmed.

"Come in and close the door behind you,"

Guillermo commanded. "Slowly. Slowly, brother dear. No sudden movements, or my knife may slip."

Nicolas complied, edging into the room.

"Back away. Toward the window. Very good. Stop."

Guillermo emitted a humorless chuckle and moved the wicked blade fractionally away from Emmaline's chin. "Finally you see the wisdom of listening to me after all these years. Is it not truly amazing how a lovely young woman may influence your judgment?"

Nicolas clenched his upraised fists. "She has nothing to do with what is between us, Guillermo. Release her and we shall decide this matter once and for all."

Flashing an ironical grin, Guillermo said, "But I find it quite a pleasant sensation to hold her in my arms. A mere prelude to what I shall enjoy with her later."

Involuntarily, Nicolas leaned forward. Guillermo pressed the tip of the knife into Emmaline's chin so that it left an indent and was only a fraction away from drawing blood.

"Do not even contemplate such folly," Guillermo muttered. "Resign yourself, Nicolas. You are about to witness degradation and eventual death. Just as you were the cause of such agony to my mother, I shall be the cause of hers."

Nicolas tasted the sourness of rising panic. "What do you want from me? Is it our father's holdings? Take them, they are yours. Is it my life? Very well. I give it to you. Just release Emmaline."

"Oh, no," Guillermo said, smiling, and the eerie light of madness brightened his eyes. "Her only release is death, at my pleasure. Just as my mother's death was at yours."

Fighting to keep his voice calm, Nicolas said tightly, "Consuelo died by her own hand."

"Goaded by you. When I am finished with this one, she too will prefer death to life." He let loose a bestial snarl, and a drop of saliva dribbled from his lips. "You think me cruel? I learned all from you, dear brother, and the manner in which you murdered my mother. If you regret this girl's death, you will have only yourself to blame."

The bindings of Nicolas' detachment suddenly broke loose. His dark eyes blazed fury.

"You are mad, Guillermo," he shouted savagely, "just as your mother was mad. Her depraved mind twisted until it snapped. She was evil, yes, evil! Her heart was rotted and putrid. She infected you with her disease. Blame her for the worms that writhe through your soul. Blame her for the devil you have become, for you learned it at her breast."

With each word Nicolas spoke, Guillermo's expression had contorted the more, until his face was an unrecognizable, tortured mask. Abruptly, his cold purpose snapped. Roaring, his lips curled back and his eyes white-hot, he shoved Emmaline roughly away and charged toward Nicolas, his lethal knife raised.

His force sent Emmaline staggering and she fell, striking her head against the wall. Bright lights flashed behind her eyes and she sank to the floor.

Momentarily stunned, she saw the action in the dim-lit room through a haze. One of them charged, and when the other leapt aside, the charging man's momentum carried him far past the man he attacked. Then the sound of breaking glass caused her to gasp. The charging man had crashed through the window! His scream echoed through the night, until suddenly, chillingly, it stopped with the sound of a sickening thud. One of the half-brothers was dead.

But which one was it, Guillermo or Nicolas? Frantically, she sought to clear her head, to see clearly, to call out Nicolas' name and hear his answering voice reassuring her.

The survivor was leaning on the windowsill, looking down to the lane. Then he turned and started toward her. Her heart pounded in her throat as he bent over her and tore off her restraints.

"Emmaline! Dearest! Are you hurt?"

That voice, mixing tenderness and strength and love! Emmaline cried out and threw her arms about him.

"Oh, Nicolas, thank God! I could not see . . ."

Gently, he touched her forehead and Emmaline winced. "You've had a nasty bump. Does aught but your head hurt?"

"No, indeed, I feel no pain whatever now that I know you are safe."

He searched her face until assured that she spoke the truth. Then, lifting her to her feet, Nicolas swept her into a fierce embrace.

"Oh, Emmaline," he whispered, his voice ragged, "I have been such a fool. I can no more cut you from my life than I can cut out my own heart. You are my heart, Emmaline, and my soul and my life."

As much as his words fired her love, his subsequent kiss burned ever more searingly into her. She reveled in his power, in his embrace that was more eloquent than any words.

"You cannot marry Cecil," he said passionately at last. "Nor anyone else upon this earth. No one could love you as deeply, as intensely as I love you, Emmaline."

"Oh, Nicolas," she sighed happily. "Nor could I love anyone even half as mightily as I love you."

His face lit with a joyous light. "Do you mean it, darling? You will marry me?"

"Oh, yes, Nicolas. And you had better marry me just as swiftly as you have proposed."

In reply, he kissed her once more, leaving no question in Emmaline's mind as to his answer.

Across London, in the verdant setting of Vauxhall Gardens, the fireworks display burst upon the darkness with brilliant flashes of color. In Quillbottom Lane, Emmaline could have sworn she saw them, too.

Epilogue

In the shade of the patio awning, Emmaline sat back and sighed with contentment. The Andalusian mountains spread out before her in a shimmering vista, the late-afternoon sun crowning the hills with a golden halo. A refreshing mountain breeze gently fanned her. Reaching languidly for the goblet of fruity wine at her side, she let her eyelids fall shut. Her smile radiated sheer bliss.

Moments later, Emmaline felt a kiss, soft as the fluttering wings of a butterfly, brush her cheek. She opened her eyes in delight.

"There you are, darling," she said softly. "How I have missed you! You've been gone an entire hour."

Nicolas sat beside her on the patio settee and took her hand. "Have I become the neglectful husband already?" Smiling, he raised her fingers to his lips, gently kissing them one by one. "I am devastated with remorse. Do you forgive me?"

Emmaline pretended to consider. "Perhaps I shall, and perhaps I shall not."

His kisses proceeded tenderly, slowly, across her palm and up to her wrist. "Have I no power to persuade you?"

Emmaline quite lost her train of thought, the delectable sensations that Nicolas provoked overwhelmed her ability to reason. Since their first night together, after their elopement, her reaction to him had been ever thus. While he worked at tantalizing her now, she reached up with her free hand to caress his sun-bronzed cheek.

"Spain agrees with you, my darling," she murmured fondly.

Although she did not say so, Emmaline was ever gratified to gaze into his dark eyes. All traces of haunting uncertainty, of guarded vigilance, had vanished, replaced by a tenderness that often blazed into passion. She rejoiced with humble thanksgiving that she might have played a part in his transformation.

"I am so glad," she said fervently, "that you have returned."

With one final lingering kiss, Nicolas released her hand. "I nearly forgot. We have received a letter from Aunt Minerva."

"Splendid! What has she to say?"

"I've not opened it yet. You read it to me while I pour more wine."

Eagerly, Emmaline broke the seal and unfolded the thick vellum.

" 'Dear ones,' " she began reading aloud. " 'With fondest hopes this finds you in good spirits.' "

"If only she knew," Nicolas murmured with a devilish smile, and Emmaline laughed.

"Behave yourself. 'As you might imagine, *tout le beau monde* still reels from the scandal so graciously provided by the family Garwin. Most everyone has delayed departure from the city, reluctant to miss the next tidbit of gossip we may toss out. You might be interested to learn, Nicolas, that your reputation as a man of mystery has grown, as has yours, Emmaline, by association. All that the *ton* knows is that you both disappeared at the same time. I quite naturally have chosen not to inform them of the details. How ever so much more delicious to listen to them speculate.' "

" 'Tis good to know that dear Auntie has not changed," Nicolas commented.

" 'Your cousin Cecil is quite beside himself with joy, and more irritatingly addled than ever. He and

Rosetta plan a wedding for the winter season. (Which you both must attend, if only to stir the gossip pot.) Noting how disgustedly youthful and ecstatic Rosetta appears warms my heart.' "

Emmaline looked up from her reading. "I am so happy for them both."

She went on, " 'The house is emptying at a steady rate. Not only family, but staff as well. I do hope Floss is serving you well in Spain, Emmaline. Be certain to curb her impertinence before it becomes too deeply ingrained. I speak from experience, as Andrews is a lost cause. Humble has requested to be put out to pasture, or more specifically, to a country cottage where he may grow roses in heavenly deafness.

" 'Much to my chagrin, I must own that I miss even Verity. She has proven quite the mysterious minx herself. I had a note from her only last week. Apparently, she decided to get away from the travails of a too-active social life and repaired to the country, where she has taken a house for the summer—oddly enough, quite near to Bevindale. She ever babbles on at length, even in her letter, but the gist of it is that she is finding country life both restorative and invigorating. My instincts tell me there is more to that tale, but I am content in remaining unawares.' "

"Verity in Bevindale," Emmaline marveled. "What a surprising turn of events. Whatever can she find to fascinate her there?"

Nicolas shrugged. "Knowing Verity, one cannot help being baffled."

"Hmm. Well, Aunt Minerva says, 'Speaking of Bevindale, I shall be journeying there myself at summer's end. By then, our charming vicar should have his new project well under way. How poignant of him to suggest—in the most delicate terms, of course—how gauche an impoverished relative by marriage would be. I was only too happy to contribute to the social, moral, and financial status of Bevindale and the vicar. I must say, his eyes did light up reverently when I mentioned the sum I had in mind. But then, when I declared how the money was to be used, he turned the most bilious shade of green. I thought my idea quite brilliant, if I do say so myself. Where better to provide shelter for orphans running the streets of London than in the good country air of Bevindale? And who better to administrate the orphanage than the vicar himself, with his vast sympathy for pitiful orphans?''

They both burst out laughing.

"Oh, but that is too perfect," Emmaline cried. "Imagine Uncle surrounded daily by guttersnipes!"

"Auntie has ever been a connoisseuse of poetic justice."

"Indeed! She adds: 'I intend to keep a judicious eye on his work. For my own gratification, of course. As for myself, I've scarce a moment to catch my breath, finding myself, if I may be so immodest, the preferred guest in the *ton*. As you well know, my health is frail, so I must take care. I did read the tea leaves yesterday and saw clear evidence of another wedding in the offing. Possibly this refers to Nan and her hackney driver, if downstairs gossip is accurate. Now that you two are out of London, perhaps the poor fellow can avoid being coshed on the skull every other week.

" 'But who can tell about affections? I have grown quite fond of being the focus of *haut ton* scandal. I may even give Lady Melton competition by developing a *tendre* for a suitor one-third my age.

" 'I long to see you and know I shall in good time. Be well and happy, my darlings. Lovingly, Minerva.' "

Emmaline folded the letter and set it aside, to be reread and savored later.

Nicolas raised his glass to her. "That we all may be well and happy."

Emmaline touched her goblet gently to his. "We need no tea leaves to assure us of that."